THE SEARCH

OTHER BOOKS AND AUDIO BOOKS

BY CLAIR M. POULSON:

I'll Find You

Relentless

Lost and Found

Conflict of Interest

Runaway

Cover Up

Mirror Image

Blind Side

Evidence

Don't Cry Wolf

Dead Wrong

Deadline

Vengeance

Hunted

Switchback

Accidental Private Eye

Framed

Checking Out

In Plain Sight

Falling

Murder at TopHouse

Portrait of Lies

Silent Sting

Out Lawyered

Deadly Inheritance

THE SEARCH

CLAIR M. POULSON

Covenant Communications, Inc.

Cover image: *Something doesn't feel right...* © PeopleImages, courtesy of istock.com

Published by Covenant Communications, Inc.
American Fork, Utah

Printed in the United States of America
First Printing: August 2017

23 22 21 20 19 18 17 10 9 8 7 6 5 4 3 2 1

ISBN: 978-1-52440-300-3

To Lynn and Julie Poulson

PROLOGUE

The attack took place on a well-lighted street during a pounding rainstorm in the early evening. The shopping public had holed up in various stores along the street when Allyah Kravitz and her boyfriend, Arrigo Benini, ran from a café with newspapers held over their heads in an ineffectual effort to keep the rain off.

When they reached Arrigo's dark-blue Nissan Pathfinder, Arrigo punched his key fob, and the doors unlocked. He opened the passenger door for Allyah, and suddenly a fully automatic rifle opened fire. Arrigo's body flew against the Nissan. He had time to shout, "Run, Allyah," before the barrage of gunfire tore the life from him.

Momentarily stunned, Allyah stood with wide-open eyes watching a dark, short man approach through the rain, the AK-47 held in front of him. His eyes were on the bloody figure on the ground. Allyah could not miss the strong resemblance of the killer to her boyfriend, and her stomach clenched with fear. She backed away from the Nissan as the killer once again opened fire, riddling Arrigo's body. She reached the café and opened the door to slip inside, but she paused when she heard the killer's voice.

"So long, little brother. You don't defy your father and live." Then he turned, locked eyes with Allyah, and said, "You . . . you are no better than him."

As he turned the AK-47 on her, she swiftly ducked through the doorway and dropped to her knees, scrambling through the tables as a barrage of bullets shattered the door and windows. Screams filled the café as other patrons dropped to the floor, some out of sheer panic, others from the deadly effect of the spray of bullets.

Allyah didn't have time to check on the victims, but she feared that others had died. She made it to the kitchen and out the back door, followed by a dozen other people. There was a lull in the shooting, then once again, there was a short burst of rifle fire. Allyah heard a loud explosion and glanced back to see the reflection of flames in the falling rain above the café.

She scrambled across the alley and then ran hard, turning up an adjoining alley. For two or three minutes, in a state of panic, Allyah ran, tears mixing with the rain. She made it across two streets and ducked into another alley just as she spotted a black Mercedes speeding toward her. She dropped behind a dumpster just a few yards into the alley. She could hear the car slowing, then a voice that sounded hauntingly like her murdered boyfriend. "You can run, Allyah, but you cannot escape. The Benini family will not be betrayed." Another barrage of bullets exploded in the darkness. Her heart was in her throat. They had found her. She couldn't escape.

But as suddenly as the latest round of fire had begun, it ceased, and loud laughter broke through the storm. "That will teach you, Allyah Kravitz," the same voice shouted. And the Mercedes roared away.

For five minutes, she stayed where she was, trying to calm herself. Finally, she crept from behind the dumpster. A flash of lightning lit the narrow street, and she saw a body lying in the mouth of the alley directly across from her. "Oh no!" she cried softly as she entered the dark street, looked both ways, and crossed to the other alley. Another flash of lightning lit the body. It was a tall man with long black hair, wearing a dark coat. She shuddered, pulled out her iPhone, and turned on its flashlight. She crept closer, praying that whoever had taken the bullets meant for her was still alive. She stooped over him, sickened at the blood that was covering the ground, the wall, and the man's coat. She didn't need to feel for a pulse.

She gasped and stood back up, willing her legs not to buckle as she backed away. There was nothing she could do. She shut off the light, put her phone back in her pocket, and hurried up the street. When she'd left the chaos safely behind, she stopped, pulled out the phone, and dialed 911. When her call was answered, she said between sobs, "A man was just murdered. He is lying on the street. Someone in a black Mercedes shot him. The same man also killed Arrigo Benini."

The dispatcher asked for the address. She gave the name of the café and said, "I don't know where I am now, but I can't be too far away from there."

She was told to stay where she was and wait until she saw a police car, and then she was to flag it down and show them the body.

"No, I can't. They're after me too." And with that she ended the call and shut off her phone. Despite the unrelenting rain and thunder, she could hear distant sirens, lots of them. She had to keep moving.

Allyah was terrified, she was heartbroken, and she didn't know what to do except run. She knew who had killed Arrigo. He'd spoken to her only once of his family, the Benini crime family. He'd walked out on his father a year ago. "They don't know where I am, but if they ever find me, they'll kill me. My father will probably send my brother, Nino, after me," he had told her. "He is my older brother; we look a lot alike except he is full of hate. If you ever see him, run, for he is a killer."

She'd heard his words, but they didn't really sink in. Not realizing how truly dangerous his family was, she'd blown it off with, "They haven't found you so far. I'm sure you're safe now."

"I can only hope," he'd said.

That had been about a month ago. He hadn't mentioned them again. Nor had she. But she knew it was Nino who had gunned her boyfriend down. She'd looked into his eyes just before she escaped through the door of the café. She also knew Nino was not alone, that someone else had been driving the black Mercedes. She'd heard the car continuing to move as the man in the alley had been gunned down.

Allyah walked until she was on the outskirts of the city, constantly on the outlook for the black Mercedes. She had seen very few vehicles, due, she was sure, to the storm. Exhausted, soaking wet, cold, and fatigued, she finally spotted an old house with the front door hanging open. Weeds grew along the walk and in the cracks. She approached it carefully, but when it still appeared empty, she entered. There was an old bed in one room. It had no mattress, but there were filthy rugs on the floor. She piled the rugs on the springs and climbed on the bed.

The bloody scenes she had witnessed kept running through her head, and tears flowed until she could cry no longer. Finally, from sheer exhaustion, she fell asleep.

When she awoke, sunlight streamed through the dirty window. Allyah sat up, threw her legs over the edge of the bed, and stretched. She was sore all over but didn't think she had any serious injuries. She did discover a small lump on one knee as she checked herself over. She pulled up her pant leg. Her knee was black and blue, but it wasn't bad. She'd had worse from falls on the volleyball court.

Allyah, a senior in high school, was a star player. In fact, it was following a game that she bumped into Arrigo in the school parking lot as she walked around the back of a large van. He'd apologized, and she'd apologized.

"I know who you are," he'd said as the two of them stepped into the light of a nearby streetlamp. "You're Allyah. Wow, you're really good. Without you, your team would have lost tonight."

"You saw the game?" she'd asked as she looked at him. He was a good inch shorter than her lanky six foot one.

He'd smiled. "I did."

"Do you have a younger sister on the team?" She could tell that he was older than she, and she was sure she'd never seen him in school.

"No, my roommate's sister," he said. He told her the girl's name and then added, "They told me you were the best on the team."

"She's not so bad herself," Allyah had answered.

"Are you hungry?" he'd asked, a sparkle in his dark eyes.

"I'm always hungry," she'd responded with a grin.

They had been almost inseparable since that night. But now his family had caught up with him, and his twinkling eyes and infectious grin were gone forever.

She pulled the phone from the pocket of her coat and turned it on. She had several missed calls. They were all from her best friend and roommate, Mya Wissing.

Allyah called Mya. "Hi, sorry I didn't make it home last night."

"Are you okay?" Mya asked. "I heard on the news that there were some people shot to death and more injured last night at the café Arrigo was taking you to. When you didn't come home, I was worried sick. And then when you didn't answer your phone, I was even more worried."

Tears sprang into Allyah's eyes. Mya was not only her best friend and roommate, but she was like a big sister. The two of them had roomed together since an airplane crash had killed both of Allyah's parents. Her family had immigrated to America when she was only five years old. And when she lost them, she was alone. Mya, who had been her friend for several years prior to that, had become all the family she had.

"Are you okay?" Mya asked when Allyah didn't answer right away. "Are you still with Arrigo?"

"No." She was fighting back the emotions. "I'm in trouble."

"Where are you? You're not in jail, are you?"

"Not that kind of trouble." She stopped and paced through the abandoned house, shivering from her still-wet clothing and from the fear of Nino finding her when he discovered he'd killed the wrong person.

"Allyah, what aren't you telling me?" Mya asked sternly. "You need to tell me now. I'm at work, but if I need to, I'll see if my boss will let me come and get you."

The dam broke. Fresh tears spilled from Allyah's brown eyes. She wiped at them with her long black hair. It took a minute before she was able to say, "Arrigo is dead. I saw who killed him."

"In the shooting on the news?" Mya asked.

"Yes."

"Where are you?"

"I don't know."

"I'm coming for you," Mya said. "Get me an address. I'll pick you up and take you home."

Twenty minutes later, Mya picked Allyah up a block from where she'd spent the night. When Mya pulled up, she stepped out of the car and hugged Allyah tightly. Mya was short, plump, and blonde. Allyah was tall, slender, and dark. But despite their differences, the two of them were inseparable.

"Where's your purse?" Mya asked after they got in the car.

"I don't know. I had it when I was walking from the cafe. It could be anywhere. I'm glad my phone was in my pocket and not my purse like it usually is," she said.

Mya parked in front of their apartment. "I need to get back to work," she said. "You be careful. Lock the door and stay inside." Mya didn't pull away until Allyah was inside the apartment.

Allyah showered, put on fresh clothes, and was brushing her long black hair when the doorbell rang. Her blood pressure spiked. She looked around for a weapon of some kind. The only thing she could come up with was a broom. She grabbed it and walked slowly to the door. The bell rang again, followed by a firm knocking.

She stood frozen with fear and not sure what to do. Her impulse was to run, but there was only one door to the apartment. She was trapped. Then a deep male voice called through the door. He identified himself as a police officer. Allyah left the chain on but opened the door the few inches it allowed, ready to slam it shut again. The man on the other side was displaying a police shield in one hand while holding her purse in the other. "Miss Kravitz?" he asked.

"That's me," she responded faintly.

"I need to speak to you for a moment."

Allyah opened the door, and the officer entered.

"Detective Martin White," he said as she shut the door behind him. He was shorter than she but well-groomed and soft spoken. "I need you to tell me what you saw last night when a young man by the name of Arrigo Benini was gunned down on the street. You were there. Witnesses saw you, and your purse was found near the back door of the café."

They had her purse. They knew she'd been there. "I—I c—can't," she stammered.

"Calm down, Miss Kravitz, and just tell me what you saw," he said. "Here, let's sit down." He sat near her, his blue eyes kindly and his voice filled with sympathy. "I'm sorry that you saw the horror last night, Miss Kravitz. It must have been terrible."

She nodded but didn't answer, and he smiled at her. She shifted in her seat. Finally, she asked, "Did—did people in the café die?"

"Yes, sadly two are dead; a dozen others are in the hospital," he answered.

"Did you find a man a few blocks away who had been . . . shot?"

His eyes narrowed. "Was that meant to be you?"

Allyah nodded as her eyes filled with moisture. "I'm in terrible danger. He'll come after me when he finds out he didn't kill me. And he will find out."

"We'll protect you," he said. "But first I need to know exactly what you saw."

"I was there. I saw my—my . . . him get shot. I ran into the café and escaped." He knew, she could see it in his eyes, that she was holding things back, that she didn't want to tell him what she knew.

"Was Mr. Benini your boyfriend?" he asked perceptively.

She looked at the floor and nodded. "Yes," she managed at last.

"Who shot him?" Detective White asked.

She pulled her eyes up and met his as a sudden surge of anger shot through her. "It was his brother, Nino. I'm sure his father sent him to kill Arrigo."

"And to kill you?" he asked softly.

"I guess," she said with a shudder.

Over the next few minutes, Detective White drew Allyah's story from her. Finally, he said, "I need you to come with me now. Pack a few things. You're not safe here. You're talking about a small but powerful Chicago crime family. They will find you here."

Reluctantly, she did as she was asked. Allyah never returned to the apartment.

CHAPTER ONE

Two years later

The heat in Phoenix was almost unbearable as Jayden Spalding climbed from his black Hummer and then let his gray German shepherd, Bullet, out. It was late in the evening on this mid-August day, but he had not yet had time to run. He was taking that opportunity now. Jayden was very fit and intended to stay that way. He worked out at the gym regularly, lifting weights and keeping his martial arts skills honed, but he hated running on treadmills. He preferred doing his running in the open air, even when it was stifling hot. Part of the reason he preferred the outdoors was the company of his three-year-old dog who loved to run with him.

Jayden fitted a blue bandana around his head to keep the sweat from pouring from his thick, reddish-brown hair. Then he patted Bullet on the head and started along a paved trail. At six foot six, Jayden had a long stride, and he covered the ground rapidly. Twenty-eight years of age, he was in the best condition he'd ever been in. After Jayden's two yearlong deployments in Afghanistan, the heat in Phoenix really didn't seem all that overbearing. In fact, he relished it.

The only time since he'd left high school ten years before that he hadn't been in peak condition was while he was serving a mission for the LDS Church in Russia. He had done what he could, but he missed the runs and the workouts.

He carried his cell phone with him but left the other tools of his trade in the Hummer, including his 9mm Beretta and small .22 caliber backup weapon. He was fresh off a case that had taken him out of state and hampered his exercise routine. But he had successfully tracked down a man who had left his wife and business partner a month ago, leaving her destitute and the company close to bankruptcy. He'd found the man spending the ill-gotten gains in Florida. Jayden brought him back to face embezzlement charges and to square things with his soon-to-be ex.

Jayden stepped up his pace after the first mile. By the time he'd finished two miles, he was drenched with perspiration, and it felt good. He and Bullet pushed on. Then his cell phone rang.

He pulled it out, looked at the screen, and reluctantly slowed to a walk. Whenever he wasn't in his office, his phone calls were automatically forwarded to the cell. "Spalding Investigations," he said, trying to control the panting, "Jayden Spalding speaking."

"Mr. Spalding, my name is Nadia Fairchild," the caller said. She had a clear alto voice, but Jayden detected emotion there. That was to be expected—anyone who called him for help probably had trauma going on in their lives.

"Miss Fairchild," he said, "are you the Nadia Fairchild that plays for the Phoenix Mercury?"

"You know who I am?" she asked.

"I do. I'm a big fan."

"Thanks," she said. "I need help."

"Do you need help with your three-point shots?" he asked.

"What?" she said, clearly puzzled. "Well, I suppose a few pointers wouldn't hurt, but that's not what I'm calling about."

"Sorry, I couldn't resist. You're a great basketball player. What can I do for you?" He knew she was LDS. She was tall, about six two, and had long, dark hair. He couldn't quite conjure up her face, but he'd seen it on TV and on the Internet. And he'd seen her play in person. She was very pretty—that he did remember.

"It's about my mother," she said. "She's missing."

"Missing? I guess you misplaced her." He hoped his humor wasn't offending her. He just couldn't help it. There had been those occasions when it had cost him a client, but usually it helped them relax. "I'm sorry. That wasn't appropriate. Does your mother live here in Phoenix?" he asked, serious, but still panting a little. He'd been running hard.

When she spoke, some of the tension seemed to have drained from her voice. "No, but she lives close. She's the head coach of the women's basketball team at Central Arizona College in Coolidge. Can you find her?"

They always asked him that. Usually he could. But it wasn't something he could guarantee. "I'll certainly do my best."

"I was told that you're the best. I'm so worried about Mom and one of her players." There was a slight pause, and she asked, "Mr. Spalding, are you all right? You sound, I don't know . . ."

"Out of breath? I am," he said. "I've been trying to outrun Bullet."

There was a sharp intake of breath. "You're being shot at?"

"Oh no, my dog's name is Bullet. He runs pretty fast. Now, are you saying that someone else is missing too?" he asked. "How could one girl misplace two people in the same day?"

She chuckled. "I heard you were a ham. I need to see you. Can you meet me now?"

"My place or yours?" he asked. "I'd prefer mine, but whatever you want works for me."

"Do you mean your home?" she asked.

"Oh, goodness no. I'd never invite a beautiful stranger to my house. I was thinking my office."

"I'll come to wherever you ask me to," she said.

"That's great. Let's make it my office. Do you have the address?"

"No."

"I'm listed in the phone book. You can find my address there or online." He paused just a beat, and then he added, "Or I can just give it to you." Before she had a chance to react, he recited the address.

"Are you there now? I know it's after regular office hours. But . . ." Her voice trailed off.

"I'd never try to outrun Bullet in my office," he said. "I need a head start, and there isn't room inside. But I can be there in twenty minutes, Miss Fairchild."

"Please, you don't have to call me that. Just call me Nadia."

"Great name," he said. "My name's Jayden. So now we're on an even playing field."

"I think I can make it in fifteen minutes. Is that okay?" she asked. "I'll wait for you in the parking lot."

"That will be great. I'll hurry, but it will take me at least twenty minutes. I don't need a speeding ticket."

She was chuckling softly as he ended the call. He put the phone away and ran hard for his Hummer.

***

When he parked in the parking lot behind the building that housed his office, he spotted a small red Jaguar. An attractive woman was unfolding herself from it. He headed toward her, feeling self-conscious. He was still damp from perspiration, wearing old sweats. He'd meant to pull off the blue bandana before he left his car, but he'd forgotten.

She was in white slacks and a light-blue blouse, and she wore her long, dark hair loose. "Are you Mr. Spalding, I mean Jayden?" A hopeful look lit up her dark, red-rimmed eyes. She tossed her head, throwing her long, black hair over her shoulder and out of her face.

"Yes, I'm Jayden," he said as he reached her and held out his hand.

She eyed his dog suspiciously, but when it made no threatening moves toward her, she accepted his hand. "I'm Nadia. Thanks for agreeing to meet with me. It looks like I interrupted a workout session. I'm sorry."

"Bullet and I were just having a little run." He took her by the arm and directed her toward the back door of the office building. "It's not a problem, other than I'm kind of sweaty. But I guess you know about sweaty."

She grinned, lighting her otherwise worried face. "I like sweaty," she said, "and I think I'm going to like you." But then the grin faded.

When they reached the door, Jayden opened it and stood back while she went in. She was followed by Bullet, and Jayden took up the rear.

"He's allowed in the building?" Nadia asked skeptically. "It is a male, isn't it?"

"Yes, he's a he, and he goes wherever I go," Jayden said with a grin. "Would you argue if it was your place?"

She shook her head, her hair flowing gently as she did. "I don't think I'd argue with either one of you," she said with that smile he already was beginning to like.

"I wish everyone we met felt that way," he said. "But we are sort of a matched pair, me and Bullet, wouldn't you say?" Before she could comment, he added, "My office is on the second floor. The stairway is over there." He pointed and let her lead the way. Bullet padded along beside him. When they reached the top of the stairs, he again took hold of Nadia's arm to direct her past a couple of other offices and stopped at his. He opened the door and ushered her inside. "Welcome to my elegant office," he said. He didn't have a plush office, but it was roomy and serviceable. He led her past the reception area and into his private office. Comfortable, padded chairs stood in front of his desk. He offered her one, and before seating himself, he filled a small metal dish with water and placed it beside his desk, where the dog began to lap it up. "Can't ignore Bullet's needs," he explained. "He has a nasty way of reminding me when I forget. I have scars to prove it. Want to see?" She blushed. "Of course you don't."

Once he was seated, he picked up a pen and gave her his *it's time to get down to business* look. "Okay, let me explain about how I work and what my rates are," he said.

"I'll pay whatever it costs," she said, causing him to think about the flashy red Jaguar. WNBA players didn't make the big bucks that their male counterparts in the NBA did, but he guessed they did okay. "I just want you to find my mother."

"I'm guessing you're of the opinion that your mother wants to be found," he said as he shoved a contract across the desk. She nodded, glanced over it, signed, and then pulled a checkbook from her purse.

He slipped the check she wrote into the center drawer of his desk and put a small recorder next to a yellow legal pad on his desk. "Do you mind if I record this interview?" he asked. "My memory isn't what it used to be. I'll take notes, but I want to make sure I don't miss anything."

"That's fine," she said as the big gray dog walked over to the door and plopped down, making himself comfortable. "I really do like your dog."

"Thanks," Jayden said. "He's a good friend and an invaluable assistant. And his memory is better than mine. Course, he's only three. What can I expect?" He turned the recorder on, and then, pen in his hand, he asked, "What's your mother's name?"

"Layda Fairchild. She's six feet tall, weighs around 150 pounds, and has shoulder-length black hair. Her eyes are brown."

"Thanks. You're a mind reader. I wish I could do that. Do you have a picture of her?" Jayden asked.

"Only on my iPhone," she said. "Can I text it to you?"

"That would be great. I can make copies if I need them." He scribbled his cell number on a business card then pushed it toward her.

She pulled her phone from an oversized black leather purse, worked with it for a moment, and then said, "There, you should have her picture. It's fairly recent."

He checked to make sure it was there. "She's an attractive woman," Jayden said, "just like her daughter."

"Mom is Latino-Caucasian mix," she said with a blush.

"That's where you get your glossy black hair and olive skin," he said. "Lucky you. Me and my pale, freckled skin? I burn if I don't protect myself. I'd trade, but you probably like what you have."

Nadia's dark skin showed another touch of blush. "Thank you, I'll keep my own. But your complexion looks good on you. I like freckles; I've never had a single one."

"If I knew how, I'd share with you."

"I also get some of my complexion and dark hair from my father. He is half black and half white. He's . . ." She paused.

He almost asked which half of her father was white and which was black, but he stopped himself. He was already overdoing it. He needed to get and stay serious. "You were going to say something else," he prompted.

"I was going to tell you about my father, but it doesn't matter. It's Mom I'm here about."

Jayden cocked an eyebrow. From the look that crossed her face, he thought maybe it could matter. "Nadia, let me decide what matters. That's what you're paying me for. Please, tell me about your father."

She slowly shook her head and looked at the window to her left. Jayden waited. Finally she said, "He and Mom don't get along. They're divorced."

"Was it an amicable divorce?" he asked.

Nadia looked at him with slightly narrowed eyes, flicked a lock of hair behind her shoulder, and then said, "No, it wasn't. It was ugly. Is that enough about him?"

"Nadia, where does he live?"

Her eyes grew even narrower. "I don't see how that can help you."

"I don't either, but I need to know," he said gently.

"I don't know where he went after he was released."

Jayden saw little red flags popping up. "Released? Where has he been?"

"I'm ashamed to tell you."

"Nadia, you're my client. And I hope you'll be my friend. You have nothing to be ashamed of."

"You don't know that," she said with a snip. "But if you have to know, he was in prison."

"What was he in prison for? It could be important," he stressed, ignoring her anger.

Nadia's smooth olive face went pasty, and her dark eyes widened. "Are you thinking he might have done something to Mom?"

"I have to consider it," he said. "You're paying me to find her, and I have to consider every possibility in order to succeed."

"Okay, but don't think badly of Mom. She loved him. I guess I did too, but he went to prison when I was only six. I don't have a lot of memories about him—except for the fights they had." Jayden gave no response. He waited, and finally she continued, "He did several things, Detective."

"Jayden," he reminded her gently.

"Sorry. He robbed a bank. He beat a cop up—pretty badly. And—uh—he—uh—he and his friend . . . kidnapped a little girl and held her for ransom," she said with downcast eyes.

The little red flags were now large red flags, the kind that enraged bulls in Spain. "How long has he been out of prison?" Jayden asked.

"A short while. Mom was notified that he was being released on parole a month ago. I think she said he was getting out two weeks after that."

"Nadia, what happened to the little girl?" Jayden asked, his eyes steady on hers.

"The FBI caught him and his partner. The little girl wasn't physically harmed. That's all I know, and that's only because I made Mom tell me that much when I was old enough to understand the seriousness of what he'd done."

Jayden nodded and then asked, "Nadia, does your mother have a lot of money?"

"She makes a good salary, but she's not rich, by any means. I know she saves a lot because when she was raising me, we didn't have much but she saved what she could," Nadia answered. "That's the only way we made it. She didn't get child support because my father went to prison."

"I know you told me already, but tell me again. What does your mother do?" he asked.

"She's a college basketball coach."

"It sounds like you're a natural. She probably played ball too."

"She did," Nadia agreed. "So did my father."

"And they must both be tall," he said.

"They are. I guess I got my height from them. There have been lots of times that I wished I wasn't so tall."

"Hey, there's nothing wrong with being tall," he said. "I am, and the only time it bothers me is when I slam into someone's chandelier. They always put those things too low."

She grinned. "I've bumped my head a few times too, but it's not that. Short girls like tall guys. But short guys, they don't give me a second look. Even average size guys don't."

"That's their loss," he said.

She blushed again. For someone with such pretty olive skin, she did that a lot, and he found it quite attractive. "Thanks," she said. "You seem like a great guy."

"I wouldn't go that far," he quipped. "Now, back to your mother. What did she do when you were growing up?"

"For the first several years, she worked as a waitress. At the same time, she was going to college. She got her degree, and then she got a job as a high school coach. She coached both basketball and volleyball, but she still didn't make a lot, and she had student loans to pay off."

"Is she still in debt?" Jayden asked.

"Oh no, she paid the loans off before I graduated from high school, and she helped me when I was in college until . . ." She stopped, and once again, a look of pain crossed her face.

"Until what?" Jayden pressed gently.

"You won't understand, but, well, I went to college in Utah. I played basketball for Southern Utah University. I met some really nice girls. They taught me about their church. I was interested, but when I joined, it upset my mother. She said I'd have to pay for my own schooling if I was going to be 'one of them Mormons,'" Nadia explained. "I was barely eighteen and well into my first year. It was hard, but with a scholarship and part-time job, I made it through school."

"You're 'one of them Mormons,' huh?" he said with a smile, but he didn't give her a chance to respond. "Well, you see, Nadia, I understand very well. I also had friends who were Mormons. That was in high school. And believe it or not, I played a little basketball myself."

Her face brightened up. "I believe it. You're so tall and athletic."

"I wasn't good like you are. I was just tall. But as I was about to say, I also eventually joined the Church. My parents wouldn't allow me to get baptized until I was eighteen, but I went to church and did everything I could while I waited. In my parents' defense," he said, "they never refused to let me go to church or participate in Young Men activities."

"Jayden, this probably sounds, I don't know, silly, I guess, but I'm glad you're LDS. That tells me that you pray for help in solving cases."

"That's a fact," he said. "I could never do what I do without the Lord's help. Back to your family, you said you talked to your mother recently?"

"We're close now. She's never taken an interest in the Church, but when I told her I was going on a mission after college, she helped support me. I think she thought the Church would turn me into some kind of monster. When it didn't, she softened. Believe it or not, Jayden, she told me after my mission that she didn't miss the money she sent me. Maybe someday—" She broke off. "Anyway, we get along great now, and I'm really worried about her. I love my mother."

"Of course you do. That's the kind of girl you are. What is your dad's name?" Jayden asked as he got the interview back on track.

"Ulisses Fairchild. Mom had talked about having her last name changed back to her maiden name, but she's never done it."

"How old is he?" he asked, ignoring the quip that had come to his mind.

"He would be about fifty now. He's older than Mom. She was only eighteen when she married him."

"How old is she now?"

"She's forty-three," Nadia responded.

"Are you their only child?"

"I am."

"Well, at least you'll always be the pick of the litter," he said, and she smiled. "Okay, so describe your father to me."

"He's big," she said. "I mean even taller than you. He's six eight, I think. And he isn't fat. He must weigh three hundred pounds. His hair's going gray. He has a scar on his face." She touched the corner of her left eye. "It runs from here to his chin." She trailed her finger in a jagged line down her face. He is very dark, much darker than me."

"Nadia, either you have a really good memory, or you've seen your father recently," Jayden guessed, cocking an eyebrow.

She flushed. "You're right, but please don't tell my mother when you find her. She would never understand. After I joined the Church, I thought a lot about the principle of forgiveness. I thought I hated him, but mostly it was Mom that hated him, and she sort of passed that on to me. On my mission, I saw some pretty hard people change. And I saw a lot of forgiveness." She smiled. "There are some pretty amazing people in Russia. It's hard to believe, but there are."

"I know," Jayden said with a little smile. "I served my mission there too."

"Wow! You didn't!" she said brightly.

He spoke to her in Russian, and she responded in the same tongue. Both of them laughed. For a couple of minutes, they talked about their respective missions.

But then she switched back to English. "I knew I had to forgive him, Jayden, no matter what he thought about me."

Jayden smiled at her. "You visited him in prison, didn't you?"

She nodded. "Yes. It was hard, and I only visited him a few times. The first time was about two years ago, right after my mission. He refused to see me. I wondered how I could ever forgive him if he wouldn't even talk to me. It made me bitter, but that only caused me to be unhappy, and I didn't want to be unhappy. So I went back about a year after that, but not until I felt like I really had forgiven him. That was something I had to do despite what he did or thought."

"And that time you saw him?" Jayden asked.

She curled a lock of long hair around her finger. "I did. He said he was sorry for what he'd done, that he'd changed in prison. He said the reason he didn't want to talk to me at first was that he was ashamed."

"What made him change his mind?"

"He wanted me to forgive him. I told him I already had, and he asked if I thought my mother could ever forgive him. I said I didn't know, that she was pretty bitter. That made him a bit angry. I guess he expected that she should. Anyway, I saw him two or three times after that. I can't say I ever felt like we'd forged a relationship, but at least we could talk."

"So did you know he was getting out of prison before your mother got her notification?" Jayden asked.

She shook her head and made a couple more wraps of the lock of hair. "The last time I was there was maybe two months ago. He didn't say a word about it." She paused. "He did ask about Mom. He asked a lot of questions about her. Now I wonder why. At the time I thought he was honestly sorry about what had happened to them. Anyway, along with other things, I told him that she'd gone to school and gotten a degree and that she was coaching in college."

"Did he ask you where she was coaching?"

"Oh!" She gasped. "Yes, he did. But he seemed different. Surely he wouldn't . . ." She let her thought trail off and released the captive lock of wavy hair.

"I'll have to check on him," Jayden said. "You understand, don't you?"

She nodded her head, rubbed her eyes, and then said, "I hope he didn't do something to Mom. It was so hard to forgive him before. I . . . I . . . I don't know if I could do it again."

"I hope it wasn't him. I will find her though, Nadia, if I possibly can. Has he contacted you since he was paroled?"

She shook her head and again captured an errant lock of hair and began to twist it. "He knows my cell phone number. I don't think I ever gave him my address, although I may have. I don't remember."

"That's probably not important. There are ways to find people's addresses." Jayden paused for a moment. He looked at her, wondering how much twisting that beautiful lock of hair could take. Finally, he said, "Nadia, if he did take your mother and if he knows you play for the Mercury, maybe it is *your* money he wants." The idea had come to him suddenly, and he really didn't like it at all.

Once again that pretty olive face went pasty. "But I don't make *that* much."

"He probably doesn't know that. Is that all the income you have?"

Slowly she shook her head and twisted that poor tormented lock. "My grandfather, Mom's father, is very wealthy. He bought my car for me and has given me some money. But . . ." She paused, thinking deeply. "My father knows that Grandpa is rich," she said quietly. "I wonder if he's tried to contact him."

"Tell me about your grandfather, and I'll find out," Jayden said.

Nadia told Jayden that her grandfather was widowed and lived alone in Galveston, Texas. "His name is Marley Ferrel," she said. "He's in his late sixties now. And like the rest of us, he's tall. Almost as tall as you."

"I like tall," he said with a grin.

She grinned back and dropped her eyes shyly. She gave Jayden her grandfather's address and phone number and then said, "He still works. I don't think he'll ever retire. He owns his own company. I guess you'll need his work number as well." She rattled that off from memory.

"Thank you, Nadia," he said. "I gather you and your grandfather are close?"

"We are," she said. "He's always treated me like I was his own. He calls me his little girl. And you know what? I like it when he does that."

"He sounds like a wonderful man. What kind of company does he own?"

"They mostly build sailboats," she said. "There's a lot of demand for them in Galveston. But they also build some other kinds of boats, even an occasional yacht."

"I'll contact him," Jayden promised.

"I was going to call him, but should I wait until you do?"

"No, you can call him. He would probably want to know about your mother if he doesn't already," Jayden suggested. "He would probably rather hear it from you than some crusty old investigator."

Nadia shook her head. "I don't know. They don't get along real well. He was against her marrying my father—adamantly against it. Mom says that he told her that there was something about my father that wasn't good, that he and Grandma both sensed it. When Dad got arrested, he called her and told her she should have listened to him. That really grated on her. But you need to understand, Grandpa is a self-made millionaire. He worked hard to get there, and he didn't do it by being soft. He always says exactly what's on his mind, regardless of what others may think. Anyway, she was offended, and it made an already poor relationship even worse."

"That's too bad," Jayden said. "If it's okay with you, then, maybe I'll call him first."

"Please do. Back when she first married Dad over Grandpa's objections, Grandpa and Grandma told her not to come to them if she needed money. I think after Dad went to prison, Grandpa and Grandma would have sent us money, but Mom was too proud to ask, and Grandpa was too proud to offer. Instead, he was always giving me money and stuff."

"Is that red Jaguar of yours 'stuff'?" he asked with a grin.

Nadia chuckled. "To me it was a lot more than that. I love that car, but not because it's expensive or because it's flashy or even because it catches the eyes of a lot of guys—even some of the short ones. I've had guys ask me out and then ask if we can take my car."

"Really?" Jayden said, feigning shock. He didn't mention that he'd had that very thought. He wouldn't mind sitting next to her in that hot little automobile. But if he ever did get the chance to ask her out, he would offer to take the Hummer. He didn't really think that would ever happen, but a guy could dream.

"Yeah, really, but not often. I mean, you know, guys don't ask me out very often. I'm too tall."

"You're just right," Jayden said, and he meant it.

That cute blush rushed up her cheeks again. She grabbed that lock of hair and twisted as she said, "No, Jayden, I don't like my car for all those reasons. I like it because Grandpa gave it to me, and I love him."

"Your Grandma Ferrel is dead?" Jayden asked in an abrupt shift.

"Yes, and it broke Grandpa's heart when she died. It was while I was in Russia. Mom didn't go to her funeral." She shook her head. "My mom can be so stubborn." She frowned. "She's just like Grandpa, but she won't admit it."

"Did your grandmother have a dark complexion too?" he asked.

"She did. She was Hispanic. And she was a beautiful woman. She and Grandpa loved each other a lot. I wrote to him and told him how sorry I was. It was after I got off my mission and went to see Grandpa and tell him how sorry I was about Grandma that he and I drew even closer than we already were. He always tells me that I remind him of Grandma. I don't think he'll ever get over her. She died of cancer."

"I'm sorry," Jayden said sincerely. "Back to your father for a minute; do you by any chance have a picture of him?"

"No, when they got divorced, Mom destroyed every picture she had of him. Sorry," she said.

"No, that's okay. Now, tell me about the player of your mother's who's also missing."

CHAPTER TWO

"Her name is Naylyn Pierza. I've met her a few times. She's nice, but she's really quiet and, well, maybe shy. Whatever the reason, she doesn't like to talk about herself. But my mother says Naylyn is hardworking and dedicated, one of their best players, even though she's only a freshman. The other girls like her well enough, although they don't really associate with her outside of basketball. She's also tall, just an inch shorter than me," Nadia said. "Oh, and she's really intelligent, an honor student."

"Describe her to me," Jayden said.

"Well, let's see. She has brown eyes, light-brown hair, which she wears quite short. She's beautiful—and I don't mean an average beauty. She is stunning."

"Do you know anything about her family?" Jayden asked.

"No, Mom says Naylyn doesn't like to talk about her family. All I know is that her parents were killed when she was sixteen and she lived with an uncle and aunt until she got out of high school."

"Any siblings?"

"I don't think so. If there are, she never told Mom about them."

"How did she come to play for your mother?" he asked.

"She was a walk-on. She just came into Mom's office one day, said she was enrolled in school and that she'd like to play basketball. Mom let her try out. She was athletic. Mom put her on the team, and she says she's never regretted it."

"I wonder," Jayden began, stroking his chin thoughtfully, "if she could have been the real target of the kidnappers, if that's what happened."

"She's poor, I know that," Nadia said. "So I can't imagine."

Jayden considered what she said, but he still didn't discard the idea. It was worth looking into.

Jayden and Nadia talked for a few more minutes, then he stood and said, "I guess that's all for now. I'll get to work on this. Call me if you think of anything that might help or if anyone contacts you about your mother. That is most important."

"I will," she said as she also stood.

Bullet joined them from his position by the door. He rubbed his long, gray back against Nadia's leg, and she stroked his head. "He's beautiful," she said. "But I haven't seen any German shepherds his color. He looks like he could be related to a wolf."

"He does, doesn't he? But he's not, unless it's way, way back. I have his registration papers. I got him when he was a puppy. The fellow that sold him to me gave me the pick of the litter." He grinned at Nadia. "He wasn't an only child." She smiled. He added, very seriously, "Of course, even if you had a dozen siblings, you'd probably still be the pick of the litter."

She reached over and slugged him on the shoulder. "You think?"

"I'm pretty sure," he responded, his face deadpan. "Bullet was the biggest, and his color made him stand out from the rest of the litter. I've never regretted picking him. He's very intelligent. I've spent a lot of time training him, and a dog handler from the Phoenix PD has helped. Bullet is amazing. He is totally loyal to me. He would protect me to the death."

"I like him," she said as she once again petted the soft, gray coat of fur.

"It looks like the feeling is mutual. Bullet doesn't always warm up to strangers like he has to you," he said.

"Bullet." She looked down at the dog. "How did you come up with that name?"

"His color. He's the color of lead. But that's not all. I could see that first day when he was with the litter, that he was strong and fast. It seems to fit."

"Well, I've got a practice in a little while, so I better get moving. Thanks for seeing me. And please, Jayden, find my mother," she pleaded as she reached for the doorknob, turning her head away as if she didn't want him to see the tears in her eyes.

But he knew. And he admired her for it. Never in his short career had he been hired by someone who had left him feeling like he'd just met someone special.

As soon as Nadia was gone, Jayden sat at his desk and reviewed his notes. Then he picked up his phone and dialed the number Nadia had given him for her grandfather's home. He didn't answer, so he called the business number. The call was answered by a receptionist, who transferred him.

When Nadia's grandfather answered, it was with a deep, "Hello. This is Marley Ferrel. How may I help you?"

"Mr. Ferrel, my name is Jayden Spalding. I was just speaking with your granddaughter, Nadia," he began.

The deep voice broke in. "She's a wonderful girl. Are you dating her?"

"Oh no," Jayden said with a chuckle. "Why do you ask?"

Ferrel chuckled. "Because if you were, I'd have a lot of questions for you. When that girl marries, I don't want her to make the same mistake her mother did. But since you're not dating her, please state your business."

"I am a private investigator," Jayden began. "I specialize in—"

Mr. Ferrel cut him off. "What does she need a private investigator for? Is she in some sort of trouble?"

"She came to me with a concern about her mother, your daughter."

"Her mother," he said, disappointment evident in his voice. "What has she done now? I hope she isn't planning to marry another no-good scoundrel like that worthless Ulisses Fairchild."

"It's not that," Jayden hastened to explain.

"Well, if it was, I could understand Nadia hiring a private detective. Her mother needs help when it comes to picking men."

"Mr. Ferrel, Nadia came to me because I specialize in finding missing persons, and—"

Once again, Nadia's grandfather broke in. "Who's missing? Wait, is it Layda?" he asked with a touch of alarm in his voice.

"Yes, your daughter is missing. Nadia will be calling you about it."

Mr. Ferrel spoke again. His voice was softer and seemed a little sad. "Layda's missing? Are you sure? Maybe she and some boyfriend decided to take a few days to themselves."

"Yes, I'm sure. Your granddaughter told me that her mother and one of her ballplayers left a basketball game last night in Coolidge where she coaches. The last time anyone claims to have seen them, the two of them were walking together out toward the parking lot."

"Mr. Spalding, is it?"

"You can call me Jayden."

"All right, Jayden it is. Jayden, don't get me wrong. I love my daughter. We just, well, I think we're too much alike. We clash," he said. "But I suppose Nadia told you about that."

"She did," Jayden agreed. "She says her mother can't see it."

"Why are you calling me if Nadia is going to?" Mr. Ferrel asked, suspicion conveyed through the slow way he asked the question.

"Well, it's like this," Jayden began. "I understand you're a wealthy man, Mr. Ferrel, and if by any chance someone has kidnapped Layda, I couldn't help but wonder if it might be about ransom. Nadia isn't rich. So I wondered—actually, she and I both wondered—if the person responsible might call you and demand a ransom."

Silence reigned for a full minute. Jayden waited, wondering if such a call had already been made, that there was already a ransom demand in place. When Mr. Ferrel finally broke the silence, he said, "Layda and I might be at loggerheads most of the time, but if I get a call, I'll pay the ransom. Young man, I don't want you thinking for one minute that I won't. But I have not had such a call."

"Mr. Ferrel, will you let me know if you do?" Jayden asked.

"Please, Jayden, call me Marley. And yes, I will. I'll do anything I can to help my girls. And I might add, if my little girl sought you out and trusts you, I do too. She's not like her mother. She has a level head. Are you in Phoenix?"

"Yes, sir," Jayden said as he smiled about the *little girl* reference.

"That would be *yes, Marley*," the wealthy man rebuked. "How much do you charge? I will be glad to pay if—if you're any good at what you do."

"Nadia has already given me a retainer, Marley," Jayden said. "But you can check me out if you'd like. You'll learn that even though I'm relatively young, I am good at what I do."

"Well, like I said, if my granddaughter came to you for help, that should be a good enough reference for me. She is a bright girl. I trust her judgement." There was just a slight, deep chuckle on the phone. Then he added, "Unless it's a young man wanting to marry her. In that case, I'd have to check for myself. Are you married, Jayden?"

"Well, no, but—" Jayden began.

"Just asking. Are you a Mormon?"

"Why do you ask that?" Jayden asked, taken aback.

"Well, you see, my granddaughter is, and she's made it very clear that if she ever marries, it will only be to someone who is what she calls a 'Mormon elder.' And if that's what she wants, then I'll see that she gets her wish. So I take it you aren't one?"

"Actually, I am. In fact, Nadia and I served church missions in the same place in Russia. Of course, I'm older, and I was there before she was," Jayden explained, not sure why he was offering this much information.

"Well, if it comes to it, you sound like just the sort of fellow she's waiting for. Be good to her, Jayden. She's the best there is," he said with a quiver in his deep voice. "And, Jayden, I mean it. I'll help any way I can to find my daughter. In fact, I think I'll catch a plane to Phoenix in the morning. Nadia probably needs my support."

"You can talk to her about that when she calls you," Jayden said. "She had to hurry to practice, but she'll call. Thanks for your time, sir. I better get to work on finding your daughter."

"Marley!"

"Yes, sir!"

"Just a minute, Jayden, and please, you don't have to call me sir. I think I quite like you."

"Thank you, Marley sir," Jayden quipped.

"Yes, I do like you. You have a sense of humor. I might tell you a little secret. When I've asked Nadia what she's looking for in a husband—after she tried to convince me that she's not looking—she says he has to be at least as tall as her, a Mormon elder, and have a sense of humor. So far, you're two out of three," he said.

"Hey, Marley sir, don't cut me short. I'm six foot six."

"Three for three! I better make sure my little girl realizes that. I really do think you are a fine man."

"Just for my information, Marley, does she also want a man who is not only tall but dark and handsome?" Jayden asked, only partly in jest.

"Not that she's said. Why do you ask?"

"I'm neither dark nor handsome. I'm sort of red-headed and freckled."

"I think she would overlook those things." Marley chuckled. "Now, Jayden, I'm afraid I can't say that her father, Ulisses Fairchild, is a fine man. Far from it, I'm afraid. If he weren't in prison, I'd suggest that he could be the one that caused my daughter to go missing. And he'd probably call me for money to get her back. I think he resented my wealth, even though I didn't inherit one penny of it. I worked for it—but that's a concept he never understood. But since he's an inmate, it couldn't be him."

"Marley, Ulisses is no longer in prison," Jayden revealed. "Layda got a letter from the prison authorities a month ago, informing her that he was to be released on parole in two weeks from the date of the letter. So that being the case, he has been a free man for about two weeks."

"Find *him*, Jayden," Marley said, his voice deep and demanding. "He may well be the key to finding Layda. And I guarantee that if he calls me, I'll let you know. He's a bad character, and he's kidnapped before."

"That's what Nadia told me. I'll try to find his parole officer and go from there. Thanks for your time."

"Don't let me down, Mr. Spalding."

"It's Jayden, Marley sir. I'll do my best."

Jayden hung his phone up and looked up the number for the parole office in Phoenix. Ten minutes later, he was connected with an officer by the name of Desmond Booker. "I'm told you're the parole officer for a recently released inmate by the name of Ulisses Fairchild," Jayden began.

"Yes, sir, I sure am," a booming voice replied. "He was released two weeks ago, and I met with him last week."

"That's good to hear, Mr. Booker. I'm sorry to be calling after hours, disturbing you at home, but it's important that I track him down. When is he supposed to meet with you again?"

"This morning," Booker answered.

"Like in the morning that just passed?" Jayden asked. "Or the one coming up in a few hours?"

"*This* morning. He missed his appointment at ten today," Booker said. "I don't think I caught your name."

"I'm Jayden Spalding. I'm a private investigator here in Phoenix. I specialize in finding missing people," Jayden told him.

"So what's your interest in Ulisses? Surely you aren't looking for him. He's only missed the one appointment, and I expect he might come in tomorrow."

"Actually, I've been retained to find his ex-wife, Layda Fairchild," Jayden explained. "She coaches the women's basketball team at Central Arizona College in Coolidge. She and one of her players left the gymnasium following a game last night. They haven't been seen since."

"Mr. Spalding, this is a major concern to me. Are you aware of why Ulisses was in prison?" Booker asked.

"When I learned that from my client, red flags popped up all over the place," Jayden said.

"As well they should," the officer agreed. "I'll immediately put out a BOLO for him. And I can also get a warrant for his arrest just for missing his appointment."

Jayden didn't need to have the acronym explained. A BOLO was a request for all officers to be on the lookout for a person. That and an arrest warrant were, under the circumstances, the best he could ask for. "Do you have an address for him?" Jayden asked.

"He was living in a homeless shelter but promised that he'd have an address by the time he came in today. You know how that turned out," Officer Booker said.

"Do you have an address for the homeless shelter?"

Officer Booker said, "Not here at my home, but I do at the office. I think I'll go in now and find it so I can have an officer check the shelter tonight."

"That's great," Jayden said. "Will you let me know the address too? And if someone locates him, I'd like a call no matter what time it is."

"I'll see that it happens. Give me your number, Detective," Officer Booker requested.

"Oh, and one more thing," Jayden said after giving him his cell phone number and the number to his office. "Do you have a picture of Ulisses?"

"That I do. Would you like me to send it to you? I could fax, e-mail, or text it. Isn't it great, all the tools we have nowadays?" The man chuckled.

"It sure is. Trouble is, guys like Ulisses benefit from all the technology as well. Luckily though, a lot of them aren't smart enough to use it."

"I think Ulisses is a smart man. Anyway, I'll get what you need. Of course, you'll have to wait until I get to my office, but I'll hurry. It won't take too long."

"A text when you can get to it would be fine," Jayden said.

"I'll do that then. I'll get on it as soon as I put the BOLO out."

Jayden looked at the clock on his office wall. It was almost eight o'clock. He wanted to drive to Coolidge, which was only about a forty-five minute drive, but by the time he got to the college, it would probably be too late to speak to the people he wanted to there. So instead, he booted up his computer and began a search. He wanted to get as much done as he could tonight. He hated to admit it, but this client was one he wanted to impress, juvenile though that might be.

One can learn a lot if he or she knows how to use the vast recourses of the Internet world, and that was something Jayden was an expert at. His first search would be to learn what he could about Layda's ball player, Naylyn Pierza. He spent fifteen minutes and found only the most basic information. She was from Oakland, California, was twenty years old, and played basketball for Central Arizona College. The only new information was about Oakland, but he had been unable to find anything more.

He wasn't ready to give up though, so he tried Facebook. Naylyn didn't have an account. The same thing was true of Twitter. That seemed strange. It was highly unusual for young women in this day and age.

Jayden next looked up the team roster. He searched each of the girl's names on Facebook and found a profile on all of them. That added to the mystery of Naylyn not having one. He even found one for Layda. When he looked at the girls' lists of friends, most of them included each other, but Naylyn's name did not appear anywhere. He did find pictures of her on some of the other girls' pages, but they were only in group pictures. There was none of her alone.

He copied and printed several of them. Then he cut out just her and enlarged the pictures on his copy machine. He studied her face. Just like Nadia had told him, she was a beautiful girl with short, light-brown hair and dark eyes. Now that he knew what she looked like, he wasn't likely to forget it.

He sat and thought for a minute. He looked at the time again. It was well past ten. He decided to try one more thing before heading for bed. He created a fake profile for a tall, dark young man, single and eager to meet young women, especially tall ones. He added a few pictures of his fictitious person in different poses, all of which would likely be alluring to young women. He added a couple of friends to the profile. He indicated that he was from Phoenix and then sent out friend requests to every member of the team. *It may be a waste of time, but you never know*, he thought. It was worth a try. If someone accepted his friend request, he would mention the coach, say that she was his aunt and that he was trying to get in touch with her. At the last minute, he decided to add an e-mail address. He spent several more minutes creating his fictional character an e-mail account. He added the address to his phone and computer.

That done, he logged off of the computer, shut the lights off, and headed to his Hummer. Bullet jumped in, and then Jayden did the same. He hadn't gone but a few blocks when he received a ding on his phone telling him he had a new e-mail. He pulled to the side of the road. The new one was to his fake account and was from one of Naylyn's teammates. The girl's name was Lorena Husman. She had accepted his friend request, but she'd used the e-mail address to type a short, terse message. It read: *Who knows where sweet Coach Fairchild is at, and who cares? I'm no longer on the team. She cut me two days ago even though I'm the best player she had. The witch. She'll wish she'd kept me on.*

It was chilling and not something to be overlooked. Even though he was anxious to get some sleep so that he could get an early start the next day, he decided to learn more about Miss Husman. This could be murder, not a kidnapping. The thought made his blood run cold.

Jayden pulled into his garage, shut the Hummer off, and sat there for a moment, as he often did. He had a nice house, but it was bigger than he needed and carried memories that haunted him. A wave of sadness rolled over him. The house had been a wedding present for his wife. She'd helped him pick it out before they were married. They spent the night of their wedding there then left for their honeymoon. When he came back, he came back alone. He'd lost her in an accident. She'd been hit by a truck as she'd stepped out ahead of him to cross a street. She'd been laughing, walking backward, teasing him. The look of horror on her face when she saw the truck a millisecond before it struck her would haunt him the rest of his life, as would the sight of her being thrown high into the air, finally landing on the hard pavement, her body twisted, bleeding, and broken.

Even though their time in this house had been so short, he still felt her presence there. Her artistic touch lingered in every room. He hadn't changed a thing in those past two years. Several times he'd almost listed the house for sale, but when it got right down to it, he couldn't do that. She was a part of this house. Whenever he came home, it was her that he thought about.

He finally opened the door of his Hummer and tried to brush the tragic memories aside as he stepped out. He walked straight to his computer in a nook at the far side of the large living room. He booted it up and went to Facebook, where he opened Lorena's page and began to study it. She had indeed been a team member until just a few days before. She ranted long and explicitly about her discharge from the team. She particularly railed about what a bad coach Layda was. She also mentioned Naylyn.

Jayden didn't learn anything more about Naylyn's background from Lorena's page, but he did learn that the two did not like each other. She referred to Naylyn as the coach's pet and as *the girl from nowhere.* He made a few notes, and then he continued on down her page. She had pictures of a man who Lorena called her boyfriend.

His name was Davon Karp, and the pictures showed a man who was not handsome by any stretch of the imagination. He had a round face with bulging blue eyes; dark-brown hair in a short ponytail; bushy, brown eyebrows; a long, slightly crooked nose; and several scars. He was clearly a tall man. Jayden didn't like the look on the man's face in many of the pictures. The pictures of him with Lorena were the only ones where he could see a spark of humanity.

He switched to Davon's Facebook page and took in a deep breath at what he saw there.

CHAPTER THREE

Davon Karp was a twenty-six-year-old ex-con. He bragged about his time in prison right there on his profile. It didn't mention what he'd been in prison for, but it did say that he was currently a welder, and it gave the name of the place where he was employed. It was in Coolidge. Jayden added the address to the list of visits he had to make in the morning.

Jayden got up and walked around his house for a moment in an attempt to shake off the exhaustion. Bullet watched from the spot where he was laying just beyond the opening to the nook. He didn't put his face back between his paws until Jayden had popped open a can of Sprite, reentered the nook, and sat back down at his computer.

He opened another Internet site he was familiar with and soon learned that Davon Karp had a long, violent history. Among his criminal skills were those of being a burglar, a drug dealer, and a frequent brawler. He had two DUIs and several drug-possession convictions along with a couple of felony convictions for selling drugs. He'd done time for his third conviction for distribution of illegal drugs. His time in prison had been while Ulisses was there. Jayden didn't have any way tonight of learning if the two had known each other. He could look into that later. Davon had been paroled about a year ago. Another call to the state parole office was added to his growing agenda for the next day.

Jayden checked his e-mails once more but found nothing in response to the profile he'd put up earlier. Then, on an impulse, he looked up Nadia's Facebook page. The pictures he found there cheered him up. There was something about her . . . After studying them for a minute or two, he sent her a friend request. Thoughts of his late wife made him feel guilty, but with an effort, he shrugged the feeling off. He had to allow himself to get on with his life.

He put his computer to sleep and let Bullet out into the large backyard to attend to his business. After Bullet came back in, Jayden set his alarm, double-checked all the doors to see that they were locked, and headed up to his bedroom.

He was only about halfway up the stairs when he noticed that Bullet hadn't followed. He went down the stairs and called for the dog. He heard a low growl from the area of his front door. His hand went to the butt of his 9mm and his eyes to a monitor above the door that was fed by the camera outside.

Bullet acted this way if a stranger approached. The figures Jayden watched on the screen were just a few yards from his door, and both men were strangers. But they were not dressed like criminals. Dark suits, shiny black shoes, conservative ties, and a slight bulge beneath their shoulders gave them away. Why would the FBI be coming to his house, especially so late at night?

One of them rang the doorbell as Jayden watched them on the monitor. He didn't answer the door right away. He let one of them shout, "FBI. Open up."

Still he waited. For all they knew, they were getting him out of bed, and he wanted to see some proof that they were who they claimed. Bullet, beside him, continued to growl until Jayden put a hand on his head and softly said, "Stand down, Bullet."

The big dog immediately ceased the low-throated growl, but his eyes continued to focus on the door, and his body was as tight as a spring. Finally, one of the agents knocked on the door and again ordered it opened. Jayden's system was state of the art. He stepped to the wall, pressed a button, and spoke into a small speaker mounted there. "Let's see some credentials," he said.

One of the men pulled out his shield and shoved it up toward the camera, which he had just spotted. The other pulled a gun from beneath his coat. The shield looked authentic. So did the handgun. Still, Jayden decided to be cautious. He spoke into the speaker again. "Your names, gentlemen?"

"Hey, enough with the games," the officer with the weapon in his hand said. "Just open up, and do it now."

"Your names, please," Jayden insisted.

The two looked at each other, and then the taller and older of the pair, the one who had been knocking, said, "Special Agent Colten Andrews."

He then glanced at the other one on his monitor who said, "Special Agent Duncan Press."

"Thank you. You can put the weapon away, Agent Press, and then I'll open the door," Jayden said, getting more curious and, frankly, more worried about the presence of the two special agents.

The shorter man put the pistol back beneath his suit jacket, but Jayden didn't push the open button until the agent had withdrawn his hand. Then there were a series of clicks, and the door slowly began to swing open on its own, humming softly. "Come on in, gentlemen," Jayden said. "It's nice of you to come and check on my well-being. I'm honored, and as you can see, I'm fine, so you won't need to stay."

Before even coming through the door, the younger, more aggressive agent said, "You can cut the cute stuff, Spalding."

Agent Andrews entered first, looking cautiously at Jayden, and then his younger partner slid in beside him. "What's with the firearm?" Agent Press asked as his hand went back into his jacket and his eyes settled on Jayden's 9mm.

"It's licensed," Jayden said as he again punched a button and the door silently closed. "Since you seem to need to do something besides check on my welfare, maybe you can tell me what I can do for you at this ridiculously late hour?"

"I said to cut the cute stuff," Special Agent Press reminded him with a glare.

When Jayden made no comment, Special Agent Andrews said, "Pretty sophisticated system you have here."

"A guy can't be too careful. Would you like to sit down, or is what you have to say brief?"

"We'll sit," Andrews answered. Both men kept glancing at Bullet, whose eyes shifted continuously from one officer to the other.

"He won't attack unless I tell him to," Jayden said blandly. "Of course, if someone makes a threatening move, he won't wait for my signal. He'll just go for the jugular. Would either of you care for a soda or a drink of water?"

"We're fine," Agent Andrews answered for both of them. Press's face was dark, displaying narrowly restrained anger. As soon as the three men were seated, Agent Andrews said, "Tell us about Naylyn Pierza."

"What about her?" Jayden asked, puzzled. That wasn't what he'd expected. Of course, he hadn't really known what to expect.

"You were exploring several pages on Facebook in which she was pictured," Agent Press said darkly.

"What are you guys talking about?" Jayden began to put it together in his mind. Her name must be closely monitored for some reason. They must have been notified and made it here in record time.

"You know exactly what we're talking about. What is your interest in her and in Lorena Husman?" Special Agent Andrews asked.

Jayden decided it was time to let them know who he was. "My credentials are in my computer nook. I'll get them if you'd like. But I'm a licensed private investigator. I specialize in searching for missing persons."

"But why those two?" Special Agent Andrews asked.

"I've been hired to locate a woman by the name of Layda Fairchild, who came up missing last night."

"Coach Fairchild?" Press asked.

"That's right. As it happens, Miss Pierza was with her when she was last seen, and neither woman has been seen since. My job is to find them."

The two men exchanged glances laced with suspicion. Then Special Agent Andrews asked, "Who hired you?"

Jayden shook his head and smiled. "You know I won't tell you that."

"Let me guess," Special Agent Press said. "It would be Miss Lorena Husman. Why would she care about Coach Fairchild?"

"You two seem to know quite a bit about the ladies we are discussing. And if so, then you must know that Miss Husman wouldn't care one whit if something happened to Miss Pierza or the coach," Jayden said.

"Perhaps you need to come with us," Special Agent Press said darkly. "Your interest in Miss Pierza is not warranted."

Jayden narrowed his eyes and looked first at Press and then at Andrews and back at Press again. "I don't think so, gentlemen. I don't have time for your games. I have a missing woman to find. If Miss Pierza is with her when I locate her, then I'll certainly let you know if you'd like. But you both know you have nothing to take me in on. I'm licensed and acting within the scope of my authority."

"I think we do," Special Agent Press said.

Jayden glared at him. The agent looked like he was about five ten and was probably a couple of years younger than Jayden. The other officer was probably ten or twelve years older and about six feet. Press stood up, and so did Jayden. He towered over the FBI agent. Bullet, the shortest one in the room but probably the most lethal, rose from his place on the carpet and stepped between Jayden and Special Agent Press. A low growl rumbled from his throat, catching the full attention of the officer.

Special Agent Andrews also stood.

"I'll show you gentlemen to the door. I think we're finished here." Jayden's words came out much more calmly than he felt.

Andrews shook his head. "I think we need to calm down and back up a step here." He looked at his partner. "We don't need to go to the office to speak with Detective Spalding. Let's just sit down and figure this thing out."

Jayden was getting very irritated. "What's to figure out? I've told you all I know about Naylyn Pierza. I was looking on Facebook in an attempt to turn up clues to her whereabouts and by extension to Coach Fairchild's location. You see, if I find one, I have reason to believe that I'll also find the other. It's as simple as that. My main interest is in Coach Fairchild."

"Let's sit down," Special Agent Andrews said again. "I think your dog would like that."

"He does get rather protective," Jayden said. "And frankly, I don't think he trusts the two of you, so it would be wise not to raise your voices. He might take it wrong."

"You're a big man," Andrews noted. "I suspect you're capable of taking care of yourself."

"That's right, far better than you know. But if you insist, then I agree. We should sit." Jayden looked at his German shepherd and said, "Stand down, Bullet."

The growl instantly ceased, and the dog plopped back down on the carpet, but not for one instant did his attention stray from the two FBI agents. Once all three men were again seated, Jayden said, "I think you should tell me what your interest in Miss Pierza is. You knew she was missing before you ever came here, didn't you? You thought you'd come here and find her in my house? I assure you she isn't here. You may look around if you like."

The chip on Special Agent Press's shoulder was still firmly in place. "Yes, I think we should."

"No, I don't think so," Andrews said to the younger agent. Then he addressed Jayden. "We didn't know for sure that she was missing, but we suspected as much. That's why we came."

"Now you know what my interest is, what's your interest in her?" Jayden asked.

"That's none of your business," Special Agent Press said.

Jayden felt heat developing beneath his collar. "I am searching for Coach Fairchild. I have every reason to believe she was kidnapped. If Miss Pierza is someone you are interested in, then it makes me wonder if she's the one who took the coach. If she's a dangerous person, I'd like to know."

"Suffice it to say that we need to speak to her," Special Agent Andrews said firmly, once again looking at his partner with a scowl.

"Her background is very lean," Jayden said. "I think you two know a lot about her, and you really ought to level with me. I don't like going into a situation blind."

"You don't need to worry about her," Special Agent Andrews assured him. "If she's been kidnapped, then that becomes the jurisdiction of the FBI. But no one has reported a kidnapping of either her or Coach Fairchild. You need to give us the name of the person who hired you. That person should have reported it."

"That person doesn't know for sure that anyone has been kidnapped either. That person only knows that Coach Fairchild is missing and that she was last seen with Miss Pierza. You both know that when someone comes up missing, no police department in the country will do anything about it until twenty-four hours has passed. That is about now," Jayden said.

"But you think they were kidnapped," Special Agent Press said, his green eyes fiery. "Maybe you would at least tell us why you think that."

Jayden forced a smile. "I'd be glad to." But before he got another word out, his cell phone rang. He jerked it from his pocket and looked at the screen. It was Nadia's number. "I have to take this," he said. "I'll fill you in on what my thoughts are in a moment."

He stepped from the room and went into his kitchen as his phone continued to ring. He finally accepted the call and said, "Nadia, is something wrong?"

"Yes," she said, tears in her voice. "I'm sorry I woke you up."

"You didn't wake me," he said. "I have guests. Tell me what happened."

"It's my father." Her voice began to tremble.

"What about your father?" Jayden asked as his nerves came to attention.

"He called me a minute ago. I thought that I had developed at least a little bit of a relationship with him by visiting him in prison," she said. "But I guess Mom's right. He's a really bad man."

"Nadia, calm down and tell me what he said," Jayden instructed her gently. At that moment, Special Agents Press and Andrews appeared in the doorway to the kitchen. "Gentlemen, this is a private conversation," he growled. "Please go back to the living room."

Agent Press said, "I don't think so. You're hiding something, and you better come clean."

"Which I will, but I have a client on the phone right now, so please, let me finish this conversation."

Special Agent Andrews took hold of his partner's arm. "Come on, Duncan. Let's give him a minute."

"Jayden, what's happening there? Who is with you?" Nadia asked in the phone.

"Two FBI agents. But my conversation with you is none of their business," he said as the agents finally retreated. "Okay, they went back in the other room. So what did your father say?"

"Why are they there, Jayden? Is it about my mother? Do they know she's been kidnapped?"

"They came here because they somehow figured out that I was doing some checking on the girl that was with your mother. I'd been on Facebook trying to learn as much as I could about the team. They had no business coming, and I'm not sure what they want. But about your father," Jayden insisted.

"He threatened me," she said. "He says his parole officer is angry with him because I told the officer some lies and now he's got the police looking for my father."

"Nadia, that makes no sense at all."

"Yeah, I know. I don't even know who his parole agent is, and I frankly don't care. Dad told me that if I didn't call the agent back and retract my lies that he'd come to my place and kick the—well, you get the picture. Jayden, he sounded really angry. He scared me."

"What did you tell him?" Jayden's nerves slowly relaxed from attention to parade rest.

"That I didn't know what he was talking about. He called me a liar. What do you think is happening?" she asked, fear evident in her voice.

"I don't know for sure, but I could guess," Jayden said. "I talked to his parole officer, and your dad didn't show up this morning to his appointment, so the officer was going to get an arrest warrant in the morning. But he already put a statewide bulletin out for officers to be looking for

Ulisses, and if they see him, they're to detain him. The parole officer has the authority, even without a warrant, to put a seventy-two-hour hold on your dad for not complying with the terms of his parole. So I'm wondering if he somehow learned that he's being looked for and is blaming you instead of me."

"Maybe," she said. "But I'm paying you, so in a way, he's right. What can I do?"

"I'll call Booker and see if he'll have the cops sit outside your place. I'm quite sure he will, and if your dad shows up there, he'll be arrested. So keep your door locked, and call me if you need to. And I mean call anytime, Nadia. Don't worry about waking me up."

"Okay, thanks. Just talking to you helps more than you know. I'm so glad you're helping me."

"So am I. All right, I need to finish with the FBI right now," Jayden said.

"Jayden, do they know it's me you're talking to?"

"No, they keep telling me that I need to tell them who hired me to find your mother. But that is none of their business."

"Maybe I should talk to them," she said. "I don't want them mad at you."

"I can handle it, Nadia," he said. "I'm a big boy."

"I know that, but I still think I should. Maybe they can help."

"I was just about to tell them about what I've learned so far, but I'm going to keep your name out of it. They must know they're both missing. And for some reason that I don't understand, they are very interested in Naylyn," he explained. "I've been on the Internet most of the time since you left my office. I can't find much about her beyond the little bit you told me."

"I'll talk to one of them," she said.

"If you're sure," Jayden replied. "You don't have to."

"I'm sure," she said.

Jayden stepped into the living room. "The girl on the phone is the daughter of Coach Fairchild. She wants to talk to one of you. But be gentle with her. She's going through a tough time."

Jayden gave the phone to Special Agent Andrews, the calmer of the two. Andrews took it and spoke into it.

Jayden sat down and listened to half of the ensuing conversation. Special Agent Andrews seemed very interested in what Nadia had to say.

From the half of the conversation Jayden could hear, it appeared that the agent would have questions for him when he finished talking to Nadia. He was right.

When the call was over, Andrews said, "I suppose you were going to tell us about your client's father."

"I was, but there's more that I can tell you than what Nadia was able to."

"You could have told us about her before," Agent Press said as he ran a hand through his short red hair.

"Not without her permission, I couldn't," Jayden said.

Special Agent Andrews broke in, "Miss Fairchild told me that her father, who only got out of prison two weeks ago, called and threatened her. She didn't tell me why he was in prison or how long he'd been there. She said you could tell us about that."

"He'd been in prison since she was six, and she's twenty-four now. You do the math," Jayden said.

"Eighteen years," Press said.

"Very good," Jayden said snidely and then wished he hadn't. It was just that the agent was really pushing his buttons.

"Tell us what he did to wind up in prison for that long," Special Agent Andrews asked, even as he gave his partner a *let me handle this* look.

"Ulisses Fairchild is a kidnapper," Jayden said.

Both agents nodded knowingly, but they hadn't been able to keep the surprise from their eyes.

CHAPTER FOUR

THE APARTMENT WAS QUIET, BUT Nadia Fairchild could not fall asleep. She couldn't shake her father's angry, threatening words from her mind. It frustrated her because she had reached out to him in prison and thought that they had developed a relationship. But his phone call that night had validated her mother's warnings. Ulisses was a rotten and dangerous man. Thankfully, officers had been positioned outside the apartment to intercept him if he came looking for her, and that gave her a measure of comfort.

Nadia tossed and turned. Finally, she lay still, willing herself to fall asleep. She was finally succumbing when a noise brought her upright in bed, her heart pounding. She tried to isolate the source of the sound. Then she heard it again. Someone was jiggling the doorknob of her apartment! *My father!* Fear surged through her. He must have gotten past the officers. She prayed that he hadn't hurt them. She had to find a way to protect herself in case he managed to get through the door and into her apartment.

She slipped as quietly as she could from her bed, dressed only in a pair of pajamas. She considered putting her robe on, but just then, someone pounded on the door. Where had she left her purse? There was a small canister of Mace in there that her mother had encouraged her to carry. Would it even work? She'd had it for over a year and never tried it. But where was her purse? She silently prayed that God would protect her.

She panicked as the pounding increased. Maybe she should grab a kitchen knife, a long one. She stumbled into the kitchen and turned on the light; there on the counter was her purse. Frantically, she opened it, dumped the contents on the counter, and quickly located the little canister. Should she grab a knife too? But she didn't want to stab her own father. Perhaps she could talk sense into him, and if she failed, she'd use the Mace.

She turned and left the kitchen when the door suddenly gave way and slammed inward against the wall. Splintered wood flew across the room. Her panic increased and thoughts raced through her mind at the speed of light. But before she could do anything—like flee to a closet to hide—a voice called her name, "Nadia, I see I found you." *It wasn't her father's voice.*

A man a little shorter than she with a nylon stocking pulled over his head advanced toward her. She kept her right fist closed tightly, gripping the little Mace canister. When should she use it? How close did he need to get before it would be effective?

She backed away, toward the kitchen door. He slowly continued closer. "Nadia, your father sent me to get you. You will need to come with me. You can make this easy, or you can make it hard. He said that I was not to hurt you unless you resisted."

She slowly shook her head. "Who are you?"

"*A family friend*," he said in a voice that was both sinister and cold.

"Please go. Dad can call me if he wants to see me," she said, her voice so shaky that she wasn't sure he could even understand her.

She bumped into the edge of the kitchen doorway, and it spun her to the side. The man lunged and caught her by her left arm. He jerked her back into the center of the room. She tried to get the hand with the Mace up. But suddenly, he struck her in the face. She fell to the floor, and the canister fell from her hand. Then he was on top of her with a growl.

Nadia was in great shape. She was wiry and strong. She fought back. She clawed at her attacker's eyes as he pulled her to her feet. She kicked him in the shin, but nothing seemed to affect him. Even though he was shorter, he was fast and strong. He jerked her close and threw both hands around her. She struggled and screamed. His face came close to hers, and she bit him. His nose tasted like blood as she clamped her mouth closed with all the force she could muster. He screamed and shoved her back. Flesh came loose along with part of the stocking. She spit it out as she fell to the floor.

He lunged again, howling in rage and bleeding profusely. She scrambled backward like a crab and spotted the Mace. She reached for it and managed to close her hands around it even though he punched her in the face again, shooting pain up her head and down her spine. She swung her arm around, hoping she was close enough to be effective, and pushed the button. A mist sprayed out, and her attacker howled even louder. He stood up, frantically rubbing at his eyes through the nylon. She jumped to her feet, closed in on him, and sprayed again. He tried with both hands to ward off the spray, but she was determined now, and she held the button down.

Finally, he turned and lunged for the busted door, but he was at least partially blinded and he ran into what was left of the doorjamb. As he began to fall, she eyed the opening, intent to rush past him. Her own eyes were stinging from the Mace, and her vision was blurred. Determined, she blinked, found the opening, and lunged toward it. She bumped into someone who threw his arms around her.

"It's okay; I'm a police officer," the man said as she struggled in his grasp.

A second person shoved past them, and she was freed from the first officer's grasp. She could make out, through her blurry eyes, the second officer struggling to subdue her attacker. But with manic force, the intruder broke loose and plunged outside. The two officers collided with each other as they attempted to go after him. By the time they had regained their feet, the attacker was nearly to the street.

Despite the stocking over his head, the man's vision had to have been affected, but it appeared that he could see well enough to run to the street. A car pulled up and stopped. The driver leaped out, grabbed him, opened the back door, and shoved her attacker inside. A second later the driver was back in his seat and the car roared down the street. One of the officers reached the car in time to grab the rear door handle, but the car's motion threw him free, and he rolled onto the pavement, again tripping his partner.

They both got up and pulled their pistols, but by then, the getaway car was turning into a side street. A second later it was out of sight. Both officers began to talk into the radio mics on their lapels as they walked back toward her. She was still standing in the doorway, trembling. "Sorry, miss. He got away. But he had help," one of them said. "I'm Officer Mills, and this is Officer Callahan. Are you hurt?"

"I'm okay," she said despite the pain that was shooting through her left arm and face—the whole thing. "My eyes are a little blurry," was all she admitted.

Officer Callahan chuckled. "I think that guy's eyes are more blurry than yours. And there was blood pouring down his face. What did you do to him?"

"I bit him. And then I sprayed him with Mace. I'll need to get a new can. I think I emptied this one." She held it up and showed the officers.

"You need to sit down. An ambulance is coming. You need to be checked out," Officer Mills said. She did. Officer Callahan disappeared into the kitchen as he said over his shoulder, "I'll see if I can find a wet cloth for your eyes."

Officer Mills said, "I'm sorry the guy got past us. We were looking for a black man who was six eight and around three hundred pounds. This guy wasn't even close to that. A few people were coming and going, and this guy didn't appear to be any different than the rest.

"We came as soon as we discovered there was a problem. I'm sorry we were so slow," Mills continued. "But it looks like you handled yourself well. You are Nadia, aren't you?"

"That's me," she said as she accepted a cold, wet dishtowel from Officer Callahan. She wiped her tender face with it and then concentrated on her eyes. Sirens blared in the distance.

"Backup and an ambulance," Mills explained.

"I'm okay. Just a few bruises," Nadia said. "I don't need an ambulance."

"We'll let the paramedics decide that," he said firmly.

"My cell phone is beside my bed. I need to go get it. I have a call to make," she said.

"We'll find it. You just sit still. You could be going into shock," Officer Mills said.

"I'll get it," his partner said and walked briskly away. He returned a moment later. "This it, Nadia?" he asked as she reached for it. He was also carrying her robe. "I found this on a chair by your bed."

"Thanks," she said, for the first time remembering that she was dressed only in her pajamas. She laid the phone down and shrugged on the robe. She tied it and once again sat and took her phone in her hand.

At that moment, Officer Mills stepped beside the sofa, where she was sitting. "I found this." In a gloved hand, he held a bloody piece of nylon sock along with a bloody piece of flesh. "You bit the end of his nose off," the officer said.

Nadia glanced at the bloody mess he held in his hand. Dropping the phone on the sofa, she threw a hand over her mouth and fled for her bathroom, where she threw up. She heaved and heaved until her throat burned and her head pounded. She finally stood and rinsed her mouth out with water a half dozen times. Then she brushed her teeth and finally rinsed with mouthwash. As she turned to leave the bathroom, she shuddered at the horror of what she'd done: *bit the end of a man's nose off.*

By the time she'd returned to her living room, it was swarming with officers and paramedics. They wanted to begin checking her out, but she shooed them back as she walked on unsteady feet to the sofa. "I need to make a call first." She began to punch at her phone. "Then you can examine me, but I'm sure I don't need to go to the hospital."

***

Jayden felt like he'd only been asleep for a short time when his phone woke him up. The FBI agents hadn't left until well past one. As he felt for his phone on his bedside table, he saw his clock. It was two thirty. He was still groggy, and when he finally found his phone, he answered, still half asleep, without looking at who the caller was.

"Jayden, it's Nadia," the voice on the phone said. He was instantly awake. "I need you," she continued.

"I'll be there as quickly as I can." He swung his legs out of bed. "Give me your address again."He memorized her response and reached for the pants that were hanging on the back of the bedroom door. "What happened?" he asked.

"I was attacked," she said tearfully.

"Call 911. I'm on my way."

"The cops are already here. So are some paramedics."

He shrugged into his pants one-handed and reached for a shirt. "Are you hurt?"

"I'll be okay. They want to take me to the hospital. But I don't need that."

"If you're hurt, you better let them take you, but let me know if they do, and I'll come there instead of your apartment." He was clumsily buttoning his shirt as he spoke.

"I'm okay," she said again.

"Call me if they don't agree with you," he said and ended the call.

Jayden put on some shoes, slipped his 9mm into a shoulder holster, and shrugged it on. Then he grabbed a jacket and threw it on as he ran out the door. He jumped in his Hummer seconds after Bullet did, pushed the button to open the garage door, and backed out. He left the door lowering as he sped up the street. He'd helped a lot of people who were in trouble, but for some reason, the attack on Nadia felt personal.

He shrugged the feeling away. She was a client who needed his help. He kept expecting another call from her, telling him that she was going in the ambulance, but the call never came. It took him twenty minutes, driving insanely fast, to get from his apartment to hers. He slid the Hummer to a stop behind a line of police cars, their lights flashing. He leaped out and ran toward the apartment where a badly damaged door was hanging open. There were uniformed officers just outside the door, and light was flooding out.

He and Bullet ran up the sidewalk and past the officers. The moment he entered, Jayden spotted Nadia on a sofa three-quarters of the way across a medium-sized living room. She leaped up and flew to him, throwing her arms around him, sobbing.

"It's okay, Nadia. You look like you're fine," he said as he held her tight. That was a lie. She was bruised and covered with blood.

"Oh, Jayden, I was so scared. Dad sent him to get me," she said, her head tucked against his chest.

"How do you know that?" he asked.

"He told me my father wanted me to go with him," she said. "But I didn't dare. He was wearing a nylon sock over his head. He looked creepy. He said if I came peacefully, he wouldn't hurt me."

"I take it you didn't go peacefully." Jayden offered a tight smile as he gently pushed her back and looked down into her glistening, dark-brown eyes.

"I couldn't. I knew that if I did, I'd be in more trouble than if I resisted."

"Remind me to never make you angry," Jayden said with a chuckle. "You are one tough lady."

"I don't feel tough. I used all my Mace. I need more Mace," she said, her voice cracking.

"I'll take care of that for you. I carry spare Mace in my Hummer. I sometimes have clients who need it."

"I needed it." She fought back a sob.

"You must have made good use of it."

"Oh! My purse!" she suddenly exclaimed. "I dumped it out in the kitchen when I was trying to find my Mace."

"I can help with that. I'll gather stuff up and put it back in. When I get through, your purse will be lighter."

"What? How?" she asked.

"I'll get rid of the stuff you don't need," he said with a straight face.

Finally, she smiled. "Oh, no you won't, mister. That's valuable stuff."

He chuckled. "I'll just help you then."

"Thanks, Jayden. I know what you're doing. You're trying to cheer me up—and it's working."

An officer in his midtwenties stepped over. "My name is Officer Mills. I take it your dog is safe."

"Only when I tell him to be," Jayden quipped.

"Pretty dog. Officer Callahan and I were outside watching for her father. This guy said he lived in the apartments. He wasn't the first. A few people were coming and going. He was under six feet tall, and he was Caucasian. So I never gave it a second thought and let him go by. We didn't realize there was a problem until your girlfriend started screaming."

"She's not my girlfriend," he said. "She's my client—but also a friend. I'm a private investigator."

"Sorry, my mistake," the officer said with a chuckle, but the look on his face told Jayden that he didn't believe him about her not being a *girlfriend.*

Jayden realized that the way they were holding each other, it would be an easy mistake to make. He stepped back until they were no longer touching. "So what was happening when you got to her door?" Jayden asked.

Officer Mills, joined by Officer Callahan, gave a quick report.

Nadia piped up, "I was so glad to see them, but I'm afraid I wasn't very nice to Officer Mills. He grabbed me, and my mind told me he was another attacker." She turned to Mills. "I'm sorry. I hope I didn't hurt you."

He grinned. "I'm sure I have a bruised shin. Even barefoot, you have a wicked kick."

"Just be glad she didn't elbow you," Jayden said, his face very serious. "She plays for the Phoenix Mercury, and I understand she has a wicked elbow. Just ask the ladies she plays against."

His attempt at humor worked again. Nadia began to chuckle, and it sounded good to him. She punched him playfully on his shoulder. "I do not elbow other girls . . . very much. Maybe when they get in my face."

"Careful," he teased. "I bruise easily."

She laughed some more. "Yeah, I bet." With a smile still on her bruised face, she turned to the officers. "He's got a black belt."

"Actually, I'm wearing my brown one this morning," he said with a straight face. "But I have a black one you can borrow if you'd like."

He got punched again.

"Careful, I know karate," he warned her.

"That's what I was just trying to say," she retorted lightly.

Jayden was examining her face closely as they ribbed back and forth. He stepped toward her and touched a red spot that was turning dark. "You're going to have some bruises, Nadia. How many times did the creep hit you?"

"I didn't count," she said. "I was too busy trying to fight back."

"Next time, try to keep track," he quipped.

"Let's sit down. I'm feeling a little dizzy."

"You need to be checked out at the emergency room, Nadia." Jayden was more worried about her than he had been about anyone for a long time. He went to the sofa and sat down with her.

"Thanks for coming," she said, sounding more like a girlfriend than a brand-new client.

Nadia recited what had happened as closely as she could recall. She'd already told the officers and repeated it when their supervisor got there. When she finished, Jayden said, "Describe your attacker the best you can."

Officer Mills had wandered over and heard the last question. "He had a nylon sock pulled over his head, but Nadia didn't tell you she bit the end of his nose off. We found it after he got away, and we'll keep it as evidence."

"I threw up," she said, "and cleaned my mouth out." She wrinkled her nose in disgust. "It was nasty, but I think it gave me the upper hand."

"You fight dirty." He chuckled. "I'm glad I don't play ball against you."

That got him a third punch. "If you don't behave, you'll be as bruised as I am."

"Like I was just saying . . ." He smiled at her. "Now, describe him to me."

She'd already been over all this before as well, but she said, "Caucasian. He wasn't heavy, and he was three or four inches shorter than me. But he was strong. He was wearing a tan shirt and tan pants. I didn't notice his shoes."

"They were bloody," Jayden said matter-of-factly. "There's blood all over you and all over your floor. He had to have gotten some on his feet." She lifted a fist, and he grabbed it. "That'll do. We don't want these cops to haul you off to jail for assaulting me, now do we?"

"I guess not," she said.

He wrote down the description she'd given him then put his notebook in a jacket pocket and pulled out his phone. "It's my turn to wake someone up." He punched in a number on his cell phone, and while it rang, he said, "We need to find you a place to stay. Why don't you get some things together." And to the officers, he said, "Maybe someone could start checking emergency rooms in case our man shows up seeking medical help."

His phone continued to ring. "I'll get your purse together while you pack."

"You aren't touching my purse," she said in mock ferocity as he helped her to her feet, holding the phone to his ear.

CHAPTER FIVE

Parole Officer Desmond Booker was sound asleep when his phone woke him up. He slipped out of bed—trying not to disturb his wife—grabbed his glasses, and hurried out of the bedroom as it continued to ring. He answered the phone while at the same time turning on the hallway light. "This is Booker."

"I'm sorry to disturb you, but this is Detective Jayden Spalding," he heard the PI say.

"Has my parolee turned up?" he asked hopefully.

"I'm afraid not, but someone who claimed to be a friend of his visited his daughter a while ago," the PI said.

"Is she okay?" Booker asked.

"She'll be all right. He attacked and beat her, but she's a scrappy gal. He got away, but he won't be smelling too well for a while. She bit the end of the guy's nose off right through the nylon sock he was wearing."

"And he mentioned Ulisses?" Booker asked.

"Yes, he was supposed to take her to her father," the PI reported. "I'm thinking that he wanted to use her to get money from her grandfather, but I don't know for sure. Do you know who any of Ulisses's associates are or if he has any former cellmates who are out on parole that might be willing to help him?" Jayden asked.

"So she didn't get a good look at him?" Booker asked.

"We know he is Caucasian and maybe five ten or eleven. The officers that also briefly had an altercation with him before he escaped in a getaway car said he was probably late twenties to early thirties."

"Did any of them get a look at the driver of the getaway car?"

"Just a second, let me ask."

Booker could hear mumbling in the background, and then Jayden came back on the phone.

"Okay, they saw him as he got out of the car and shoved the attacker in. The officers were in pursuit. They could only say that the driver was very big. They're pretty sure his hair was black and quite long. Nadia sprayed her attacker with Mace and got some in her own eyes, so she couldn't see well, but she was also sure the driver was big."

"Probably Fairchild. Can you give me a few minutes? I'll call you back as soon as I see if I can find something," Booker said. He again wished he was in his office, but he already had a thought niggling in his mind. He did have a list of his entire current case load there at home. He went into his study and found the list. He was overloaded, as most officers were, so it was a longer list than he would have liked. He ran his finger down the names and stopped on one. Lester Skiles. He remembered Lester. He'd been part of Booker's caseload for about two and a half months, and he'd been paroled from the same prison as Ulisses. It might be a stretch, but he had a thought, and following it up might be worth the effort.

Officer Booker picked up his phone and made a call to the prison. He knew the staff would be limited this time of night, but he figured there would be someone in their main office that could find the information he needed. He asked the question that was on his mind. He had to wait for several minutes, but he smiled grimly when the answer came. He gave his thanks and disconnected.

He dialed another number and sat back in his desk chair.

***

"Detective Spalding here," Jayden answered.

"I have an idea who your client's attacker might be," Desmond Booker announced. "A man by the name of Lester Skiles is the right race, height, and build. But here's the kicker—he was Fairchild's cellmate before he was released two months ago."

"Good work," Jayden said. "Do you have an address for him? My dog and I might drop by the creep's place."

"I'll go with you," Booker said. "He lives right here in Phoenix. One of the advantages of his being on parole is that I have the right to go in without a warrant, even bust a door down if I have to."

"Sounds like fun." Jayden was going on barely an hour's sleep, but he wasn't about to miss a chance to get a lead on the kidnapper and have

Nadia's attacker arrested. "I have to help Nadia find a hotel room where she'll be safe first. The attacker kicked her door down."

"Do you think you could meet me at my office in an hour? I'll have a couple of Phoenix officers meet us as well." Booker chuckled. "They like it when they can bust into some con's house. They're always happy to help."

"I'll be there," Jayden said, and the call ended.

The officers were finished at Nadia's place, and she had packed a suitcase and put stuff back in her purse. "Who was that on the phone?" she asked.

"That was your dad's parole officer, Desmond Booker. I'm going to meet him in an hour. One of your father's former cellmates is also a parolee he's supervising. He's the size and color of your attacker, so Booker and I are going to go have a talk with him."

Nadia's face froze. "Are you sure he's the guy that attacked me?"

"I don't know, but he's our best guess right now. We'll know it's the right guy because he'll be short a nose."

She shuddered. "What if he's not home?"

Jayden explained about what Booker could do and why. Then he said, "If we can catch him, he might be able to lead us to your father and possibly your mother. It's the best lead we have right now."

"Why, if my father already kidnapped my mother, did he want to take me as well?" Nadia asked.

"Perhaps he knows you and your grandfather have a close relationship. Maybe he thinks your grandfather would pay more to get you back than he would for your mother."

Nadia nodded. "He's an awful man."

"Yes, he is, but so is his friend, if he's the one that attacked you. We'll see what the guy has to say."

"Don't let him hurt you," Nadia said in a plaintive voice.

"I'll be fine. I'll have Bullet, and I'll grab my black belt. You know I do deal with people like this from time to time. Depending on how this goes, I may be driving to Coolidge tomorrow. I'd like to talk to several people up there. Do you have what you need from your apartment?"

"I think so. The manager said he was going to board the door up until he could get a new one installed," Nadia said. "So I think my stuff should be safe. And I've got enough clothes to last me a couple or three days." She grinned at him. "And I even got rid of some of the junk in my purse."

"I could have done that for you," he said.

"No, I got rid of *junk*. You'd have gotten rid of *stuff*. You wouldn't have been able to tell the difference."

As Jayden picked up her suitcase, he said, "You're probably right, but I'll bet you would never have missed what I threw away."

She picked up a small travel bag and her purse, grimacing as she did so. He noted it but said nothing. She had dressed a little while earlier, and she looked nice, other than the large bruises on her face. She seemed to be favoring her left arm as they started down the sidewalk.

"Nadia, did he hurt your arm?" he asked as they approached his Hummer.

"Yeah, a little. He yanked on it pretty hard. Thank goodness I don't have a game for a couple of days. But I do have practice this afternoon."

Jayden opened his Hummer and put her suitcase in the backseat with Bullet.

She hung on to her bag and purse. "I'll keep these with me and meet you at the hotel." Jayden had located a hotel and reserved a room for Nadia while she was changing her clothes and ridding her purse of junk. "I'd feel better if you rode with me," he said.

"I'll follow right behind you," she promised. "I'll need my car to go to practice and to go to the airport day after tomorrow."

Jayden knew she was right, but he didn't like the idea of her being alone right then. And he worried that someone would follow them. If it was just him and his Hummer, he'd be able to keep a lookout, but that would be much harder if they were traveling in separate vehicles.

"It'll be okay, Jayden."

He didn't want to frighten her, so he finally said, "Okay, but you need to stay right behind me. Where's your car?"

"It's parked around back of the apartments," she said.

"Jump in, and we'll drive around there."

He opened the door for her. She climbed in, favoring that left arm more than he liked to see. It continued to worry him, but he said nothing more about it. He did, however, grab a small Mace canister from his glove box and hand it to her. She thanked him and dropped it into her purse as they drove around to the back.

"I'm parked in the back side of the lot about halfway down there." She pointed. He slowly drove down between the other cars, looking for her small red Jaguar. She suddenly gasped. "It has a flat tire. I'll have to change it."

"We'll change it," Jayden said, but a quick glance told him that there was more than *a* flat tire. All four tires were flat. He stopped right behind the Jag. "Let me check it out. Stay here."

He walked around the Jag. All four tires were more than just flat, they were ruined. Each of them had a big slash in the side. Anger flared in his chest, but he quickly cooled it, walked back to the Hummer, and retrieved a flashlight.

"Did someone let the air out of them?" she asked, nearly in tears.

"Nadia, I'm sorry, but they've all been slashed. You'll need new tires," he said, turning the flashlight on.

"What are you doing?"

"Looking for blood."

"Ooh," she moaned. "You think he came back here afterward and slashed them?"

"Honestly, I don't think so, but I want to be sure. You stay here. It won't take long. If you need something to do, call the number that Officer Mills gave you," he suggested.

She nodded and got the phone out of her purse.

Jayden's investigation didn't take long, and when he got back in the Hummer, he said, "No blood, but that doesn't mean he didn't slash them before he broke in."

"Or Dad did it," she said darkly. "Okay, I guess what's done is done. The officers are on their way, but I told them that you had to meet Desmond Booker and why. They said I should let you take me to the hotel and they would get back with me later today."

"I'll see if I can get someone to put some new tires on it for you," Jayden offered as they drove.

She looked over at him sleepily in the semidarkness. "No, I'll take care of that. You have more than enough to do. I want you to find my mother."

"If you're sure," he said. "I'd be glad to do it for you."

"I know you would, Jayden, but I can do it."

At the hotel, Jayden lifted her suitcase out and started toward the door.

"I can get it from here," Nadia said.

"I'll see you to your room. I still have plenty of time before I need to meet Booker," he said firmly.

He told Bullet to stay in the Hummer. When he put her suitcase in her room and turned to leave, she said, "Jayden, be careful, please." She took a couple of tentative steps toward him as she spoke.

"I will," he said, looking deeply into her gorgeous brown eyes.

She suddenly reached up and kissed him on the cheek. "For good luck," she said and blushed.

They looked at each other for a moment, each with their own thoughts. Jayden didn't know what hers were, but he was thinking that when he finished with her case, it would be difficult not to see her anymore. He'd like to be more than mere Facebook friends with her.

He shrugged the feeling off, chalking it up to the fact that he'd barely had any sleep.

***

Outside Booker's office, the large African-American officer eyed Jayden's vehicle. "We'll go in my car. That Hummer of yours kind of stands out."

"I have another vehicle, an old beater Chevy, that I use when I don't want to be noticed. I should have brought it," Jayden said.

"No, that's fine. Come with me. The PD officers will meet us a block from Lester's apartment."

"Only if you're okay with my dog in your car," Jayden said.

They found the officers easily, and Booker asked them to watch the backdoor of the ratty dump of an apartment. It was actually a duplex. Lester's was the one on the left. They parked their vehicles on the street, and the PD officers headed around the back. Desmond and Jayden headed for the front door, Bullet trailing behind. There were no lights on in either of the duplexes, but there were old, rusty cars parked in small carports attached at either end. The one beside Lester's duplex was small and gray, not at all like the one Nadia and the officers described.

The parole officer knocked hard on the door and then rang the bell. He stood to the side of the door while Jayden stood on the other, one hand on Bullet's head. Jayden was certain he heard movement inside. "He's in there," he said softly.

"Lester Skiles, it's Officer Desmond Booker, your parole officer. Open up. I need to talk to you."

"No way, man," someone shouted from inside. A moment later a shot rang out and a small hole appeared in the center of the door. Booker and Jayden pulled their weapons and retreated toward the car, but they didn't get there before shooting commenced in back of the duplex. Booker took off at a run, and Jayden followed right behind, his alert canine assistant bounding along.

The shooting continued as they circled the duplex. Around back, they could see the two officers peering over a pile of old lumber in the dim light from a bulb over the back door. One of them lifted his gun into sight, and a flurry of shots rang out from the back door of the house. Wood splinters flew in all directions. During another momentary lull, Jayden could hear running steps inside the house. Bullet whined, and Jayden took hold of his collar.

"He's heading for the front," Jayden shouted. "Stay with me, Bullet." Then he ran back that way, his long legs carrying him swiftly. He and Lester saw each other at the same time. Lester fired a quick shot from the front step. The bullet whistled past Jayden's ear. He dropped to the ground and shouted, "Drop it, Lester, or I'll have to shoot." Then to his excited German shepherd, he said, "Stay, Bullet."

Lester, who was in the open now, halfway to the street, fired another shot, kicking up dirt a foot to Jayden's left. He aimed at Lester, but before he squeezed the trigger, a shot from over his head rang out. The con screamed and fell to the ground.

"Cover me," Booker ordered. "I'll check him out."

The officer slowly moved forward, his pistol aimed at the man on the ground. The other officers joined Jayden and started forward as well. The man on the ground suddenly lifted a hand and fired. Booker took the bullet in his shoulder, and the force knocked him to the ground. The two PD officers opened fire, and a moment later, the shooting was over. Booker was trying to sit up, his gun still firmly in his right hand. Bullet had shot from beside Jayden and was now gripping one of the felon's arms.

Jayden sprang to his side, glanced at his dog, and said, "How bad is it, Booker?"

"Feels like a flesh wound," he said through tight lips. "Did you get him?"

"The PD officers did. And Bullet has him by the arm. He's down for the count. Let me look at that wound."

He tore the sleeve of Booker's shirt. What he saw was much worse than Booker had thought. It was oozing blood in a steady flow. The big officer looked at the shoulder, grunted, and said, "I'm fine. Help me up."

"You must not have seen it clearly," Jayden said. "It's deep."

"I'm okay. Help me up," Booker insisted.

Jayden reached for him and pulled the officer to his feet. Sirens sounded nearby. People lined the street in nightclothes. Lights shone in every residence up and down the street. Even the duplex next to Lester's regurgitated its residents. A rough-looking man with a barrel belly and no shirt raced toward Lester, an equally rough-looking woman with a similar build following him. The officers ordered them to stand back. Bullet let go of Lester and advanced menacingly on the pair. They glared at the officers, looked at the dog, and stepped slowly back to their door. Jayden stepped next to the downed man. One of the officers told him Lester was dead but also pointed out that the con was missing the end of his nose.

"It got bitten off earlier," Jayden said. One of them made a comment about Bullet, but Jayden said, "It wasn't my dog. He met a lady with a vicious bite."

Jayden had no doubt Lester was dead. Bullet's actions told him that. He turned his attention back to Booker. He took him by the arm when he saw that the parole officer was wobbling on his feet. "Sit down," Jayden said, "before you fall." One of the other officers told them that an ambulance was on the way.

It showed up in about five minutes. As soon as the paramedics went to work on Booker, Jayden gave them room. The pair next door had gone inside. Bullet stood near their door. Jayden was anxious to look inside Lester's apartment. He needed to be sure that Nadia's mother wasn't in there. He told one of the other officers what his concern was, and one of them joined him. He called Bullet, and they searched the house. If anyone was hiding, the dog would find them, but he showed no interest at all.

Jayden found no evidence that there had been anyone else in the house. When he went back outside, he lifted the blanket that had been thrown over the dead man. He explained to the officer standing watch that he was trying to see if he could find a connection to Ulisses. He pulled out the parolee's wallet. He rustled through it and found a slip of paper with the name Ulisses and a phone number on it. He wrote the phone number in his notebook, and finding nothing else of interest, he replaced the wallet.

Next, he took out the man's cheap cell phone and flipped open the cover. The officer told him he would probably need a search warrant to look in it, to which Jayden responded, "Maybe you would, but I don't. I just want to see what calls he's made." It was a cheap phone and didn't require a password, so Jayden soon had the recent calls on the screen. There were only a dozen listed. Three of them were the same number as the one on the slip of paper. He wrote down all the numbers.

Once he was done, he handed the phone to the officer. The ambulance had taken off while he'd been in the house. So Jayden reported that he was going to the hospital. He drove Booker's car with Bullet riding shotgun.

When he arrived, he was told that Booker was in surgery. No one could give him an estimate of how long it would be before the surgery was completed.

He checked his watch. It was after seven, and he was hungry. He was also tired, but he didn't have time to go back to his house and rest. There was too much to do, and time was ticking away far too quickly. He had a missing woman to find. He drove home, parked Booker's car in the driveway, fed Bullet, fixed himself a quick breakfast, and ate. When he was done, he opened his phone and dialed the number he'd found in the wallet. The call went to voice mail after about six rings. He closed the phone, told Bullet to come with him, and headed for Booker's car. He drove to the parole office and explained to another officer about Booker. Then he left the key to Booker's car with the man and drove his Hummer onto the street.

By then it was eight thirty. He thought about calling Nadia before heading for Coolidge, but he had a feeling she'd be asleep, and he didn't want to disturb her.

Five minutes later, his phone began to ring.

CHAPTER SIX

"Spalding Investigations, Detective Spalding speaking."

"Detective, this is Marley Ferrel. I flew in a little while ago from Texas and then rented a car and drove to Nadia's apartment. I am worried about her. There's police tape around the doorway, and there is a sheet of plywood nailed over it."

"Nadia's fine," Jayden reassured him. "As you can see, she had a problem in her apartment, but she handled it very well, and she's okay. I moved her to a hotel room."

"What happened?" her grandfather asked anxiously.

"A man busted the door open and attacked her, but she is a plucky girl. She bit his nose and sprayed him with Mace. Some police officers outside the building saw what was happening and went to help her, but the guy got away."

"Are you sure she's okay?"

"She has some bruises and her arm hurts, but she says she can go practice this afternoon."

"Where is she? I need the name and address of the hotel," Nadia's grandfather said. But before Jayden could respond, he asked urgently, "Why were cops outside the apartment? Had she received a threat of some kind?"

"She did, and she called me," Jayden said. "I had Ulisses's parole officer get the police to station some officers there for the night to watch for him."

"Was the threat from Ulisses?"

"It was," Jayden said. "I wasn't taking any chances."

"But someone got past the officers?"

"It wasn't their fault. They were watching for Ulisses or at least someone who fit his description. The attacker wasn't even a little similar."

"Okay, I'm going to go check on my little girl," Marley said. "Where is she?"

"I'll meet you there." Jayden gave him the name and address of the hotel. "I'll fill you in when I see you."

After ending the call, Jayden chuckled to himself. Marley's *little girl* was six foot two. But the nickname left no doubt in Jayden's mind that Marley Ferrel was very fond of her.

He got to the hotel before Marley. Parking his Hummer, he rolled the window down a little, told Bullet to stay, and then he waited by the entrance. In about five minutes, a silver Nissan with a rental sticker drove up. The driver parked and unraveled himself from the car.

The man was probably an inch shorter than Jayden's own six foot six but not nearly as heavy; actually, he was quite slender. He was an impressive man with light skin, a thick head of white hair, and silver-rimmed glasses. He was dressed immaculately. He didn't look like he'd just gotten off an airplane. His pants were perfectly creased, his light-blue sport shirt unwrinkled.

He approached the door, and that was when Jayden stepped toward him and held out his hand. "Good morning. You must be Mr. Ferrel. I'm Jayden Spalding."

The fellow accepted his hand, and they shook. His grip was strong, and as they shook, Marley's ice-blue eyes looked intently at Jayden. When he pulled his arm away, he said, "I approve, even if you do have a short memory."

"Approve of what? And what makes you think I have a short memory?" Jayden asked.

"I approve of *you*, Detective," the distinguished gentleman said. "And you already know that you are to call me Marley."

Jayden nodded his head, a serious expression on his face. "Thank you, Marley sir, and I'm just Jayden. I have a feeling that Nadia may still be asleep. It was late when I got her here and she got settled in."

"Then I guess I'll take a chance on waking her up. I need to see her, to make sure she's okay. Not that I don't trust your word, but well, you know, she's my little girl."

"She's in room 810," Jayden said. "I'll go up with you, if you don't mind."

They crossed the lobby and entered the elevator. Jayden quickly filled Marley in on the events of the previous night, and as the elevator made its way up, Marley said, "I thank you for looking out for Nadia. She's a special girl."

"I can see that," Jayden said.

"And even though her mother and I have a strained relationship, I still care about Layda. I know that she and Nadia are close. I want you to find her as quickly as you can," he said, giving Jayden a firm look with those ice-blue eyes.

The elevator slid to a stop, and the door opened. To Jayden's surprise, there stood Nadia, her long, black hair glistening, her eyes sparkling, and her bruises partially covered with makeup.

She broke into a grin. "Jayden, Grandpa, what are you guys doing here?"

Before Jayden could say a word, she rushed into the elevator and threw her arms tightly around him and then released him. They stepped off the elevator before she gave her grandfather a hug, and Jayden noticed that she winced as she tightened her left arm around the older man. She was hurt worse than she was willing to admit.

Marley said, "Well, I see where my little girl's priorities are," but he was smiling at her.

She blushed and said, "I guess you've met my, ah, my private investigator, Jayden Spalding."

Marley nodded. "He seems very competent, but are you okay? I can see bruises under all that makeup."

"I'm fine, Grandpa. I was lucky. I was just going down to eat. Would you two like to join me?"

Both men agreed, and Jayden pushed the down button on the elevator. While they waited for it to descend from the upper floors, she said, "Jayden, did you find the guy who broke into my apartment?"

"We did," he said. "He won't be bothering you again."

"Thank you, Jayden," she said. "Tell me about him."

The elevator doors opened just then, and Jayden followed the two of them in and pressed the button to shut the door. There were two older women on the elevator. Jayden smiled at them and then silently faced the door—like it's customary to do when riding on an elevator. But Nadia took hold of his arm and said, "So is the guy that attacked me in jail?"

"We're on an elevator. Don't you know you shouldn't talk on an elevator?" he teased. "We'll talk about it at breakfast."

"But I *want* to talk on the elevator. So tell me what happened," she insisted, worry in her eyes.

Her grandfather, who was on the other side of her, said, "He's not in jail; he's dead. He tried to shoot it out with Jayden and the other officers."

She gasped in unison with the other ladies in the elevator. Jayden realized that Marley Ferrel was a man who spoke his mind, and he wasn't shy about it.

"I'll explain when we get down," Jayden promised.

"Did anyone else get hurt?"

Her eyes, and those of the other ladies, looked at Jayden expectantly. The elevator stopped, and three more people entered. Jayden again hit the button to close the door. When they started moving again, Nadia asked, "Did they?"

"He did shoot the parole officer, but he's going to be okay. I checked in at the hospital before your grandpa called me. He's in surgery," he said to the rapt attention of an elevator full of folks.

"Did the shooter shoot at you?" she asked.

Jayden felt awkward. "He missed me—both times. He wasn't a very good shot."

"Who shot him? Did you have to?"

"Nah. I was too slow. The others did it."

"And he's dead?"

"Yes, ma'am. Bullet checked him out and confirmed it," he said with a straight face. There were questioning looks throughout the elevator.

"Are you sure it's the guy who attacked me?" she asked, trembling slightly and gripping his arm.

"I'm sure," he said as the elevator came to a stop on the main floor. The doors opened, but no one stepped off.

"How can you be sure?" she asked.

Jayden looked around at his little audience and finally said, "He was missing the tip of his nose. Somebody I know bit it off in the night."

"Ooh," she moaned. "It *was* him."

The elevator was full of wide eyes. Jayden ushered them all out. "That's all folks. It was nice to meet you all. I enjoyed the ride with you."

They all looked at each other, but no one dispersed.

"Well, with that morbid tidbit, let's go have some breakfast," Jayden said, and he took Nadia gently by the arm and led her through the door. The others followed. Jayden could see questions in their faces, but he was firmly committed to saying nothing more in their presence. They had already learned more than anyone would normally hear in an elevator.

Having already eaten, Jayden sipped on a glass of juice and told Nadia what had transpired at her attacker's duplex. When he'd finished, she said, "That's awful. But who is he? And why did my father send him after me?"

"I think you already know that." Jayden pulled his phone from his pocket and said, "He had a slip of paper in his wallet with a name and phone number on it. The name was Ulisses. I tried to call, but it went to voice mail. I'll try it again now."

He waited while it rang. He was sure it was going to go to voice mail, but to his surprise, it was answered after the fifth ring.

"Is that you, Lester?" the voice asked.

"No, my name is Jayden Spalding. I'm glad I reached you, Ulisses. I'm afraid I have some rather unpleasant news for you."

"Who are you? Where did you get this number?" The voice didn't deny being Ulisses.

"I just told you who I am. I got the number from Lester Skiles," he answered.

"Why did Lester give it to you?"

"Don't be angry at Lester," Jayden said evenly. "He gave his life trying to keep me from getting it."

"You . . . killed . . . him?"

"I didn't say that."

"But you made him give you my number. Why did you do that?" Ulisses asked.

"Because you and I need to talk," Jayden said. He heard the line go dead. "He hung up on me."

"Was it my dad?" Nadia asked anxiously.

"He wouldn't say, but he thought I was Lester when he first answered. And he didn't say he wasn't your dad." Jayden shrugged. "I imagine he's in a state of shock at the moment. Maybe he'll be more polite when I call him back in a few minutes."

"Let me have that number," Marley said. "I'll call him right now. Maybe I can get him to talk."

Jayden shrugged again, read it off, and watched Marley make the call. Nadia and Jayden sat quietly. Jayden didn't really think that Ulisses or whoever it was would answer the phone again.

But after a moment, Marley said, "Ulisses, this is Marley Ferrel. What have you done with my daughter?" He listened for a moment and then said, "You don't really expect me to believe that, do you? She's missing, and I have every reason to believe you had something to do with it. You better come clean right now, or so help me, I'll hunt you down, and when I find you, you won't like it." Marley's face was growing dark, and his eyes were narrowed in anger. He listened for a moment, and then he said, "Why did you send your buddy Lester after my granddaughter?" Another quiet moment. "Don't tell me you didn't have anything to do with that. First you call and threaten her, and then you send that worm to beat her up. So help me, Ulisses, you better come clean, or you'll end up in the mortuary with your little buddy." He frowned deeper and then said, "Don't you dare hang up on me."

But he did.

"Did he deny everything?" Jayden asked.

"Yes, but I don't believe him for a minute. What are you going to do now, Jayden?" Marley asked.

"I need to drive to Coolidge and check with some people over there, but first, I want to make sure that Desmond Booker is going to be okay."

"I'll come with you to the hospital," Nadia said. "Grandpa, you can come with us, or you can go up to my room and take a nap."

"I don't need a nap," he said gruffly. "I slept just fine on the plane."

"Then we'll all go," Jayden suggested. "Nadia, have you found anyone to replace the tires on your car yet?"

"No, but I can call around while we're driving," she said.

"What happened to your tires?" her grandfather asked with narrowed eyes.

"Somebody cut them up," Jayden said.

The narrowed eyes grew narrower yet. "They are all flat?" Marley asked.

Before Jayden could make another comment, Nadia explained.

Then Marley said, "You two go ahead to the hospital. I'll take care of your car, and then I'll meet you back at the hotel. You'll drop her off back here, won't you?"

"Yes, Marley sir. I will do that."

Nadia looked at Jayden and said, "Marley sir?"

"It's his way of showing that he respects me." Marley's eyes began to twinkle.

She shook her head. "Grandpa, you don't have to buy me new tires."

"I want to, and I will," he said firmly. "I think your plate is full. I have all day."

"Thank you," Nadia said.

"He's right, you know," Jayden said. "Your plate is full. Aren't you hungry?"

She'd nibbled at her food, but that was about it. "I thought I was, but I keep thinking about that nasty, horrible nose of Lester's, and it makes me sick to my stomach. And I'm so worried about Mom. Maybe by lunch I can eat a little better."

As they got up to leave the restaurant, Jayden asked, "What time is your practice?"

"I have to be there at two," she said.

"Can you really practice? I've noticed how you wince whenever you use your left arm."

Color filled her cheeks, and tears filled her eyes. "I have to practice. If I can't, they'll put me on the injured reserve list, and I don't want that to happen. The team needs me."

"Jayden, why don't you have them check her arm while you're at the hospital?" Marley suggested. "And don't you be stubborn about it, young lady," he said to Nadia. Marley scooped the ticket off the table. "I'll take care of this. And as soon as you know something about Mr. Booker, let me know."

A moment later, the three of them walked out into the blinding sunshine and searing heat. Marley followed them to the Hummer, where the big gray German shepherd was sticking his nose through the large crack above the window that Jayden had left for him.

"What's that in the back of your car?" Marley asked.

"That's my assistant," Jayden said with a grin. "His name is Bullet."

"Was he with you when you caught that guy?" Nadia asked.

"Like I said, he confirmed that Lester was dead—of course, not without chewing on him a little first."

***

Inside the hospital, the pair found Desmond Booker in a room on the third floor, but he was still a little groggy. "So they patched you up, did they?" Jayden asked.

Booker turned toward him. "Yeah, but they won't let me out of here now. I have work to do. Who is this young lady?" he asked gruffly.

"This is my client, Nadia Fairchild," Jayden said. She looked at Jayden and smiled.

Booker said, "So you're Ulisses's daughter. You must have gotten your beauty from your mother."

Jayden grinned, and Nadia said, "My mother is a very pretty lady. I hope we can find her soon."

"That's why I need to get out of here." Booker grimaced. "If one of my parolees took her, I need to help find her."

Jayden took a moment to explain about his phone call to Ulisses a little earlier. "He denies having anything to do with Nadia's mother and says he has no idea why Lester Skiles would have bothered Nadia, that he had nothing to do with that. Of course, we know different."

"Did he tell you where he is?" Booker asked.

"He wouldn't even admit he *was* Ulisses. But I know it was," Jayden said.

"What are you thinking, Jayden?" Booker asked. "Do you think he took Nadia's mother or not?"

Jayden glanced at Nadia. She was slowly shaking her head. He wasn't sure what that meant, but he had a feeling she was thinking what he was. He said to Booker, "I think it's possible." He explained his reasoning then said, "He told Nadia's grandfather that he didn't know anything about Layda being missing. He could be lying, but I think I still need to take a serious look at other possibilities."

"Wouldn't he or someone else have made a ransom demand for my mother by now?" Nadia asked as she began to twist a strand of her hair.

"I don't know, Nadia. If a demand came, it would most likely be to your grandfather," he said. "Especially if your father is behind all this."

Nadia suddenly began to sob. "What if she's dead? What if someone murdered her?"

Jayden said, "We've got to think positively. I'll do everything I can to find her. I need to go to Coolidge as soon as I can get there. After we can get an X-ray on your arm, I'll head up there."

"I don't need an X-ray," she insisted. "I know Grandpa means well, but I'm really okay. Please, just take me back to my hotel and get on your way. I am so worried about Mom I can hardly stand it."

An hour later, Jayden and Bullet arrived in Coolidge.

CHAPTER SEVEN

Jayden drove directly to the campus police headquarters. He and Bullet went inside, and a receptionist—a student, Jayden judged from her age—said, "I'm sorry, sir, but that dog can't come in here."

"My name is Detective Jayden Spalding, and I need to talk to someone about the disappearance of your women's basketball coach and one of her players," he said, ignoring her comment.

"I'm sure that can be arranged, but like I said, you can't bring the dog in," she said firmly.

"He's a service dog," he said. "Where I go, he goes."

"You don't look blind."

"I'm not blind, and I didn't say he was a Seeing Eye dog. He is a service dog, and it's his job to keep me alive," he explained.

"I don't know," she said, looking flustered.

"Listen, I nearly died this morning, and so did he."

"You nearly died?" she said. "I'm sorry. Do you have some kind of condition?"

"My dog and I have the same condition that you have," he said, and her eyes grew wide. "My body is not immune to bullets. Bullet and I had a close escape. Now, please, could I speak to the police chief?" He looked at her name plate. "Please, Janelle." Bullet tugged on the leash.

The poor girl was more confused than ever. She kept looking from Bullet to Jayden and back again.

"Just direct us to his office, and we'll get out of your hair," Jayden said.

"But the dog, is his name Bullet?"

"Yes, Janelle, it is."

"Why did you name him that?"

"Because he is fast, like a bullet, you know?"

"Okay, but he can't go back there," she insisted.

"Listen, Janelle, this is a matter of life and death that I need to speak with the chief about," he said.

"But the dog," she began.

"He's my partner. He wants to come with me. If you aren't going to let him, you'll need to explain to Bullet why he can't come." He looked down at Bullet and said, in a firm voice, "Bullet, this young lady says you have to stay here with her while I go back. Why don't you explain why that would not be a good idea."

Bullet, who had been sitting patiently, rose to his feet, and a rumble began deep in his throat. Janell went white and finally picked up the phone and punched in a series of numbers. "Chief Owens, there's a man here who needs to talk to you."

"A detective," Jayden interrupted.

"A detective and his dog need to see you," she said without taking her eyes off the dog. She listened for a moment, and then she said, "He says the dog has to stay here with me if we don't let him come back there. And I don't dare watch him." She listened again, and then, "He says it's a service dog." A moment later, she hung up the phone. "Okay, Detective, you and Bullet may go back." She explained which office was the chief's.

"Thank you, Janelle. Bullet and I appreciate it."

He found the door of the chief's office open, and the chief was sitting behind a desk. "You must be the detective who wants to see me."

"Yes, sir, I am. My name is Detective Jayden Spalding. I am a private detective, and this is my assistant, Bullet."

The chief rose from his desk and came around it. He had not invited Jayden in, so he came clear to the door. Bullet was sitting calmly by his side. "Is he dangerous?" the chief asked.

"Only if I am threatened or if I give him an order to attack." The deep rumbling began again in the deep chest. "Stand down, Bullet." The growling stopped.

"Come on in, then," the chief said, looking up at Jayden, who was a good eight inches taller. "Sit down." He pointed to a chair.

Jayden did as he was instructed, and Bullet sank to the floor beside him, his head in his paws, looking quite relaxed.

"I'm Chief Gary Owens. What can I do for you?" the chief asked as he took a seat behind his desk.

"I've been retained to locate Coach Layda Fairchild. I need to speak with some of the folks on campus, but I wanted to give you the opportunity to have an officer accompany me if you like. I'd also like to be brought up-to-date on what you and your officers have done and what you've learned so far on the disappearance of both the coach and Naylyn Pierza."

The chief tapped a finger on the desk. "It's a very puzzling thing. It is not like the coach to just take off like this and not make any contact with her staff."

"Do you have reason to believe that she simply took off?" Jayden asked.

"Well, I can only assume," he said.

"Assumptions can be risky," Jayden said. "Unless of course, you get lucky and the assumption turns out to be right. I'm working on the angle that the two of them were abducted, and from a conversation I had late last night with two FBI agents, they seem to be of a similar mind."

"Who would kidnap them?"

"Have you seriously done nothing in regards to those very questions?" Jayden asked with a frown of disapproval.

"I guess not. I did get a call from a special agent, but he didn't ask about Coach Fairchild. His interest seemed to be only about Miss Pierza."

"What did he want to know?"

"He wondered if anyone had contacted me about her or if anyone she associates with has heard from her."

"And you told him what?" Jayden pressed.

"No one has contacted me. And no one seems to have heard from her," he said.

"And you've checked?"

"Of course we have," he said, appearing to be both offended and nervous. "The agent wanted to know if her car was here. I told him that Layda's was missing and that Naylyn didn't have a car."

"Have you attempted to locate the coach's car?"

"It was found abandoned in the parking lot of a grocery store in Florence," he said.

"That's interesting," Jayden said. "I wonder if Layda often gave rides to Naylyn. It's something to consider, though it may or may not matter. We'll need to look at the coach's car, but right now I need to talk to several people. Would you like to have someone accompany me? I would certainly be okay with that, but I need to get after it right now," Jayden said.

"Detective Spalding, you seem to be awful sure that someone kidnapped them. I suspect as much what with the deal with her car and all, but you didn't know about that. Why do you think she was taken by someone?" Chief Owens asked.

"To make it short, Coach Fairchild's ex-husband was released from prison two weeks ago. He'd served eighteen years for kidnapping."

The chief leaned forward. Apparently Jayden had gotten his attention. "Her ex is a kidnapper?"

"That's right, and his former cellmate, who is also out on parole—or I guess I should say he *was* on parole—" The chief raised an eyebrow. "This former cellmate attempted to abduct the coach's daughter last night, shortly after her father called and threatened her."

"I take it the cellmate failed," the chief said.

"Yes, fortunately. His parole officer and I tracked him down with the assistance of the Phoenix PD. He tried to shoot his way out of his house. He injured the parole officer and was killed in the process. We have strong evidence—almost irrefutable—that the deceased man was acting on behalf of the coach's ex-husband," Jayden explained.

The chief took his glasses off and rubbed his eyes. "I'll have my secretary cancel my engagements for the rest of the day, and I'll personally assist you."

"Thank you, Chief Owens. I appreciate it," Jayden said.

The chief made a call on the intercom and gave instructions to his secretary. Then he stood and said, "Let's go. Where would you like to begin?"

"With the coach's staff and players," he said. "And be aware that even though I suspect Ulisses Fairchild, I have an open mind."

"Surely you don't think her staff or players could be involved?"

"An open mind means that I consider everyone until I am satisfied they couldn't be involved. And even though I said players, I also need to locate and speak with a former player who has indicated that she has a serious bone to pick with Coach Fairfield and who has also expressed a strong dislike for Miss Pierza."

They were passing the receptionist's desk at that point. Janelle looked at the two of them with a question in her eye.

"I will be working with Detective Spalding for a while," the chief explained.

"And with my service dog," Jayden added with a wink that made the poor girl blush.

They left the building and resumed their conversation. "You mentioned a player who was dismissed from the team?" the chief prodded.

"That's right. Lorena Husman. She's made quite a fool of herself on social media since her dismissal. She even made some veiled threats."

"Oh, I hadn't heard that," Chief Owens said.

"It gets worse. Her boyfriend, Davon Karp, served time in prison and also has a long record of offenses for which he has served several jail terms from two weeks up to six months, all since he was eighteen," Jayden explained.

"It sounds like we need to take a look at the two of them."

"They are one of the reasons I'm in Coolidge," Jayden said. "But first, I'd like to talk to Coach Fairchild's staff and current players."

The chief agreed, so their first stop was at Coach Fairchild's office, which was occupied, to the police chief's surprise, by her assistant head coach, Raven Wagner. They introduced themselves, and then the chief let Jayden take the lead.

"Miss Wagner, or is it Mrs. Wagner?" Jayden asked.

"*Miss* Wagner," the tall, striking black woman said. She appeared to be in her midthirties and wore her hair in a short afro. "What can I help you with? I don't have time to waste."

"We need to talk to you about the night Coach Fairchild and Miss Pierza disappeared," Jayden said. "Have you been filling in for her since she disappeared?"

"Just because she's chosen to take some unapproved time off doesn't mean that the team has to suffer," she said with a haughty shake of her head. "I'm trying to pick up the slack. We lost the game that night. Frankly—I don't mean to sound disloyal—but she's not been up to par lately, and the team is suffering. I've talked to the athletic director. If she doesn't come back in the next few days, he's going to ask me to take her place."

That didn't seem quite right. He could imagine her being appointed acting head coach, but ordinarily, colleges searched for head coaches before appointing anyone. And it looked to Jayden like Miss Wagner wasn't too fond of her boss.

"I'll also talk to the athletic director," Jayden said. "I believe I can convince him to give her some time before he makes any moves that could negatively affect her career."

Jayden was looking for a reaction, and he got one. The woman scowled and gave him a look that was almost strong enough to launch Bullet into action. He put a hand on the big German shepherd's head, and Bullet instantly calmed.

Wagner said, "What he does or doesn't do is none of your business. Anyway, he knows I'm better qualified to be head coach. The girls would much rather have me too."

"We'll see." Jayden exchanged a glance with Chief Owens. "I need you to tell me where you were after the game."

"You jerk," she shouted, jumping to her feet and poking a finger at Jayden. "Don't you even go accusing me of doing something to her. She's my friend. I resent the implication. I don't even need to talk to you. Why don't you get out of my office!"

"Stand down, Bullet," Jayden said as Bullet had risen to his feet, appearing ready to attack. "She's just making a lot of noise."

Chief Owens finally entered the conversation, and when he did, it was with more vigor than Jayden had witnessed to that point. "Miss Wagner. He may be a private investigator, but I am the police chief, and I asked him to assist me." That wasn't quite true, but Jayden saw no reason to correct the chief.

"Well, I don't have to put up with the way he's acting," she spluttered. "It's none of his business where I was at any time."

"It's very much my business though," Chief Owens said. "Sit down and answer his questions. And you can consider that an official order."

"I'll answer your questions," she said, "but I want him out of my office."

"He is staying right here until he says he's finished. And don't forget, this isn't *your* office, Miss Wagner. You're being rather presumptuous even being in here." Chief Owens cocked an eyebrow.

The two of them stared at each other with stone faces for a minute, but the chief won, and Raven finally sat down behind Coach Fairchild's desk.

"Go ahead, Detective," Chief Owens said to Jayden.

"Where were you from the time the game was over until the next morning?" Jayden asked, expanding his original question. This woman had raised his suspicion levels. He had mentally placed her as a person of interest in whatever had happened to Layda and Naylyn.

She folded her hands across her chest. "I take the fifth."

Jayden chuckled. He didn't hear that very often.

But of course, he was with the police chief, who said, "I think you better answer his questions."

"No way. I know my rights," she said.

Wow, did that ever get red flags popping up.

The chief tried again, but she wasn't budging. Finally, Jayden looked at Chief Owens and said, "It looks like there are some things we need to do."

"What do you suggest, short of arresting her?" the chief asked.

"A couple of things. We need to search this office and also Miss Wagner's. How long do you think it would take to get a search warrant?"

"An hour or two, I would guess," the chief said.

"In that case, both offices will need to be secured, and Miss Wagner must be kept out of them, until we finish," Jayden said. "And while you're at it, I think it would be wise to search the computers as well."

Raven burst to her feet.

"Bullet, guard," Jayden ordered.

Bullet leaped to his feet, dashed to the doorway, and planted all four paws, the hair on the back of his neck standing up.

"Wow. That's an amazing dog," Chief Owens said.

"He's smart; that's for sure," Jayden agreed.

The chief eyed the assistant head coach suspiciously as he pulled out a cell phone and made a couple of calls. Within minutes, two uniformed officers appeared at the doorway. Chief Owens gave strict orders for one of them to stand at Coach Fairchild's door and one at Miss Wagner's door. "No one is to go in or out until I give the okay, and that includes Miss Wagner."

One of the men took Bullet's place while the other one trotted to Miss Wagner's office. Raven was held in Coach Fairchild's office until Chief Owens got word from his officer that her office was now under guard. Finally, he said, "You may go now, Miss Wagner, but you need to stay available. You're not to leave campus until I say you can."

She glared at him, stepped over to the desk, and reached for her purse.

"Not so fast," the chief said as he beat her to the purse and pulled it away from her reach.

"Hey, that's my purse! Give it to me."

"It's part of what's in this room. Therefore it will be searched along with everything else," Chief Owens said.

"But it's mine. I brought it in here. Give it to me," she said, sounding more like a first-grader than a college coach and instructor.

"Well, what can I say?" The chief smiled. "If it is yours—and I don't know for sure that it is—then you shouldn't have brought it into Coach

Fairchild's office, where you had no business being. And that brings to mind another question. How did you get in? This office should have been locked."

"That is not your business. Now, again, give me that purse."

"No, and if you don't leave this office right now, I'll have to place you under arrest," the chief said evenly.

"You wouldn't," she said.

"Try me," he responded. Then he addressed the officer standing beside the door. "I'll need your handcuffs."

That was all it took. Miss Wagner bolted from the room like a frightened rabbit. After she was gone, the chief turned to Jayden. "That was fun."

"Very suspicious behavior," Jayden said. "There's clearly bad blood between the two coaches. I need to find out where Miss Raven Wagner was when the two ladies went missing."

"How do you intend to do that?" the chief asked.

"I need to talk to the other players, the former player, and anyone else who was hanging around after the game, such as custodial staff," he said.

"I need to work on the search warrants," Chief Owens said. "If you'd like to find some of the people you just mentioned, go ahead. I'd like to work with you, but the search warrants come first. I'll get another officer here to assist you as soon as I can. Two heads are always better than one. In the meantime, you go ahead. I'll call you when I get you some help and when I have the search warrants ready."

"In that case, I think I'll head to the gym and see if I can find out about the practice," Jayden said. "Come on, Bullet."

CHAPTER EIGHT

Jayden, a former ball player himself, had an idea where to find out about the women's practice times, and that was to find the men's coach. Ten minutes later, he was seated in Coach Jimmy Ashcroft's office. He had already learned that there would be a practice for the women in a couple of hours. He planned to be there as soon as it started, even though he didn't look forward to another encounter with Coach Wagner.

Coach Ashcroft was a tall, slender man with light-blond hair cut in a butch. His blue eyes reflected his concern about Coach Fairchild and her player. "Layda is a good coach," he said. "And she's a good person. She and my wife are friends. I can tell you this for a fact, Detective: she would never just up and leave. There is more to this disappearance than the two of them running away."

"What do you think may have happened?" Jayden asked.

"It's like I told you. My wife and Layda are good friends, and they talk a lot. Layda was over a few nights ago. My wife, Sandra, told me after Layda left that she was very worried about her ex-husband getting released from prison," Coach Ashcroft said. "I assume you already know about him."

"I'm afraid so."

"Yeah, anyway, I think he might have done something. But why he'd take Naylyn as well doesn't make sense," he said.

"Are you aware that they were together when they went into the parking lot?"

"Yes, I'd heard that. Miss Pierza doesn't have any family, and Layda had taken her under her wing." The coach scratched his chin and looked toward the far wall for a moment. Jayden waited. Finally, he said, "Maybe Miss Pierza was at the wrong place at the wrong time."

"That could very well be the case," Jayden agreed.

"Detective, I hate to have to mention this, because I just told you that Layda is a good person and a friend to Sandra and me, but, well, she didn't have the greatest judgement in the world when it came to men."

"So I've heard," Jayden said, and then he waited expectantly.

Coach Ashcroft took a deep breath. "We've already talked about her ex, but are you aware that she recently broke up with another fellow?"

Jayden slowly shook his head. "No, do you know him?"

"Oh yes. I don't like him, and neither does Sandra," he said with a frown. "He's a history professor here at the college, but believe me, he's a different sort of character. He's a couple of inches shorter than Layda." He paused. "You know what Layda looks like, right, Detective?"

"I've been shown pictures."

"So you know she's a beautiful woman." He rubbed his short-cropped hair. "I guess there's only one way to say this. Pedro's quite homely. I know that sounds crass, but he is. His full name is Pedro Delgado. He's seriously overweight, and he has these tiny little pig eyes with thick round glasses. He wears his black hair in a long braid. His face is severely pockmarked. But it's his eyes that I don't like. There is something lurking there, something—well . . . evil, I'd say. He uses foul language in every sentence. On the other hand, he's a smart guy. Some of my players who've taken classes from him say he's a good teacher, despite the colorful language. And they say he grades fair."

"Wow. That's quite a description," Jayden said. "And you say you know him?"

"Layda likes to play cards with Sandra and me and a few other friends. When she began to date him, she invited him to our card games. He was pretty good. In fact, he was very good. I suspected him of cheating, although I never mentioned it to anyone but Sandra, and she agreed with me. One of our friends did call him on it one evening at my house. He exploded, threw our table over and broke it—our dining room table! He made a mess of things. Wine glasses were broken, the carpet was stained, and . . . well, he made a mess and hurt one of the women's arms and another's leg."

"Did you involve the cops?" Jayden asked.

"No, but only because of Layda. She was, in her words, shocked at his behavior."

"Are there any other incidents that you know of regarding his temper? It sounds like he has a bad one," Jayden said.

"I can't prove it, but the fellow that called Pedro on his cheating was ambushed by his car a couple of nights after in the grocery store parking lot. His attacker was built like Pedro, but he was wearing a mask of some kind and didn't say a word. He just appeared from behind the car and started swinging a club. He left Joe on the ground unconscious. Someone else found him and called it in. He suffered a broken skull and a concussion. His arm was also broken." Coach Ashcroft shook his head. "Like I say, it was never proven that it was Pedro. So nothing could be done."

"Did Layda continue to date him after that?"

"Oh no, but her tires got slashed one night—all four of them. And he stalked her a lot. He would show up in front of her house and just sit there for a while. Then he'd drive off. And she got these weird phone calls quite often. No one would speak, but she could hear heavy breathing on the line. She changed her cell phone and home numbers, but a couple of times after that, she got those same calls at her office here. And sometimes he would follow her home," he said.

"Did she do anything about it?" Jayden asked, looking up from the notes he'd been taking.

"Yes, finally, about four or five days ago, she called him and told him that if it didn't stop, she'd get a restraining order against him," the coach explained. "But he just laughed and told her it wasn't him."

Jayden thought for a moment. "When did the phone calls occur?"

"I know what you're thinking," Coach Ashcroft said with a smile. "Could it have been her ex-husband? But it began over two months ago. Her ex was still in prison."

"Did Layda ever mention any calls from Ulisses—that's her ex-husband—after he got out of prison? That would've been in the past two weeks."

The coach shook his head. "Nope. She was afraid of it, but I don't think it ever happened. I can't help but wonder if Pedro didn't go off on Layda that night after the ball game. I wouldn't put anything past him."

"Do you have any idea if he was at that game?" Jayden asked.

"I saw him there. He was sitting about three rows above her and the team. He had a look about his face that was, well, deadly, I'd say."

"Have you seen him since that night?"

"I haven't, but one of my players mentioned that he taught his class this morning."

"Layda disappeared Tuesday night after the game," Jayden said. "And today is Thursday. I need to talk to him. Do you have his address or phone number? And do you know where his office is?"

The coach shook his head. "But if you'd like me to, I can find out right now."

"That would be great," Jayden said.

He waited while the coach made some calls. He kept thinking about the four slashed tires—exactly what had happened to Nadia's car.

After the coach gave him the information on Pedro, Jayden asked, "What can you tell me about Lorena Husman and Davon Karp?"

***

Nadia hadn't heard from Jayden since he'd dropped her off at her hotel and headed for Coolidge. It was a little depressing—both because she was eager for good news about her mother and because, in the short time she'd known Jayden, she had found that she'd never been with a guy that made her feel the way he did. Her grandfather had teased her about him in the hotel room that morning.

"You told me what you're looking for in a man," he'd said. He held up three fingers. "First, he has to be tall, not shorter than you, at a minimum." He curled one of the fingers into his palm. "Second, he has to be a Mormon elder." He curled a second finger. "Third, he has to have a sense of humor." He curled the remaining finger. "Three for three."

"Oh, Grandpa, you don't meet a guy by hiring him to conduct an investigation for you," she said, but she'd been unable to wipe the smile from her face.

And thinking of him now as she hurried into the practice, she smiled again. But her smile slipped as a shot of pain ran up her left arm. That wasn't good. She had to play well in practice, or she'd be put on the injured reserve roster. That wouldn't be good for her or the team. She prayed with determination that she would be able to perform up to par and not let anyone see the pain she was experiencing.

She entered the locker room and said hi to her teammates. The laughter and talking suddenly ceased. "What? Did I say something?"

For a moment, they all looked at their feet. Finally, one of them told her that they'd heard about her mother and wondered if she was okay.

"I've been better, but I won't let it affect my play," she said.

Having broken the ice, the tension left the locker room, and the normal banter resumed, but a couple of the girls asked her what was being done to locate her mother. She told them the police were involved but that she'd hired a private investigator to help as well. Another asked how she got her bruises.

"Are they that noticeable?" she asked. "I tried to cover them up." She didn't explain.

Jules, a tall African-American player, Nadia's close friend and roommate when they were playing road games, asked with a grin, "This private detective, is he short, pudgy, nearsighted, old, and a retired cop?"

"No, but he specializes in searching for missing persons," she said as his freckled face swam through her mind.

Jules looked at her with a cocked eyebrow. "Then is he tall, dark, handsome, young, and single?"

Nadia felt the heat in her cheeks. She couldn't help it.

And Jules couldn't help but notice. "Oh my! He is, and he must be cute too. I can see you blush right through all that makeup. We need to talk about those bruises, girl."

"It's nothing," Nadia said. "And about my PI, he isn't most of those things you asked, but he's good at what he does. That's why I hired him."

Jules put both hands on her hips. "Okay, he isn't tall?"

"Kind of," Nadia said, wishing the topic would change and knowing that it wouldn't. She knew Jules too well.

"How tall is kind of?" her friend insisted.

"He's six six," she mumbled as she started toward the door. It was almost time for practice to start.

None of the other girls made a move toward the door, and Jules skipped past her and blocked her way. Her hands once again went to her hips. "Okay, hon, out with it. He's tall, dark, and handsome, right?

"No."

"Be specific. Do I have to ask every single thing one at a time?"

Nadia started to go around her.

"Oh, no you don't. Is he dark?"

She shook her head.

"Is he single?"

"Yes, but don't go and assume things that aren't there," Nadia said. "I hired him to find my mother, and that's all."

Jules was as persistent as a puppy. "Handsome?"

Nadia couldn't hide the smile.

"Okay, I take that smile as a yes. So he's tall, not dark, handsome, and single. I know you, girl. So tell me, and this is the big question, is he a Mormon?"

She slowly nodded. And then she said, "Are you satisfied now? He works for me, and I hired him because he is the best at what he does. I would have hired him if he was short and fat as long as I thought he might be able to find Mom."

"Sure, girl. But he's not short and fat. And that's why you're blushing. There's one more thing. Does he have a sense of humor?"

Nadia started to chuckle. "Yes, but it's a bit warped. Jules, you sound like my grandfather. He grilled me just like you are. All I can do is tell you what I told him. He's looking for my mother. End of story."

Jules started to move aside, but then she stopped. "I guess I do have another question, and then I promise I'll leave you alone. Has he had any luck finding your mother?"

"He's following some leads. He was up almost the whole night last night," Nadia said as she felt her eyes mist up. "He's got to find her. He's just got to."

"I'm sorry." Jules draped an arm around Nadia's shoulder. They started to move toward the door, the rest of the team following. "I didn't mean to upset you. This must be really hard."

"You have no idea. It's killing me. But I'll try really hard not to let it affect how I play."

"I know that," Jules said. They pushed through the locker room door, but partway down the hallway, Jules stopped. "I have another question. Is that okay?"

"You would ask anyway, wouldn't you?"

"Of course, because we're best friends," Jules said, her face somber. "After . . . what's his name?"

"Jayden Spalding."

"Good name. After Jayden finds your mother and brings her home, if he, well, you know, if he asks you out, will you go?"

That brought a smile to Nadia's sad face. "Do I look like an idiot to you?"

All the girls laughed, and Jules patted her on the back. "That's all the answer I need. Let's get in there before Coach comes looking for us."

But as they reached the door to the gym, Jules stopped again. "Nadia, if Jayden isn't dark, then tell me this, does he have freckles?"

"Yes, and reddish-brown hair," she said. "What made you think that?"

"I don't know, but he sounds just right for you," Jules said with a smile. And before Nadia could say that it simply wasn't likely to happen, Jules opened the door to the gym, and they led the rest of the team in.

For the first few minutes of the practice, Nadia did fine. Even though the arm that Lester had jerked was hurting, she was able to mask it. But later in a skirmish, when she attempted to steal a ball, a pain shot up her arm, and she missed. It angered her. She would normally have made a steal like that easily.

She tried to pick up the pace again, but when she had to dribble through traffic on the way to a layup, she had to switch the ball from her right hand to her left. When she did, the pain returned, and the ball got away from her. One of the other girls snatched it up easily.

A minute later, the coaches called all of them to the side, but the head coach, Leticia Korner, directed her question to Nadia, a worried look on her face. "What's going on, Nadia? You blew two plays that should have been easy for you."

"I'm sorry. I guess I need to pay closer attention, Coach."

"Are you suggesting this is about your mother?" Coach Korner asked. "I know she's missing, and I'm sorry about that, but you can't let that affect how you play. We have an out-of-state game tomorrow night. I need you at your best."

"I know. There's nothing more I can do to help Mom right now. I hired a private investigator. I just have to wait for him to do his work."

For a moment, Coach Korner looked at Nadia with narrowed eyes while her assistants talked to the other team members. "Is there something you're not telling me?" she asked.

Nadia felt the heat in her cheeks. She was an honest person. She hesitated, but in the end she knew what she had to do. "I have some pain in my left arm."

"And underneath all that makeup, you have some bruises. What happened, Nadia?"

"I was assaulted last night."

"You don't drink. You don't go to bars. Where were you that allowed someone to assault you?" the coach asked.

"In my apartment."

"Well. Did you know the guy? It was a man, wasn't it?" Coach asked.

"Yes, but I didn't know him."

"But you let him in?"

"No, he busted the door down and came at me."

The coach looked toward where the other players and coaches were huddled. "Jules," she called out.

"Yes, Coach?" Jules answered as she joined the two of them.

"I'd like you and Nadia to do some one-on-one for a minute," Coach Korner said. She grabbed a ball and headed to one end of the court.

"What's going on?" Jules asked, concern etched on her dark face.

"I had some trouble last night. You know, the bruises and all," Nadia said as they followed their coach. "I think she thinks I'm not up to par."

When they reached the end of the court, Coach Korner suddenly threw the ball with a great deal of force to Nadia. She caught it, but her arm screamed in pain. "Dribble. Take it away from her, Jules," the coach instructed.

The two girls played hard for a couple of minutes. But suddenly, Nadia attempted a shot but then did not carry through. Jules stole the ball from her and tucked it under one arm. "You're in a lot of pain, hon," she said.

Nadia nodded, and her eyes misted. "Let's go to the locker room," Coach Korner said. "We need to talk. Jules, you come too."

As soon as they entered the locker room, the coach said, "Let me see your left arm."

Nadia held it out. The coach took her hand, and then she tugged it. It was all Nadia could do not to cry out in pain. "Have you had this checked out?" she asked.

"I thought it would be okay," Nadia said. "I have to play."

"Nadia, I'm afraid that isn't going to happen. At least not tomorrow. Let's sit down, and you can tell Jules and me exactly what happened."

So they sat, and with tears that she couldn't restrain, Nadia told them everything. She talked about her father, about Lester, about Jayden, about Desmond Booker. She even told them about Bullet.

When she'd finished, Jules said, "Your PI nearly took a bullet for you."

"Two bullets," she sobbed. "I'm so scared for him."

"And for your mother and for yourself," Coach Korner said.

"Yes, but especially for my mother."

"Jules, you can go back to the practice. Explain that Nadia is having her arm checked out. I'll be back when we're done," the coach said. "But regardless of what our team doctor finds, we'll be playing without Nadia tomorrow. Practice accordingly."

CHAPTER NINE

JAYDEN, CHIEF OWENS, AND AN officer by the name of Lieutenant Tevin Kaiser were in the chief's office. The three men had completed the searches. There was nothing in either Coach Fairchild's office or Coach Wagner's that gave so much as a hint as to what might have happened to the missing women. However, the three men were concerned about what they had discovered in some e-mails that Raven Wagner had written to several friends. They were worrisome, to say the least.

"Jayden," the chief said, "I think it's clear that Raven has her eyes set on the head coaching job."

"I'd say that's clear. She as much as told her friends that she'd be there in a matter of weeks. The question now is whether she did something to Layda and Miss Pierza to create a vacancy. There was nothing in the way of threats in those e-mails. I wish we had her cell phone," Jayden concluded.

"I think we need to talk to her again," the chief said. He glanced at his watch. "It's time for the women's team to practice. You need to be there and talk to the girls. Tevin, why don't you go with him and make sure no one fails to cooperate. You can let them know we're conducting an official investigation. Then I'd like you to bring Coach Wagner back here, and we'll have another talk with her."

"What if she won't come?" Tevin asked.

"Then arrest her. I'm not putting up with any more of her insolence," the chief said. "Make sure she doesn't ditch her cell phone. I'll be confiscating that."

"Very well, Chief," Tevin said with a tight smile. "Ready, Jayden?"

"Lead the way," Jayden said. "Bullet and I will follow you."

Jayden was impressed with the lieutenant. He was only five eight, but he was built like a bulldog. His chestnut hair was cut short, and his green eyes shone with intelligence. He'd been the one to discover the e-mails after the chief had ordered Miss Wagner to open her e-mail accounts and social media pages. She resisted, but when the chief told her that she could either cooperate or they would simply seize the computer and send it to a lab, she relented.

The team was already starting warm-ups when Jayden and the lieutenant stepped into the gym. Raven spotted them and came scurrying over. "Now what are you doing? I think you've done enough damage for one day."

Lieutenant Kaiser addressed one of the other assistant coaches and told her to have the players sit down and to speak with Jayden, who he then introduced. "Chief Owens expects full cooperation. Detective Spalding is working with our department on an investigation over the disappearance of Coach Fairchild and Naylyn Pierza." Then to Raven, he said, "You're coming with me, Coach Wagner. The chief is expecting you."

Her eyes narrowed, and her fists balled at her sides. "This is pure harassment," she said. "The team needs me. I'm in charge now."

"No, you're coming with me."

"And if I don't?"

"If you resist, you'll be under arrest, and I'll handcuff you. It's your choice," Lieutenant Kaiser said.

Raven relented.

As soon as they were gone, Jayden spoke to the other women. "I need to speak with each of you individually. We can just go to the far end of the gym. The rest of you stay right here."

For the next hour, he talked to each of them, including the assistant coaches. Bullet stayed with the main group, and when the girls got friendly with him, he let them fuss over him and pet him. But all the while, he kept track of his master. When Jayden finished, he thanked them for their time and told them to call if they recalled something that might help. He left business cards with each of them.

Then he sat down in the bleachers with his faithful companion at his feet and reviewed his notes as the practice resumed. Not one of the coaches or players seemed to have any idea what might have happened to the missing women. Several people confirmed that the two of them left together on Tuesday night. Most of the players expressed discontent with Coach Wagner. None of them spoke of Coach Fairchild in anything but glowing terms. And not one of them seemed to have any hard feelings toward their missing teammate.

The two assistant coaches both seethed with resentment against Coach Wagner. Both told him that they could tell that she had it in her head to force Coach Fairchild out and get herself inserted. They also said she'd left the locker room before anyone else on Tuesday evening. When asked if they thought she may have resorted to violence against the coach, both of them hedged a little. In the end, Jayden came away with the feeling that Raven needed to be kept on his list of persons of interest.

Another matter he had discussed with the players and coaches was the disgraced player, Lorena Husman. Again, all of them agreed with her being cut from the team. In fact, it was actually the girls themselves who had pressed Coach Fairchild to do something about her. She was a troublemaker, and they had either met or at least seen her boyfriend, Davon Karp. They all told him that Lorena had it in for Naylyn. The impression he got was that if anyone did anything to the coach and Naylyn, it was most likely at the hands of Lorena and Davon.

The final item of his interviews was the relationship between Coach Fairchild and Professor Delgado. His name, in most of the interviews, had brought about the only criticism any of them had about their coach. He was told that she should never have allowed a relationship to begin with him at all, but when she broke it off, his anger and the way he stalked her was disturbing, and they had all witnessed it in some degree.

He made a few further notations and then went in search of the custodians. He found two men and one woman. One of the custodians, Bruce Whipple, told him, "I was working that night. I can tell you this, Detective: Professor Delgado slithered out of a snake pit. He's a big guy, that guy is, but he slithers just like a snake. He's one place one minute, and then in almost no time, he shows up somewhere else. I swear poor Coach couldn't get away from him. The night she disappeared, that was Tuesday, I saw him first in the bleachers behind Coach Fairchild. But a short time later, when I'd gone to clean up a drink that someone had spilled in the hallway, he came walking in from outside. I hadn't even seen him leave the gym. And then, after that, I again saw him behind the players."

"Did you ever hear him make any threats to the coach?" Jayden asked.

"Oh yeah, but not that night; it was at the previous home game several days ago. She was coming out of the locker room after the game. I don't know where he'd been hiding, but all of a sudden, there he was, blocking her path. She told him to step out of her path, and he said something to the effect that if she didn't come back to him, she'd wish she had."

"Was it anything specific?" Jayden asked.

"No, but I could tell she was scared."

"How did she get past him?"

"She didn't. She went back in the locker room," Bruce told him. "And then he saw me. Those little piggy eyes stared at me—made me shiver. I did just what the coach had done. I got away from him."

"Okay, back to Tuesday night. Did you see him again after the second time he was seated behind her and her team?"

"Oh yes. I'd gone out for a smoke after most of the crowd had cleared. It was the exit nearest the locker room. He came out the door past me and disappeared into the parking lot. It was only a short time later—I had just snuffed out my cigarette—when Coach Fairchild and that pretty player came out and headed into the parking lot."

"Did you see them reach the coach's car?" Jayden asked.

"No, my pager went off, and I had to go back in. But I tell you, Detective, that snake had something to do with their disappearance," he concluded.

"Can you think of anything else I should know?" Jayden asked.

"You mean like the time I saw the snake talking to Coach Wagner?" he asked.

"Yes, that could be important. Did you hear what they said?"

"No, but she was bending down with her head close to his, and they were whispering. When they saw me, she stood up and walked away from him. I went past and down another hallway a minute later, but I got to thinking about how strange those two were acting, so I went back and peeked around the corner."

"Let me guess," Jayden said. "They were head-to-head again."

"Yeah, that's right. Strange, don't you think?"

Jayden learned absolutely nothing from the other custodians. As he and Bullet walked back to the chief's office, he mentally reviewed his list of persons of interest or, he decided, his list of *suspects*.

On the top of that list was Nadia's father, Ulisses. Then there was Coach Fairchild's recently estranged boyfriend, Professor Pedro Delgado. Then there was Raven Wagner. Her movements had to be traced. She clearly hoped to gain from Layda's disappearance. And finally, two people he hadn't yet spoken with—Lorena Husman and her ex-con boyfriend, Davon Karp—could very well have committed violence against the missing women.

One more thing he had learned was that Coach Wagner had been angry when Lorena had been cut from the team. It appeared she was the only one who had defended the girl and had done so quite vocally.

He was torn between finding Pedro first or looking for Lorena. He was exhausted, and the day was wearing away. His thoughts kept drifting to Nadia. He wondered how her practice was going or if it was over. He wished she'd call. He'd call her, but he had to keep reminding himself that he was working for her. It was really only proper for him to call to update her on the search for her mother. Right now, he didn't have enough to justify a report.

Back in Chief Owens's office, he found Tevin and the chief discussing the interview they had conducted with Raven Wagner.

"Do you think she may have done something?" Jayden asked after being brought up to speed on their interview with her.

"In a word," Chief Owens began, "yes. Somewhere along the line, Miss Wagner, who at one time worked well with Coach Fairchild, turned against her."

"Could it have been over the dismissal of Lorena Husman from the team?" the lieutenant asked.

Chief Owens began to nod. "Perhaps Husman and Wagner are working together."

"That's possible," Jayden said. "But from the interviews I just conducted, I think the rift between Coach Fairchild and Coach Wagner has been going on for some time now. However, there's no doubt that Wagner was upset over Husman's dismissal."

He gave a report of his interviews. When he mentioned Bruce Whipple, the custodian, and what he'd seen, the chief said, "What could Wagner and Delgado have been talking about?"

"Exactly." Jayden grinned. "Perhaps Miss Wagner finds him attractive. He must be a very charming man."

The other men chuckled. Then the chief said, "Charming maybe, but he's one homely dude. However, if those two were having a whispered conversation they didn't want others to see, it certainly raises my suspicions.

"I see all kinds of possibilities here," Jayden said. "If there wasn't a romantic tryst between the history professor and the finagling coach, then they had to have been planning something. And odds are it concerns our missing women."

After discussing the matter for a few more minutes, Jayden rubbed his eyes. "I need to find Pedro Delgado. That snake, as Bruce Whipple called him, has some explaining to do."

"Detective, you look totally worn out. Don't you think you better get some rest? You've had a rough day."

"So have Coach Fairchild and Miss Pierza, if they are still alive. There is no time to waste."

"There is a breakroom at the end of the hallway," the chief said. "It has a nice recliner and a sofa. Why don't you go get a little shuteye while Lieutenant Kaiser and I find Professor Delgado. I'll wake you if and when we find him."

"If you can," Jayden said.

"If we can find him? We will if he's on campus," the chief responded.

"No, I mean if you can wake me."

***

Nadia was depressed. Everything was going wrong. First her mother comes up missing. Then her father threatens her. His former cellmate assaults her in an attempt to kidnap her. And to top it all off, she was now on the injured reserve roster.

She had met with the team doctor. After extensive examination, he told her that her attacker had caused damage to the ligaments of both her elbow and shoulder. He estimated that she'd be out for as much as three or four weeks. He put her left arm in a sling to limit motion.

Three to four weeks! For all intents and purposes, the end of the season was a disaster! The coach had been discouraged too. She'd told Nadia that without her, there were some teams they may not be able to beat. She'd been nice, but she hadn't been able to hide her disappointment.

After leaving the building, Nadia climbed in her little red Jaguar and cried. She finally pulled herself together and went in search of something to eat. She hated to tell her grandfather, and even more, she dreaded admitting to Jayden that she hadn't come out of the attack practically unscathed, as she had tried to convince herself and everyone else. She had prayed that this wouldn't happen, but the fact that it had didn't cause her to doubt her faith. Sometimes God simply said no. But as disappointed as she was, she knew that when God said no, it was because that was what was best for her. He saw the bigger picture. She simply had to trust Him.

Impulsively, she pulled to the side of the street and silently offered a prayer. She promised the Lord that she would bend to His will but pleaded that He would help her know what she needed to do. Perhaps, she thought as she concluded her prayer and sat in silence, she was being given a chance to be more active in the search for her mother. She received a quiet, simple confirmation that this was the case.

Feeling much uplifted, she decided to drive to her hotel. Perhaps she and her grandfather could go to dinner together—if he was still there. She didn't welcome that thought. He was a busy man, and she knew he'd be anxious to get back to work, but he wouldn't leave without telling her first. Still, she was relieved to see that his rental car was parked at the hotel when she pulled in. She parked her Jaguar beside it and climbed out.

When she got to her room, she tapped on the door. She didn't want to walk in unannounced. But when he didn't answer, she unlocked her door and opened it.

Her grandfather was sitting at the little table with his elbows on the table and his head in his hands. Her heart jumped into her throat. She ran across the room. "Grandpa, are you all right?" she asked softly as she put her good hand gently on his shoulder.

He slowly raised his head and turned his eyes up at her. She could see sorrow and pain there that shocked her. "Nadia," he said. "I'm glad you're back. How did practice go? Are you going—" He cut himself off abruptly as his eyes fell on the sling. "What happened, little girl?" There was a catch in his voicc.

"Grandpa," she knelt and put her good arm around him, "I'm fine. I can't play ball for a few days." She knew she was being overly optimistic, but she didn't want to worry him anymore. "Something has happened, hasn't it?"

He nodded, and through the sadness in his eyes, a sharp spear of anger appeared. His face grew hard, and when he spoke, she could feel that anger growing. "He called."

"Who called, Grandpa? Did Jayden call? Is he okay?"

He slowly shook his head, and she pulled her arm tighter around him.

"Grandpa!" Terror tore through her soul. "What is it? Please tell me Jayden is okay. And don't tell me that Mom isn't."

"My precious little girl," he said, tears in his eyes. That was shocking. Never in her life had she seen her grandfather cry. It brought tears to her own eyes, and they fell silently onto her arm. "No, your worthless father called," he finally revealed.

"Oh no! What did he say, Grandpa?" she asked in a broken voice, not sure she even wanted to hear.

"He has my Layda," he said. "He wants a million dollars. If I don't get it to him exactly like he says, he said—he said he will . . . kill her."

"Oh, Grandpa! No! No! No! He can't!"

"I'll give him the million dollars. I'll give him everything I've got if I have to." He hung his head again. "Nadia, I can't let him hurt her. If something happens to her and I haven't done everything I can to breach the chasm between us, I don't know what I'll do. I've wanted to make peace with her, but I'm a stubborn old fool. I have too much pride. Oh, how I wish I'd tried to reach out to her sooner. Now it may be too late."

Nadia took a deep breath. She let go of her grandfather and wiped the tears from her eyes. "Grandpa, I'll give you all my savings. Together we can get her back."

He lifted his head and then rose to his feet. "No, Nadia. I owe this to your mother. I will pay the ransom, and I will get her back." She could see the familiar determination as it seeped back into his long frame. The sadness and anger in his eyes faded, replaced with a look of absolute determination. "He said no cops, Nadia. It's got to be just me and him."

"No, Grandpa. Maybe no cops, but we need to let Jayden help us. He's smart, he's brave, and he'll help us."

"I like him a lot, Nadia, but I don't want to jeopardize Layda's life. I must do what it takes. Then when I get her back, I'll hire Jayden to hunt Ulisses down."

"Grandpa, I need to call him. He is wasting time now. He needs to be here."

He slowly shook his head. "I don't know if that would be wise."

"Please, Grandpa." She seized his hand and gripped tightly. "I trust him. Please, I need him here with us."

Her grandfather's face softened. "If I didn't know better, I'd say you were falling for that young man."

"I don't know what I feel except that I need his support. I want him to help us. Please, Grandpa, for me?"

He looked tenderly into her eyes. "You are so like your grandmother. Yes, little girl, you may call him. Have him come here as soon as he can. I expect Ulisses to call again at eight tonight. In the meantime, I need to call my bank and have some money gathered. He wants cash in hundred-dollar bills. They'll try to find out why I need it, but if they want to keep my business, they'll do as I say."

"Okay, you do that, and I'll call Jayden." She pulled out her phone, brought his name up in her contacts, and punched it gently.

It began to ring.

CHAPTER TEN

Jayden was sleeping deeply in the recliner the chief had directed him to. His phone began to ring, but he didn't hear it. Exhaustion had overcome him. His German shepherd did hear it though. He leaped to his feet and grabbed hold of Jayden's pant leg. Jayden groaned and shooed the dog away, but Bullet wouldn't be denied. He began to bark. The only way Jayden wouldn't have been rousted by the dog's incessant barking was if he was dead.

"Bullet, what is it?" he asked as he pulled the recliner up.

"What's the matter?" Chief Owens shouted as he ran to the doorway. But one look from Bullet kept him from entering the break room.

"I don't know. He just woke me up," Jayden said. "Did you find Professor Delgado?" Bullet grabbed his master's sleeve and pulled. Jayden sat up straight. "What is it, young fella?" he asked groggily.

Bullet answered the only way he knew how. He pawed at the pocket where Jayden carried his cell phone. Understanding dawned. "My phone must have been ringing," he said as he pulled it out. It was no sooner in his hand than Bullet whined softly and sat on his haunches watching his master expectantly. A moment later Jayden was checking missed calls. "There's a missed call here from my client," he said. "You can come on in now. Bullet won't hurt you."

"That is some dog you have there," Lieutenant Kaiser said.

"He is at that," Jayden agreed as his phone call went through.

"Jayden, oh thank goodness it's you. I need you to come back," Nadia said. The emotion in her voice caught his full attention.

"What's the matter?" he asked urgently, surging to his feet.

"It's my father. He's got Mom. He says my grandfather has to give him a million dollars to get her back."

"Is your grandfather there with you?" Jayden asked as he signaled for the officers to follow him. He was going to his car, and he wanted them to know what had occurred.

"He's right here," Nadia responded.

"Let me talk to him."

"Jayden, this is Marley," came a new voice. "Ulisses called a little while ago. He says if I don't follow his exact instructions, he will kill my daughter and the girl with her. He wants a million dollars. I'm working on getting the cash together now. He's calling me back at eight tonight with instructions. It isn't easy to get a million in hundred-dollar bills, but I'll get it done."

"I'm on my way, Marley," he said, leaving off the *sir*.

"He said no cops, or they both die," Marley said. "I don't know if you should be involved."

"I'm not a cop. And I am involved. By the way, how do you know it was Ulisses? Did he identify himself?"

"Not intentionally. I think he must have had a handkerchief or something over the phone. I'm still sure it was his voice. But there's another thing. There's a phrase I recall him using when he was married to Layda. He always said to me, 'See ya later, sonny boy.' It was like it was a habit. I heard him say it to other men while he was still with Layda. When he ended the call, that was the last thing he said. I think it's such a habit that he uses it all the time and doesn't even realize what he's saying."

"Did he say that when he called you in Texas?" Jayden asked.

"He sure did, and that's probably why I remember it so well. After all those years in prison, he still says it." Marley sounded tired. "Also, he called me on my cell phone. Not a lot of people outside of my business know my number. So you see, I know it's him."

"Got it. I'll see you at the hotel in a little while," Jayden said. "Call me back if you hear anything else before I get there."

Jayden ended the call and put his phone back in his pocket. He and the officers had already exited the building and were almost to Jayden's Hummer. "Gentlemen, that call was a game changer," he said.

"Is there a ransom demand?" Chief Owens asked.

"Yes, there is, but at this point, I'd appreciate it if you kept that to yourselves. As usual, the kidnapper said not to say anything to the cops or he would kill both women," Jayden said.

"Surely you won't keep it from the FBI, will you?" the chief asked as they reached the Hummer.

"Probably not, but I need to consider how to utilize them. The FBI is already looking for Naylyn, although they won't tell me why."

"Keep me posted, Jayden."

"Of course." He opened the door for Bullet.

"Who did he call about the money?" Lieutenant Kaiser asked as Bullet jumped in.

"His former father-in-law, a wealthy businessman from Galveston, Texas." He opened his door.

"I guess we should put things on hold here," Chief Owens said.

"That's up to you. I can't imagine any connection between the caller—since I know who it is—and our suspects here, but you never know." Jayden slid into his seat, but before he shut the door, he had a sudden flash. "Wait. The kidnapper was in prison with Davon Karp. I haven't yet checked to see if they were cellmates or if they even knew each other, but it's worth pursuing. And someone slashed Layda's tires as well as Nadia's. It's probably nothing, but I want to keep it in mind."

"What's the name of the man who called for the ransom?" Owens asked.

"His name is Ulisses Fairchild," he said, anxious to be on his way.

"The ex-husband of the coach?" the lieutenant asked.

"He is," Jayden confirmed.

"We'll check on Davon," the chief promised. "I'll let you know what I learn."

"Thanks. I better go. Ulisses is calling back at eight, and I need to get things prepared before that. And again, please, let me handle this."

***

"Grandpa, are you going to be able to get the money in time?" Nadia asked.

"I'll have it all right. I called two of my top men to pick it up for me. They know how to keep their mouths shut when it's needed. They will rent a jet and bring the money here as soon as they can get it together," Marley said.

The shock of the call had worn off, and Marley Ferrel was in control of his emotions and was planning and thinking like the shrewd businessman he was. For the next several minutes, he kept his phone busy. Nadia, in the meantime, was going crazy. Apparently her grandfather sensed her unrest. "Call down and have a meal sent up," he suggested. "It's almost dinnertime."

She did that, grateful for some little thing to do. While she waited for the food to come up, she started pacing. Her phone rang. She snatched it from the table.

"Nadia, it's Jayden. I'll be there in a few minutes, but I just had a thought. It might be best if you guys came to my office. I have equipment there that we can use to trace the call when he calls back. And I have other helpful gadgets as well."

"I'll tell Grandpa. He's on the phone right now," she said. "Let me ask."

"Grandpa," she said as she held her phone at her side, "can I interrupt for a minute?"

"Hold on a second," he said to whomever he was currently speaking with. "What do you need?"

"I'm talking to Jayden. He wants us to meet him at his office. He says he can trace calls from there," she said.

"Do you know how to get there?"

"I do."

"Then tell Jayden we'll meet him there in my rental car. I don't want you in your car until we catch your dad. He tried to grab you once, and I suspect he might want to try again. We can't let that happen."

"Okay," she said, and Marley turned his attention to his call again.

Nadia lifted her phone to her ear. "He says that will be okay, but I'll ride with him in his rental car."

"That's what I was about to suggest," Jayden said. "I'll be there in less than thirty minutes."

"Then so will we," she said.

"Other than this, are you doing okay, Nadia?" Jayden asked.

She looked down at the sling. "I'm okay."

"Short practice today? I didn't expect you to be back to the hotel so soon."

"I, uh, I left a little early. I can hardly wait for you to get here," she said as she thought about her grandfather's words. For only having known Jayden for less than forty-eight hours, it seemed unreal that he had worked his way so deeply into her heart. But he had. She wanted to be with him.

"Miss my dog, do you?" he teased.

"That's exactly it."

"Nadia," Jayden said, his voice serious again. "There's something you're not telling me. What else is going on?"

She felt tears well up. She was vaguely aware that her grandfather was no longer on his phone, and his eyes were on her. Just then there was a knock on the door. "Our food is here," she said. "I ordered something to eat. Grandpa and I will hurry." She watched her grandfather open the door. "I better go now. I'll see you in a few minutes."

"You haven't answered my question," he said.

"Later. I'm fine, really." She ended the call.

Her grandfather had their burgers laid out already, and he said, "While we scarf this down, please tell me about the sling you're wearing."

***

Jayden pounded his hands on the steering wheel. "Doggone it, Bullet," he said to the dog in the seat behind him who was watching with intelligent black eyes. "She won't tell me what's wrong, and there is something. I think it has to do with her practice today."

Bullet's tail beat a pattern against the back of the seat and the window. If dogs could smile, he had a feeling that Bullet would be right then.

"I know," Jayden said. "You think my heart is going pitter-patter. Well, okay, I admit it. It is. And I can't help it. That girl, she . . . well, you know, she's pretty, she's sweet, and I, well, I think I like her quite a bit."

The tail pounded harder and faster.

"What do you think, Bullet? Am I going gaga over a woman? I know, it's not like me, and I shouldn't be letting this happen after what happened to—" He broke down as he pictured his late wife's face. Finally, calm and in control again, he said, "I need to watch myself and my feelings."

The road sailed by. The thumping of his dog's tail ceased.

"I know, I need to avoid setting myself up for a broken heart," he said. "There is no way a classy gal like Nadia would ever give a second look at a freckled-face guy like me. Is there?"

Bullet began wagging his tail again.

"Anyway, I don't need a girl. I have you," he said, and he told himself he meant it.

Suddenly, his phone began to ring again. He answered.

"Detective Spalding, this is Chief Owens. There's been a development."

"What's that?" Jayden asked.

"I just got a call from an FBI agent by the name of Colten Andrews. Does that name ring a bell?"

"Yes, as a matter of fact, he's half of the pair that accosted me at my apartment last night," he said. "I did mention that to you, didn't I?" It was hard to believe that it had been less than a day since the FBI had come calling.

"Yes, you did," Chief Owens said.

"Andrews is okay, but watch what you say around his partner, Special Agent Press. He's a cocky little bugger. Thinks he's a *special* special agent. I wouldn't be at all surprised if he thinks that I had something to do with Naylyn Pierza's disappearance."

"I appreciate the heads up, Jayden. Now, you probably wonder what they called for," Owens said.

"For sure," Jayden said, not actually sure that was true. He hoped they weren't going to waste his time again.

"They've located Naylyn's cell phone," Chief Owens revealed. "At least, they think they have. They located it using its GPS feature."

"I had a feeling they were going to keep looking for Naylyn. They were very closed-mouth about it with me, but they certainly have an interest in her. What that could be, I can only theorize," Jayden said. "Where do they think it is?"

"Right here on campus. They expect to find it somewhere on the far side of the parking lot beside the gym."

"I was hoping the women still had their phones. That was one of the things I was going to work on when I got back to my office. Let me know if both phones are there as soon as you know."

"I'll do that," the chief promised.

"Let me know if Press tries to accuse you of something. He likes to do that. If he throws you in the slammer, I'll get you out," Jayden said.

"You'll get my first phone call." The chief chuckled.

"Actually, what's more likely is that they'll still try to blame me. If they do, let me know. I may need to disappear myself. I'm not letting that jerk Press toss me in jail," Jayden said. "Oh, and please, don't mention what I'm doing now. I wouldn't mind working with Andrews on the ransom demand, but Press would mess it up. He's one of those *act first, let someone else clean up your mess later* type of guys."

"You have my word," the chief said. "I'll be in touch."

Jayden had really hoped that Nadia's mother still had her cell phone. He'd already planned on trying to locate it. If her phone was with Naylyn's, then that was out of the question. That meant there was only one thing he could do—try to spot the guy when the money drop was made and then try to follow him, hoping he would lead him to the women. As much as he wanted to believe that Ulisses would release the women once he had the million dollars, he didn't believe it.

A few minutes later, he was still running scenarios through his mind as he drove into the parking lot of the office building. He looked at the time on his dash. Almost six o'clock. Where had this day gone? And yet, he had covered a lot of ground. But there was a lot of work yet to do.

CHAPTER ELEVEN

"THERE HE IS," NADIA SAID to her grandfather. She didn't know why but just seeing the black Hummer turn into the parking lot eased her tension. She opened her car door and got out.

As soon as Jayden and Bullet got out of the Hummer, she hurried toward them, her left arm clamped in its sling to her side so it wouldn't bounce. Jayden stopped and stared at her, concern written all over his handsome, freckled face. Bullet, on the other hand, ran right to her and started running around her like he'd just found a long-lost friend. She dropped to her knees, smiling. The dog stopped his antics and pushed close to her. She hugged him with her good arm and then patted his head. She became aware of Jayden standing over them and looked up. The frown from a moment ago was gone, and he was smiling.

"See, Bullet, I knew she liked you."

Nadia gave the dog one last pat on his head and rose to her feet. "Thanks for coming so fast," she said as their eyes locked.

"You are my boss," he said. "When you tell me to do something, I do it. That's the way it works, isn't it?"

"Not if you don't think it's right," she said.

"Let's get inside. I feel exposed out here," he said, and he headed with her toward the office building. "Marley sir," he said as Marley fell in step beside them. "I'm sorry it's come to this, but I have some ideas. We'll talk about them in my office just as soon as this pretty granddaughter of yours explains how she can be fine and have an arm in a sling at the same time."

Once the four of them were in the office, Bullet assumed a position near the front door. The three of them sat around a table in the room next to his private office with the door open. "Now, is that," Jayden began, touching her sling, "because of the attack last night?"

"It is." She quickly explained what had happened at the practice and what the team doctor had told her.

"So no games for a while?" he asked as Marley answered his ringing phone and stepped into the reception area. A useless space, Jayden knew, as he had no one to fill the space behind the reception desk. He'd considered hiring someone but had never gotten around to it.

"Nope, I'm on injured reserve," she said.

"I'm sorry."

"I am too, and I know it will affect the team. Not that I'm *that* good, but I like to believe they need me," she said modestly.

"I'll bet you're their best player," he said seriously. "This has got to be a blow to you and to them."

"I was mad at first, but I prayed, and I was reminded that Heavenly Father knows what's best for me. So I just want to be available to help you in any way I can for as long as possible."

"I'd like that, Nadia."

She impulsively reached over and touched his cheek where whiskers were threatening to hide his freckles.

"Okay, let's get down to business," he said, the tenderness in his eyes replaced with a deadly seriousness that could only mean that he was going to focus on the problems they had to face.

Marley finished his phone call and rejoined them at the conference table. "The money is rounded up. I had two of my best people gather it up, and they'll fly it out to us."

"Are they coming on a private plane?" Jayden asked.

"Yes, a rented one. I've thought about buying one from time to time, but I don't need a plane that often. When I do, I can rent whatever is best for the job at the time. For this matter, they'll be on a Learjet. I want that money here as soon as possible. I want my daughter back," he said with a small crack in his voice.

"Of course you do," Jayden said.

"More than you realize," Marley responded. "I have waited too long to make peace with her. I love her, and I want her back in my life. I just pray that God will give me that chance."

"That makes both of us," Nadia said.

"I'm glad you're here, Marley. Now, let's get some things set up," Jayden said. "I want to be ready to record the moment Ulisses calls again, and we don't have a lot of time." He rose to his feet and opened a large walk-in closet at the far end of the conference room. He began to pick out the things he needed.

Nadia was impressed with how organized the large closet was. She and her grandfather carried items to the table as Jayden selected them. It was a little awkward with only one functional hand, but she did the best she could.

Bullet dozed at the door in the outer office, seeming unconcerned about what was happening.

Nadia put a small box on the table and turned and looked at Jayden as he walked from the closet with a large box in his arms. "Jayden, when was the last time you ate?"

"I'm fine," he said.

"Now you sound like me. I said I was fine when I wasn't," she said with a tight smile. "So again, when was the last time you ate?"

He smiled at her. "You don't have to worry about me. I fixed myself some breakfast at my apartment this morning."

"That's what I thought." She pulled out her phone. "What kind of pizza do you like? I'm going to have some delivered."

***

Police Chief Gary Owens met the two FBI special agents the moment they walked into the department reception area. He invited them back to his office, but they declined. "No, let's find that cell phone first. You can come with us, or you can wait here. Your choice," Agent Andrews said.

"No, why don't we do this ourselves," Agent Press countered. He turned to the chief. "This is an FBI matter. We just wanted you to know that we would be on your campus. We'll let you know if we find the phone."

"Since these women disappeared from *my* jurisdiction, I need to be involved. Lieutenant Kaiser and I will both assist." He thought about Detective Spalding's warning. The PI had nailed it when it came to the younger FBI man's attitude.

He ignored Press's scowl and turned to Janelle, who was still manning her desk even though it was after hours. "Janelle, would you have Tevin meet us at the far side of the parking lot next to the gym? And then you can go ahead and lock up here. I'm sure you have studies to attend to."

"I'll let him know," she said with a smile. "And thank you, sir."

"Really, that's not necessary," Special Agent Press said again. "We can handle this just fine."

"It's okay, Duncan. I'm sure they won't be in the way," the older and wiser special agent said calmly. He seemed to be practiced at brushing off the younger agent's hard attitude.

Press followed the directions of a small GPS unit in his hand, and they headed through the lot, which, at this time in the evening, was almost empty. Ten minutes later, he picked up a Blackberry with a gloved hand and dropped it into an evidence bag that Andrews held out.

"Guess that's it," Special Agent Press said. "We'll just be on our way."

"What about the other phone?" Chief Owens asked.

"What other phone?" Press said with a scowl.

"Coach Fairchild's. She's been kidnapped. You'll need her phone too, won't you?" he asked.

"You are just as naïve as that PI in Phoenix. There is no evidence of a kidnapping. We are interested in Miss Pierza, that's all," the young FBI man said curtly.

"Why are you interested in her?" the chief asked. "She was a student on this campus. If she's done something to garner your attention, I need to know about it."

"With all due respect, Chief Owens," Agent Andrews said. "It's a confidential matter, and it will have no adverse reflection on the college. But if you have some knowledge that this is really a kidnapping, we need to know about that."

The chief and Tevin looked at each other and shook their heads. Tevin wandered back into the area where the phone had been found, and the chief said, "It just feels like a kidnapping. That's all. Maybe I'm wrong." He could see why Detective Spalding didn't want them involved in the ransom demand. "Please let me know if you do learn anything that I should know."

"There won't be anything," Press said curtly. "You can forget we've even been here. This is of no concern to you."

"But if there is something, we'll let you know," Andrews said.

Tevin was standing a few yards away, looking at the ground.

"What does your lieutenant think he's doing?" Special Agent Press asked, pointing at Kaiser.

"I don't believe that's any business of yours. This campus is my jurisdiction. Thanks for letting us know you were coming, and have a good evening," Chief Owens said, trying hard to keep his anger in check.

"You two better not interfere in a federal matter," Press warned and then followed his partner, who was already walking away.

Owens watched the two men climb in their sleek black SUV and drive out of the parking lot before walking over to where Tevin was standing. "What do you have here?"

Tevin pointed to the ground without uttering a word.

Chief Owens looked where he was pointing. "Well, I'll be. Jayden was right. Whoever took the coach and her player threw both phones in the weeds. I don't have an evidence bag on me; do you?"

"No, but I'll go to the office and get one," the lieutenant said. "And I'll bring a glove too."

"That will be great. We'll let Detective Spalding know what we've found as soon as we've had a closer look around the area. In fact, I'll do that while you run back to the office," the chief said. "The kidnapper, or kidnappers, as the case may be, probably tossed these over here. That would explain why they were several feet apart. There probably won't be anything else to find. But we'll look anyway."

***

Everything was set. Jayden had tested his equipment, and everything was working properly. He looked at his watch. It was seven thirty. Now all they could do was wait for the call.

Nadia, who had been speaking quietly with her grandfather in the outer office, walked back into the conference room. "Everything working okay?" she asked.

"Sure is. You two know what to do when the call comes in, right?"

"We do," she said, gazing at him. "You look like you're ready to drop. You ate your pizza, so it's not hunger. How much sleep have you had?"

He smiled warmly. "You're a sweet lady, you know that?"

She put her good hand on her hip and gave him a stern stare. "This is not about me. When did you sleep?" she insisted.

"Well, if you have to know, you woke me up when you called me."

"That was early this morning. And I'm sorry. How long had you slept before I woke you?"

"A little over an hour both times," he said with a grin. "So that means I've had over two hours. That should do."

"Both times? What do you mean?" She was clearly puzzled.

He stepped close to her and peered into her eyes. "I was taking a nap in the police chief's breakroom recliner when you called about the ransom. I didn't even hear the phone I was out so soundly. Bullet woke me up and pawed at my phone. That's when I phoned you back."

"I'm sorry," she said, lifting her right hand and placing it against his chest. "I needed you again."

"Nadia, I hope you will never *not* call me if you need me," he said softly.

"I'll remember that," she promised.

"That nap you interrupted was a good one. I'm rested and ready to do whatever we have to," he said. "So please, don't worry about me."

She lifted her hand from his chest and touched his cheek. "You need to shave," she said with a tender smile.

"I was actually thinking of growing a beard."

"And hide all those cool freckles?" She quickly switched gears as her smooth olive skin began to redden. "I wonder if my father will call right on time."

"I hope so," he said as he slid past her and out of the conference room. Her grandfather was sitting at the receptionist desk, his head in his hands.

"Are you okay, sir?" Jayden asked as he stopped beside the desk.

The old man looked up and said, "Marley."

"That's right. Are you okay, Marley sir?"

Marley smiled. "Whatever else comes of this horrible situation, I hope that you and my granddaughter give each other a chance. I know it's not my business, but the way you two look at each other and interact reminds me of me and my dear departed wife." He dropped his head in his hands. "I hope he calls soon."

Jayden looked at Nadia, who was looking at her grandfather with eyes filled with love and concern. Jayden went into his office.

"What are you doing, Jayden?" Nadia asked.

He paused beside his desk. "I was going to uncover my freckles. I have an electric razor in here."

She smiled then pulled a chair around behind the receptionist desk and sat down beside her grandfather, putting her right hand on his knee. "I love you, Grandpa."

He put a hand over hers and squeezed. "And I love you, little girl. I love your mother too. We have to get her back."

"We will," she replied.

As Jayden listened to them, he offered a silent prayer that their hopes would come to pass. He pulled his razor from his desk and began to shave. His whiskers were long, and the razor had to work to cut its way through them. It was taking a while. He walked toward the outer office as he worked, but suddenly a phone began to ring.

All three of them came alert suddenly, but then Jayden said, "It's my phone."

CHAPTER TWELVE

THE CALL WAS FROM CHIEF Owens.

"Jayden here, did you find the cell phones?" he asked.

"You were right about Special Agent Press," Chief Owens said. "He found the phone belonging to Naylyn, and then he scoffed when I told him that the other phone might be nearby since it could be a kidnapping. The agents made it very clear they don't consider it a kidnapping. They took Naylyn's phone and left."

"Did you keep looking?" Jayden asked.

"Of course, and we found Coach Fairchild's phone. At least, I think it's hers. It's locked, and we can't open it. I wondered if you would call her number. If it has any charge left, we'd know for sure," he said.

"Just a second," Jayden said. He looked over at Nadia. "Call your mother's cell phone," he said. "They think they found it."

She scrambled to pull out her phone.

"Okay, she's calling," Jayden said.

"It's ringing," the chief said a moment later. Then he could hear Chief Owens as he said, "Hello, Miss Fairchild."

And from a couple of steps away, he heard Nadia say, "This is Nadia."

"Okay, we found your mother's phone. I'll talk to Jayden again."

"Thank you, sir," she said.

"You're welcome, and I hope it helps us." Then to Jayden, he said, "I'm back. As I'm sure you just heard, it is the coach's phone. Would you like me to have someone bring it to you?"

"That would be wonderful," Jayden said. "Let me give you my office address."

"I think I'll do it myself. I might bring my wife with me. She says we don't go out enough, and I know a quick trip to Phoenix would be welcome," the chief said.

Jayden thanked him, gave him the address, and then said, "If we have to leave, I'll call you."

Nadia's phone began to ring. She looked at her screen as Jayden put his phone back in his pocket.

"Jules. You didn't have to call." She moved into the conference room, and Jayden resumed shaving. She was back before he had finished. "That was my friend and teammate. She's worried about me, but all I could tell her was that I was okay and would be back playing as soon as I could. She said she was going to come to my apartment and see me tonight. But I told her I wouldn't be home."

"Does she know about your mother?" he asked.

"She knows that she's missing." Nadia stepped close to Jayden and reached out her hand. "Let me help you; you missed a spot."

He relinquished his razor. She leaned close and ran it over a spot under his chin. Then she shut it off. "There, you look great," she said, handing him back the razor.

"So do you," he said. "In fact, if there's such a thing as a girl looking perfect, it would be you."

She shook her head with a little smile on her face.

"I wasn't joking," he said.

"I'm bruised. My hair's a mess. I have an arm in a sling," she listed off as their eyes locked.

"Okay, then almost perfect," he amended. She blushed, and he nodded his head toward the door. "If your father is going to call, it could be anytime now."

As they walked back into the reception area, there was a light tap on the door. Jayden reached for his 9mm, but Marley said, "That'll be my men."

"I'll answer just to make sure." Jayden slipped the pistol from his shoulder holster and approached the door. You two go in the conference room and get out of sight."

"I'll call them," Marley said. As he and Nadia left the room, he was working with his phone.

Bullet was on his feet, his teeth bared, and a low rumble easing its way up his throat. Jayden slipped next to the door with his back to the wall and reached over and unlocked the door. He waited, glancing at Bullet.

Marley called out from the conference room. "What's going on with your dog?"

"Bullet suspects something. I'll let them in, but you two stay there." Jayden slowly turned the doorknob with his left hand. He then eased the door open and saw the face of the first man. The look on his face was one of pure terror. Something wasn't right. Jayden signaled for his dog to stay beside him. Then he swung the door all the way open. Two men with suitcases stepped inside, and right behind them was a man with a gun, a man that Jayden recognized from the description of Professor Pedro Delgado. His hand was shaking as he kept the gun pressed into the back of one of Marley's couriers.

His little pig eyes met Jayden's, and he said, "Give me the gun, or this man gets it in the back."

Jayden let the gun slowly rotate until he was holding it by the trigger guard.

"Hand it to me," the professor said as he crowded the men into the room. He turned the gun toward Jayden. "Now," he ordered.

Jayden slowly extended his gun-bearing arm. Then as the man reached for it and his attention was temporarily distracted, Jayden tapped Bullet on the head with his left hand. Bullet had been trained well. He didn't even bark as he dove for the professor's gun hand at something near the speed of light. The gun flew from his hand to the floor, and the professor screamed with pain.

"Go," Jayden commanded the two couriers.

They ran into the conference room like scared rabbits. Jayden, in the mere blink of an eye, flipped the gun Delgado had thought to take away, and it was back in his hand, ready to fire. Bullet tightened his hold on the professor's wrist, and Jayden could hear bones crushing. But he didn't call the dog off. Professor Delgado was beating at Bullet with his free hand, but the dog wasn't deterred. He dragged the professor into the middle of the room, and then Jayden delivered a powerful karate chop to his chin. He dropped like a rock. Only then did Jayden say, "Bullet, release."

The big gray German shepherd let the mangled wrist slip from his mouth, but he didn't back off. He watched the man with deadly eyes, and that growl rumbled from deep in his chest again. Jayden stretched behind him with one foot and kicked the door closed. Then he dropped on his knees beside the professor. When he was sure Delgado was out cold, he said, "Stand down, Bullet."

He slipped his 9mm back in the shoulder holster, and then with quick hands, he frisked the unconscious man. He pulled a long, dangerous-looking knife from a sheath that was fastened to Delgado's right ankle. He tossed it a few feet away and continued his frisk. As soon as he was satisfied that there were no more weapons, Jayden stood up, retrieved the man's gun and knife, and slipped them into a desk drawer.

He was finally able to take a look around the room. Crowded in the doorway of the conference room were Nadia, Marley, and Marley's two employees, who still held the suitcases containing a million dollars in cash, their faces white.

He took a deep breath. "Take the money in my office." He pointed to it. "There are chairs in there. Go ahead and relax as much as you can. We are expecting a call. It's important. We'll deal with Professor Delgado as soon as we finish with the call. In the meantime, Bullet will keep him company in case he comes to before we've finished." Marley and his men stepped to the office door. Jayden said, "I suppose that after what you've been through you might need a restroom. It's over there."

Both men nodded but did not utter a single word. The fellow who'd had the gun poked in his back rushed to it immediately, dropping the suitcase he was carrying. Marley picked it up, and he and the second man went into the office.

Only then did Nadia rush over to Jayden. "Oh, Jayden, I've never been so scared in my life. Not even when that man attacked me last night."

"You were in more danger then than you were this time," he said. "Goodness. This guy was the one who should have been afraid."

"But he could have shot you, Jayden. I couldn't stand it if you got hurt . . . or worse," she said with a shaking voice.

"Hey, I had Bullet. There's no way he would have let that guy shoot me." He looked fondly at the dog that stood rigidly beside the unconscious professor. "And if by some extremely unlikely event he had shot me, that dog would have torn him to pieces. I can guarantee you that at no time were you in any danger."

Jayden raised a hand and pointed to the restroom, where the sound of someone being very sick at the toilet was carrying through the door. "That man, now he was in danger. The professor's hand was shaking so badly my biggest fear was that he would fire accidentally."

"But that . . . that horrible man, he turned the gun toward you," she sobbed. "It was you I was scared for."

"Ah, Nadia, that's so sweet." He touched her cheek briefly.

"I mean it. Believe it or not, just because I have not known you for very long doesn't mean I don't care about you. Because I do," she said with a touch of anger in her voice.

"Hey, you're making me blush," he joked.

She looked up at him, but then she abruptly turned away and knelt down beside Bullet. "Thank you, Bullet. You were amazing." She looked up at Jayden. "Did I hear bones crunch?"

"I have no idea what you heard, but I know I did."

She grinned at him. And then she said with her eyes suddenly wide, "Hey, he's moving. Shouldn't we do something about the bleeding?"

"Yes, we should. That blood is messing up my floor." Jayden retrieved a first-aid kit from his office and began to deal with the man's injuries.

While Jayden worked, Marley stepped back into the front office. "My guy wonders when we're going to call the cops. I told him I'd ask you."

"Not until we hear from Ulisses." Jayden glanced at the clock on the wall. "He's ten minutes late calling."

The bathroom door opened, and the second courier came out. He was pale, but he walked quite steadily. Marley directed him into the office as the other man took his turn in the bathroom.

Delgado woke up from his karate-induced sleep and began to curse.

"You can just close your mouth," Jayden said in a tone of voice that begged to be obeyed. "If you don't, I'll let my dog finish what he started."

The professor turned his head just enough that he could see Bullet. His eyes bulged. Not a sound was coming out, but his lips continued moving. He was obviously cursing to himself.

Jayden ignored it until he had finished his first aid. "That's better," Jayden finally said. "I don't allow that kind of language in my office, especially when there's a lady present."

Marley returned just then. "You do good work, Jayden."

"Thank you, Marley sir. I've had a lot of practice." Then Jayden looked down at the man on the floor. "I know who you are, Professor Pedro Delgado. You made the biggest mistake of your life today. Now, we have some business to attend to. I'm leaving you under the watchful eyes of Bullet. If you so much as try to sit up, that will then become the biggest mistake of your life. You're already going to lose your job and go to jail for a very long time, but if you stir before I tell you to, my dog will probably kill you. That, of course, would be your last mistake. Do I make myself clear?"

Pedro nodded ever so slightly, his little eyes not moving from Bullet.

"Good, let's go in the conference room, folks. That call should be coming in anytime," Jayden said.

"If it comes in at all," Marley said dejectedly. "So help me, if that guy so much as hurts a hair on my daughter's head . . ." He didn't say any more, but Jayden and Nadia had gotten the message.

The three of them dragged Delgado into Jayden's office, where he instructed the couriers to also keep an eye on him.

In the conference room, Jayden shut the door behind them. They all sat at the places previously designated.

Nadia said, "Who is that despicable man? He is one creepy guy, but you seemed to know him, Jayden."

"I knew who he was the second I saw him. I can call him despicable, but, Nadia," he said, shaking a finger toward her, "you should be ashamed speaking that way about your mother's old boyfriend."

"What?" she said as Marley's phone, which was on the table right in front of him, began to ring.

"Later," he said. "Now remember, total silence except for you, Marley. This will be on speaker so we can all hear."

Jayden touched a button, and his recorder began. He touched another button, and the tracer began to work. "Remember, don't let him know that you know who it is."

Marley picked up the phone. "Hello. This is Marley Ferrel."

"Oh, it is huh? Then listen up, old man. If you want to see your daughter and her friend alive, you better have that million in unmarked hundreds we talked about earlier," the caller said.

"I've got it. Are the women okay?" Marley asked, holding his fists so tight they were white.

"Of course they're okay."

"I want to talk to my daughter, and then I'll believe you."

The slightly muffled voice said, "They're fine. I'm taking good care of them."

"I need proof," Marley said tensely as Jayden watched him getting angrier by the second. Nadia looked up at Jayden and mouthed, "It's him."

He nodded that he understood. Marley nodded as well.

"You want proof? I'll give you proof. I'll leave their dead bodies where they can be found, and that'll be proof—proof that I am serious. They die if you don't do exactly as I say."

"Okay, I guess I'll have to take your word on it," Marley said. He was trying to keep Ulisses talking while Jayden attempted to trace the call.

"Yes, you will. And remember this, old man. There better be no police involved. If there are, the deal's off. And I'll know. Believe me; you won't slip any cops in without me knowing it. If you're stupid enough to do that, then you may not lose your money, but the women will die—and they will suffer."

"No cops. I got it, but you better make sure my daughter and that other woman aren't hurt. If you don't, I'll figure out who you are and chase you down. And you don't want to know what I'll do to you when I catch up with you." The veins on Marley's head were swelling like they were ready to burst.

"Won't happen. You don't know who you're up against," the caller said. "Here are your instructions. There is a garbage bin behind a Denny's Restaurant. It was dumped this morning, so it's empty now. You are to carry the money in two suitcases and drop them into the dumpster. Come alone. And I don't mean having someone close by. You be all alone. When it's done, walk back the way you came. Come back in thirty minutes, and the women will be standing by the dumpster. They'll be tied together but unhurt. Here's the address." Ulisses gave him the address and finally said, "Ten o'clock tonight. Don't be late. Don't be early. And be alone. Don't try any funny stuff. Just do as I say, and you'll get your precious daughter back." There was a slight hesitation on the line. "We know about your granddaughter, old man. You mess with us, and she's next."

The call ended. Marley's face was dripping with perspiration. Nadia was as gray as a London fog bank. "I don't know what to think," Marley said. "But I am going to do exactly as he says. And you two Mormons need to pray that it goes as he claims."

"I'm praying, Grandpa." Nadia stepped beside him and put a hand on his shoulder.

"So am I," Jayden said. "I've got his cell phone fixed on my GPS tracker. It's from the same one he used before, but he wasn't stationary while he was talking." Jayden had a map of Phoenix and the surrounding area on the table. He marked a spot with a yellow marker. "He was here when the tracker picked up on him." He marked another spot. "He was here when he ended the call."

"He's moving pretty fast," Marley said. "Even if we'd called the cops, I'm afraid it wouldn't have helped. We don't have any idea what he's driving or if he's alone. And he will have kept going. He could be anywhere in the city now. He's smarter than I gave him credit for."

"And dumber," Jayden said. "He should have used a burner phone." He smiled. "He's right here now." Jayden marked another spot on the map. Then he turned his state-of-the-art tracking device so Marley and Nadia could see it. "I'm still tracking him."

"Fantastic," Marley said.

"We could have him stopped and picked up at any time, but if we did, it might be fatal for the ladies. I doubt he has them in the car with him. But we can watch and see where he goes between now and the time for the drop and then where he goes after that."

"He may not have my mother and Naylyn with him, but someone does," Nadia said, her face gradually resuming its color.

"You picked up on that, I see," Jayden said. "Yes, he said *us* and *we*, so we have to assume he's got help."

"What do we do now?" Marley asked, his shoulders stooped and his face looking ten years older than it had the day before.

"We follow his instructions. That's the only thing we can do. We need to get the money ready," Jayden said.

"It's ready. It's in two suitcases, just like he ordered," Marley said.

"I have a little something I need to add to the suitcases," Jayden said. Jayden opened one of the boxes on the table. He reached in and pulled out a tiny gray object. "This is a transmitter. I plan to attach one to each of the suitcases. Then, even if he gets smart and ditches the phone, I can still keep track of where he is."

"That would stand out on the suitcase," Marley said.

"I have them in a variety of colors. I'll put them where they're not likely to get knocked off or be seen."

"Okay, but you can't be with or even near me when I leave the money," Marley said. "You heard him, and I won't risk it."

"Don't worry. I'll be around but nowhere near you. You'll be on your own."

A knock came on the door. Jayden's hand went to his shoulder holster and came out filled with steel. "It's too early for that to be Chief Owens. You two stay in here. I'll get Bullet and see who's there."

CHAPTER THIRTEEN

"Be careful, Jayden, please," Nadia said softly, her eyes wide with concern.

"I'll be okay," he said as the knock came again and he slipped from the room, shutting the door behind him.

Bullet was already near the door, but he was silent. Whoever it was, Bullet wasn't concerned, so it must be someone they knew. Jayden stepped beside the door, his 9mm held up in his right hand, just in case. He slowly unlocked the door and called, "Who's there?"

"It's me, Desmond Booker," came the parole officer's familiar voice from the hallway on the other side of the door.

"Okay, the door's unlocked, come on in, but do it slowly."

The door slowly opened, but until Jayden saw the bandage-swathed parole officer, he didn't relax. As soon as Booker was inside, Jayden shut the door and put his pistol back in his shoulder holster. Then he once more locked the door. "It's good to see you, Desmond. How'd you escape from the hospital?"

"I had planned to slip away without being seen, but when I explained to the doctor that I had a parolee who was up to no good, he agreed to release me. And it was none too soon. I was going stir-crazy in that place."

"Are you sure that was wise? You look a little pale."

Booker grinned. "Pale? Me? The only way you could make this black boy pale was if you bathed me in hydrogen peroxide. Seriously, I'm fine. I drove by your house, but when you weren't there, I decided to drop by here just in case you were working. I saw your vehicle in the parking lot, so I came on up. What's going on?"

Jayden pointed to the conference room door. "I have company. You're my fourth visitor in the past little while. The first two were followed by a man who was planning to shoot some folks. Bullet had other ideas. Those three are in my personal office. The others are in the conference room. Why didn't you just call me?"

Booker chuckled. "I wanted to offer to help, and I knew that on the phone you'd tell me just to go home and rest. I figured if I caught you in person, you could see that I was doing good and let me assist."

"Let's join the others, and I'll explain," Jayden said. "My client and her grandfather are in here." He opened the door to the conference room.

Jayden made quick introductions.

"It's nice to meet you, Mr. Booker," Marley said, "and I'm sorry about the injury, but one of your parolees was just on the phone. And he said not to involve the cops."

Jayden offered Booker a chair. After he was seated, he asked with narrowed eyes, "Are you referring to Ulisses Fairchild?"

"I am. He has my daughter, and I intend to get her back. And furthermore, he threatened harm to my granddaughter if I didn't do exactly as he said. I can't risk cops being involved until I get Layda and her young friend back."

"Mr. Ferrel," Booker began.

"Call me Marley."

"Marley, I'm not a cop in the traditional sense. I'm a parole officer. That technicality aside, I'll only be involved in whatever way you all advise me to," Booker said. "Why don't you tell me how you know Ulisses took the ladies and what you are doing here." He indicated to the table with Jayden's equipment spread out on it.

"Ulisses has demanded a million-dollar ransom," Jayden said as he worked to attach one of the little transmitters to a suitcase. "Each of these two suitcases holds a half a million dollars. I'm attaching transmitters to each one." He straightened up then checked his GPS tracking device. "This is Ulisses," he said as he pointed to a small, red, flashing dot. Then he explained about Ulisses's call and how they were still watching where he was going. "He seems to be circling around now." Jayden drew Booker's attention to the large map. He added another red mark and wrote the time beside it. "As long as he keeps his cell phone with him, we'll know where he is at any given time."

"That's impressive," Booker said.

"We do have a little problem. I need to call the police and get someone to take Professor Delgado off our hands."

Jayden had a lot of friends in the police department. He decided to call a detective who attended the same LDS ward that he did. He explained about the professor without telling him about the kidnapping. His friend promised to come right away with another officer. Then Jayden said, "I patched him the best I can, but Bullet sort of mangled his wrist. He'll need medical attention before he goes to jail."

His friend told Jayden that he would take care of it but that he would need witness statements from everyone. Jayden assured him that he would get them but because of something pressing going on, it might take a while.

While they waited for the detectives to arrive, Jayden explained to Booker about the little transmitters. Nadia and Marley followed the slowly moving red dot with their eyes as Jayden finished his explanation.

When he'd finished, Booker said, "He expects to get away with this, doesn't he? I take it that you have a plan to recover both the women and the money."

Marley looked up from the device. "I don't care about the money. I just want my daughter back. That's what I expect Jayden to concentrate on." He gave Jayden a meaningful glance.

"Here's what we'll do. I'm expecting the campus police chief to be here shortly with some evidence he recovered earlier this evening. He might be able to help smooth the way with the local officers without letting them know about Ulisses. I can't let Chief Owens get involved until we get the women back, but I'm hoping he'll stay with Nadia, keep an eye on things here, monitor the phone, etc. Marley will drop the money off. If you would, you could stay here too. I don't think you're ready for a lot of activity right now."

"I hate to admit it, but I am a little weak. However, I do want to help. After all, it's one of my parolees causing all this trouble. I'll stay here unless I'm needed elsewhere," Booker agreed.

"Thanks. That would be great. Now, the ransom drop is to take place here." Jayden pointed at a mark on the map. "Once he gets the money, we'll have two ways to track him: his cell phone's GPS and the tracking transmitters."

"So if he finally realizes that you could find him with his cell phone and ditches it, you can still get to him." Booker nodded. "I like it."

"I hope it works," Jayden said. "Now, the ransom drop is to be at ten o'clock sharp. Marley will put the money in the dumpster and leave. He will return thirty minutes later and hopefully find Layda and Naylyn."

"And where will you be?" Marley asked.

"I'm going to leave shortly and try to get within a block or so of Ulisses," he said. "I'll make sure he doesn't see me, but I'll also have a pretty good idea if he picks up the women from whoever he has helping him."

"He has help?" Booker asked.

"We think so, yes. And that's something else you could be doing." Jayden explained quickly about the disgraced former team member, Lorena Husman, and her boyfriend, Davon Karp. "Karp served time in prison while Ulisses was there."

"I'll find out all about him," Booker said. "It'll be good to have something to do. I'll let you know what I learn."

"You shouldn't go alone, Jayden," Nadia said with worry in her voice.

He looked at her and smiled. "I'll have my canine partner. You already know what he can do."

"I was meaning a *person*," she said. "I'll go crazy sitting here while you and Grandpa are out there in danger."

Jayden slowly shook his head. "I want you to stay here," he said firmly. "Anyway, I need two good arms. You have one. Booker has one. You'll make a good team."

Booker smiled, but Nadia didn't.

"I also want you to stay here, little girl," Marley said. "I will not risk losing you. You are the most important person in my life."

A pout formed on Nadia's face, but she said nothing more, just moved away from Jayden and sat down on the far side of the table. Jayden attached the second tracking transmitter to the other suitcase.

Just as he finished, there came another knock at the door—Detective Noe and his partner. Jayden shut the door to the conference room and had Marley, Booker, and Nadia wait in the reception area. Jayden then opened the door and let the detectives in. "We dragged the professor into my private office," he said, as he waved the men in that direction. He then introduced everyone. "Nadia and her grandfather are clients of mine. These other fellows work for Marley at his plant in Texas. They were delivering some material from his plant in Galveston that I need for their case. The fellow on the floor is Professor Pedro Delgado from Coolidge. I was asking questions about him at the college there. He hasn't told me, but I think the reason he came packing a gun is that he's angry with me. I suppose we can straighten that all out later. Right now, I want him gone."

Detective Noe nodded his head. "Like I told you on the phone, I'll need statements from all of you."

"All but Officer Booker. He came in after it was over," Jayden explained.

Detective Noe said, "When can I talk with you about this?"

"In the morning?" Jayden asked. "And I'll bring statements from everyone else then."

"I'll need contact information for all of them," Detective Noe said. He rubbed his chin for a moment and then asked, "Are these fellows from Galveston finished, or do you still need them?"

Jayden looked at Marley, who said, "Why don't I have them meet you at your station in a little while. I need them back at my plant first thing tomorrow."

"Do they have a plane to catch?" Noe asked.

Marley said, "They didn't come on a commercial flight. I have a jet waiting for them at the airport. I'll call the pilot and tell him they'll be delayed. He won't care. He's getting paid by the hour."

"Jayden, if you'll meet me tomorrow morning and bring statements from your clients, that will be fine," he said. His eyes lingered for a moment on Nadia. "It's nice to meet you. Good luck with whatever you're involved in. I can tell you this—Jayden is the best PI in town. Not all PIs get along with the cops," he said. "That's not the case with Jayden."

With that, he and his partner, who hadn't said a word, reached for the professor.

"Stand down, Bullet," Jayden said and pointed to the reception area. "Go in there."

Bullet obediently trotted out of the room. As quick as he was out of sight, Delgado, who was now on his feet with the officers firmly in control of him, said, "I'll kill you for this, Spalding. You got no business sticking your nose in my life."

Detective Noe and his partner left with Professor Delgado. As soon as the door was shut behind them, Jayden spoke to the two couriers. "When you speak to the detectives, you're not to tell them anything about what's in the suitcases you brought here. Is that clear?"

They both nodded.

"Okay, here's the address of the police station." He wrote it on a notepad, ripped off the sheet, and handed it over. He then gave each of them one of his cards and said, "Call me if you need to. But Detective Noe is a good friend of mine, and his partner is a decent cop as well."

As soon as they were gone, Jayden led the remaining guests back into the conference room. "I want to get out there. Marley, it should take you about twenty minutes to get from here to the Denny's, but I want you to leave by nine thirty to give you time to walk into the alley carrying the money."

"I can handle the money," Marley said. "Surprising as it may seem, it's not all that heavy."

"Okay, Marley sir," Jayden said, bringing a puzzled look from Booker. "Nadia," Jayden continued. She looked up at him. "There are two GPS trackers and two trackers for each of the transmitters. "I'll have one set in my Hummer with me. The other set is your responsibility. You and I will talk as we need to. You have the map here. I'd like you to pinpoint his location at all times and make sure I'm in the right area. Will you do that?"

"I'd rather go with you," she said. "But will it help?"

"A lot," he said.

"Then I'll do it. I don't want you getting lost." She offered him a weak smile.

"And I don't want to," he replied, sending her a warm signal with his eyes. Then he turned to Booker. "I expect Chief Owens here at any time. I was hoping he'd get here before I had to leave, but it looks like that isn't going to happen." He turned toward the door, but just then, there was another knock. Bullet sprang to his feet and stood near the door wagging his tail. "That will be him now," Jayden said.

"How do you know that?" Booker asked.

"He knows Chief Owens, and you'll notice the way he's wagging his tail. I'll get the door."

Jayden introduced the chief, who indicated that his wife was shopping, and then Jayden said, "I'm on my way out now. Why don't the three of you bring him up-to-date on the plan."

"Will do," Booker said. Marley merely nodded.

Nadia walked with Jayden as he headed for the door. "Jayden," she said. He stopped and looked at her. "Good luck." She gave him a smile.

"Thanks," he said, and with that, he and Bullet were out the door.

***

Nadia stood watching the door after Jayden and Bullet had left. Her heart was heavy. She examined her feelings that seemed to be developing in regard to him. She hardly knew Jayden. Perhaps she was only in awe of his personality and his determination to find her mother. He was a likable guy. But even though they shared their religion, they lived in very different worlds. Still, she felt a connection that couldn't be denied. She worried about him in a way she wouldn't have done if she didn't have that connection. She knew he was capable—more than capable—and so was his dog, but she worried anyway.

Footsteps sounded on the polished hardwood floor, and a hand fell gently onto her shoulder. "Don't worry," her grandfather said as she turned toward him. "He's as good as they come. He knows how to take care of himself. I know you like him, and I don't blame you. But try not to worry so much."

"Is it that obvious?" She pulled a face. "I don't even know how I feel."

"Little girl, you look at that man the way your grandma used to look at me. I know that look. And Jayden looks at you just the same way."

"But, Grandpa," she said with a catch in her voice. "I only met him yesterday. How could I get these feelings so fast? And how could he? It doesn't happen."

He smiled and pulled her into a gentle embrace. "Not very often, but I can see what's happening between the two of you. It's real, little girl. Don't fight it."

"Thank you, but I don't want to rush myself." She kissed his cheek. "I need to get back in there and watch the GPS tracking things."

She sat down at the table and watched. Her father's GPS wasn't moving anymore. She pinpointed the location on the map. "Maybe this is where he's holding Mom," she said without looking up.

"If we knew for sure, we'd get some backup and move in, but we don't. We can't risk it." It was Booker speaking. "We have a plan, Nadia. We need to stick with it."

Chief Owens nodded in agreement.

"I'm going to call Jayden." She dialed his number and waited.

"Hi," he said, and the way he said that one little word sent shivers all over her body.

"Hi," she said back, wondering if he felt any shivers. But then she got down to business. "Dad has stopped. I marked the spot on the map."

"I see he has," Jayden agreed. "What is the approximate address?"

She studied the map. Booker leaned in next to her and studied it as well. Just then there was a loud rap on the door. "Jayden, somebody's at your door," she said as her stomach took a tumble. "Who could it be?"

"I don't know. Stay on the phone with me. Let Booker and Owens handle it. They know what to do," he said.

She looked at Booker, who was already moving away, pulling his gun with his good right hand. Chief Owens had his gun in his hand as well. "Jayden said you guys would know what to do," she said. "He wants me to stay on the phone with him."

"We've got it," Owens said. He and Booker left the conference room, shutting the door behind them. Marley sat next to Nadia in the chair that Booker had just vacated.

And then she again spoke into the phone. "I've got the address, Jayden." She read off the nearest intersections.

"Okay, I'm just two blocks from there. I'm going to leave my Hummer, and Bullet and I will approach on foot," Jayden said.

"Jayden, don't let them see you."

His chuckle warmed her but didn't decrease her worry.

"I'm an expert at this. This isn't my first time. I served in Afghanistan when I was an army ranger. I'll call you back shortly."

The call ended, and she sat looking at her grandfather. She told him what Jayden had told her.

"Hey, this investigator of yours is smart. He'll be okay. But he won't do anything yet. He just wants to see if he can determine what they are doing and if your mother and Naylyn are with him."

She nodded. "I know. I wonder who was at the door."

In a few seconds, the door to the conference room opened, and she knew.

"Marley, Nadia, these men are with the FBI. Special Agents Colten Andrews and Duncan Press," Chief Owens said. "They're looking for Jayden. We explained that he's out on a job."

"You people are up to something." Press squinted suspiciously. "I demand to know what it is."

Marley was looking nervously at his watch. "I need to go too," he said.

"Go where?" Press asked.

"I have a delivery to make." He grabbed a suitcase in each hand and headed for the door.

"You aren't going anywhere," Special Agent Press said as he blocked the conference room door.

Marley's eyes narrowed, and his face darkened. "Unless I have broken a federal law, you better get out of my way."

"What's in the suitcases?" the FBI man asked.

"It's none of your business," Marley said. "You guys are entirely out of order here."

"Duncan, lighten up. He's right. We have no reason for stopping him—unless you know something I don't?" Special Agent Andrews said.

The younger agent glared at the older one. "I want to know what these people are doing." He waved a hand at the table. "This is a lot of fancy equipment I see here. What are you watching, Miss Fairchild?"

She looked at Booker, who had moved back beside her for support. He took the initiative. "I took a bullet last night from one of my parolees. He beat this young lady up. Her father is also one of my parolees, and these people are trying to help me find him."

"Ulisses Fairchild?" Andrews asked.

"That's right. He's my former son-in-law, and I want him corralled," Marley said, the anger in his voice and on his face evident. "He called and threatened me, and I believe he was behind the assault on my granddaughter. Now, I've got to go."

"Not so fast." Special Agent Press again blocked the door, this time the one to the outer hallway.

Chief Owens spoke up. "Let him go; then we'll all sit down and explain exactly what's going on."

"I don't think so," Press said.

"Let him go," Andrews ordered with clear authority in his voice.

Press glared at him but stepped out of the path. A moment later, the door closed behind Marley. Chief Owens locked the door. Then he said, "Why don't we all sit down and talk about what's happening."

As soon as they had all pulled chairs up from the wall of the outer office, Chief Owens began, "We have a situation here."

CHAPTER FOURTEEN

It was a moonless night but still very warm. There were streetlights in the vicinity, which was filled with industrial buildings. Jayden moved quickly but cautiously toward the spot where Ulisses's GPS indicated he was stopped. A lot was running through his mind as he slipped along—foremost was the text Nadia had just sent him. He couldn't believe the bad luck in having the FBI agents show up at his office. He hoped Booker and Owens could keep them under control, but he knew Special Agent Press was headstrong, and if he found out there had been a ransom demand, he would want to take over. Jayden could only pray that the more even-headed senior agent would see that interference at this point would only endanger lives.

Jayden knew there wasn't anything he could do that he wasn't already doing. Bullet was staying close and being as silent as a mouse. He walked on noiseless pads. It was a comfort to have him along. He hoped to be able to spot Ulisses and whoever was with him, and more than anything, he prayed that the women were here. If he found them, he'd call for backup and end the whole thing right there. He suddenly pounded his head and whispered to Bullet, "I don't know why I didn't think of this sooner. If Nadia knew where I was, she could tell me how close I am to Ulisses."

The dog looked up at him, his gray face barely discernable in the dark alcove they'd slipped into. Jayden pulled out his phone and punched in Nadia's number.

"Jayden, are you okay?" she asked urgently. "Have you spotted my father yet?"

"Yes and no," he whispered. "I'm fine, but I haven't located your father. I need you to do something for me. Do you have the Find My Phone app on your iPhone?"

"Yes. What do you need me to do?"

"Find my phone," he said. "I have the app too."

"Jayden, are you sure you're okay? You're talking on your phone. You haven't lost it," she said.

"Oh, *that's* why it isn't in my pocket. Good grief." He allowed himself a quick, quiet chuckle. Then he said, "I need you to know where I am and then tell me how close I am to your father's phone," he whispered. "If I'd had another GPS tracking device, I'd already have you watching where I go, but I don't."

"Got it. I'll need to end the call, but I'll call you back from your office phone as soon as I locate the signal."

"That's my girl, but first, tell me, has Agent Press arrested anyone yet?"

"No, but I think he'd like to. Thank goodness his partner has a level head. Press tried to keep Grandpa from leaving with the money."

"Did he know it was money?"

"No, Grandpa told him it wasn't his business. And Andrews said to let Grandpa go."

"Where are the agents?"

"In your reception area, talking to Chief Owens and Mr. Booker," she reported. "I'm in here alone at the moment."

"Have you heard any gunshots?" he asked wryly.

"No, did you think I would?" she asked with urgency in her voice.

"I'm just pulling your leg. What about shouting?"

"Not that either."

"Have you heard anyone leave?"

"No."

"Okay, I was hoping those guys would stay out of the way. Let's end this call, and you can attempt to find my phone. I need it really badly."

She chuckled as he ended the call.

***

It only took Nadia three or four minutes to find the location of Jayden's phone using the app. Then she took another minute to locate it on the map. He was almost on top of her father according to the map, but of course, the map was small when compared to what she was able to see on the screen showing Ulisses's phone. It was still stationary. After comparing the map on her phone with the GPS on her father's phone, she knew exactly how to tell him to proceed. She called Jayden.

"Did you find my phone?" Jayden asked.

"I did," she said. "I'll keep the phone open and direct you as you walk. And, Jayden . . ."

"Yes, Nadia?"

"Don't take any chances," she said softly.

"You have my word," he whispered.

She followed his movements and directed him closer to where the signal from her father's phone was originating. "Jayden, you're really close. You better stay out of sight."

"Bullet just told me that there's no one nearby," he said. "I don't like the looks of this."

"Why not?"

"I'm standing at the corner of a large building with an empty lot in front of me."

"What are you going to do?"

"I'm going to keep moving, but that means I have to cross the empty space," Jayden said as she became aware of the conference room door opening behind her. She glanced back. The first person through the door was Special Agent Press.

"My dad and his friends might be watching," she said into the phone.

"Might be watching who?" Press asked as he closed in on her.

"Is someone with you?" Jayden asked as he stopped in a small alcove in the old building he'd been passing.

"Special Agent Press just joined me," she said. "He wonders who I'm talking to."

"Then tell him," he said.

"I'm talking to Detective Spalding," she said to the FBI agent.

"What's all this?" he said, pointing to the phones and GPS tracker on the table. "Where is he?"

Jayden could hear what the agent was saying. So he said, "Nadia, let me talk to that guy."

"Where are you, Spalding?" Press demanded. "If this is a kidnapping case, then that puts me in charge."

"Who said anything about kidnapping? I'm a private detective working a case which, it so happens, is none of your business. Now quit interfering and give the phone back to Nadia."

"I think you're trying to catch the kidnappers," Press went on. "I know you're working a kidnapping. If you don't let me in on what is going on right now, I'll hold you personally responsible when someone gets hurt."

"Special Agent Press, listen to me. Right now, all we know is that I'm closing in on a criminal. I'm helping Desmond Booker. Now give the phone back to Nadia."

"He's really mad," Nadia said with a tremor in her voice a moment later.

"Not as mad as I am," Jayden said. "I'm about to step out into the open here. Bullet's right beside me. Tell me where to go."

Behind her, Nadia could hear Special Agent Press arguing with Andrews, Booker, and Owens. Her own temper suddenly spiked. A man she had come to care for was in danger, and she needed to concentrate in order to help him. "Hey, Chief Owens, Mr. Booker, I need to have you guys take the FBI back in the other room before they get Jayden shot!"

Special Agent Press refused to budge until his partner said, "Duncan, get back in the other room." His voice left no room for argument, and Press finally stepped out of the conference room. Booker slammed the door and left Chief Owens to deal with the FBI. He locked it from the inside and then stepped over to Nadia.

"Is he okay?" Booker asked. She nodded. "Then do whatever it is you were doing."

"Jayden, you can start now." She watched as Jayden's phone moved at an angle away from her father's phone. "He's back to the left a little bit. You should be able to see him by now."

"No, there's only open space here," he said as he continued to move. "Is that better?"

"Yes, keep going straight now. Are you sure you don't see anyone? Could he be hiding somewhere?"

"Not here," Jayden said. "There's nothing to hide behind."

"Okay, just a few more steps," she said. Suddenly Jayden's phone moved rapidly forward. He stopped so that the two phones were at the same exact place. She held her breath. He was only stationary for a couple of seconds, and then he was hurrying back the way he'd come.

She waited for him to speak. When he did, she could hear the discouragement in his voice. "I've got his phone," he said. "He ditched it. Now I have no idea which way he may have gone."

"Oh no, I so hoped you'd find my mother," she said dejectedly. "Where are you going now?"

"Back to my Hummer. I need to get off my phone. Your grandfather should be calling before long. What are the FBI guys doing now?"

"I don't know. Booker locked them out of the conference room."

"Okay, let me talk to Booker." And then he added, "Hey, Nadia, it'll be okay. We'll find your mother. You hang in there. And there's one more thing."

"What's that, Jayden?"

"I think you're cute. Give the phone to Booker."

The words left her stunned but with a smile on her face and a blush in her cheeks.

"I don't know what you just said to this girl, but she's blushing," Booker said. "You like to kid with her, don't you?"

"I wasn't kidding. I was serious." Then he said, "Booker, Ulisses finally got smart and dumped his phone. I have it with me. We'll analyze it later, but right now, if you're feeling up to it, I need you to help Nadia watch the tracking units. I expect a call from Marley any moment now."

"I'm fine. I think that arrogant FBI guy, Press, got my adrenaline flowing, and it hasn't let up yet," he said. "I'm nearly jumping out of my skin with energy."

After Jayden got back to his Hummer, he and Bullet got in. The vehicle was still hot inside, even though it had been dark for quite some time. Jayden stepped back out and had Bullet join him while the air conditioning cooled the car. He was tense, listening for his phone. It finally rang. He took the call quickly, and Marley said, "I just left the money in the dumpster, and I'm getting out of here now. Do you still have a bead on Ulisses?"

"If by a *bead*, you mean am I still following his cell phone signal, then the answer is no," Jayden said. "He dumped his phone. But I found it, so I have it now."

"I guess he finally wised up," Marley said. "Well, all we can do is hope he brings my daughter and her friend like he said he would. I'll stay away a reasonable distance, and then I'll come back in thirty minutes and see if the ladies are here."

"I'll join you," Jayden said. "As soon as you pick a place to park and wait, give me a call, and I'll go there. In the meantime, I'm headed in the general direction of the drop site."

He got off the phone and back in the Hummer, Bullet beside him. He was silently praying that Ulisses and whoever was helping him would live up to their end of the bargain. Marley had done his.

Jayden's phone rang again. "Jayden here," he said when he recognized Chief Owens's number on the screen.

"I'm about to lose it with Special Agent Press," Owens said. "We told them what we had, but we made sure they knew it wasn't a confirmed kidnapping. We told them Marley's a rich man and would rather lose the money than take a chance. Andrews says they'll wait, and if we get the women, they'll go after Ulisses. Press says they need to go to the drop site now, since we admitted we were leaving money."

"Do they have the address of the drop site?"

"No, but they've seen the map. So they know about where it is."

"Do what you can. If they show up there, they could ruin the only chance Ulisses is going to give us," Jayden said.

"I'll do my best. I'm going to hand the phone to Booker. He wants to talk to you," Chief Owens said.

"Jayden, I've been so busy trying to keep that young FBI agent from messing things up that I haven't been able to follow up on Davon Karp yet. The senior agent seems to have the other one in control now, so I'll work on that," Booker said. "Although I'm not sure I can learn anything this time of day—or night."

"Thanks. I have another call coming in. It's probably Marley." He switched to the other caller. It was Marley, and he gave Jayden the address where he was at. "Got it," Jayden said. "I'm not far away."

He climbed into Marley's rental car just as the trackers started beeping. The cash had been picked up and was moving.

Nadia called. "They have the money, Jayden. You're probably watching it too," she said.

"I am. Keep an eye on it. It's possible that the two suitcases could be split up," Jayden told her. "If that happens, I can only follow one of them, so it will be important that you keep track of the other one."

He wanted to leave right away, but he knew that they should wait for the full thirty minutes. The second they reached that time, Jayden, who had left his car running with Bullet in it, said, "You go to the drop site and get the women—if they're there. I'm going to try to close in on whoever picked up the money."

Back in the Hummer, he sped away, praying that the women had been returned. Whoever had picked up the money was going fast, but Jayden was going faster. Suddenly, he had an idea. He called Chief Owens's number. As soon as he had the chief on the phone, he said, "I wonder if the FBI would be willing to help now. We could sure use a chopper if they have one."

"Hang on, I'll talk to them," the parole officer said. Jayden continued driving as fast as he dared. Finally, Booker came back on. "Special Agent Andrews wants to talk to you."

"Put him on," Jayden said. When Andrews spoke, Jayden cut him off, "Sorry we've been so hard to get along with. But we didn't have time to waste. I could use your help now, if you want to."

"Booker said you need a helicopter," he said. "Is it Mrs. Fairchild's ex-husband in the vehicle you're tracking?"

"We think so, but we haven't seen him. The guy that demanded the ransom had his voice muffled, but both Nadia and her grandfather said it could be him. But he might not be alone."

"Do you think you'll get the women back?" Andrews asked. "Miss Pierza is very important to us."

"In all honesty, whether it was Ulisses Fairchild or not, I don't hold out much hope that the women will be where he promised they'd be."

"If you have a recording of him claiming he kidnapped them, I can get a chopper."

"Oh, yeah, we've got that all right," Jayden said.

"May I take one of the trackers?" the agent asked.

"Yes, if it will help."

"Consider it done. I'll let you know when we have a chopper in the air," he said.

"Thanks. Would you hand the phone back to Booker?" As soon as Booker came back on the line, Jayden said, "Give the tracking device to the FBI agents. I'll continue to follow the other one. I think they'll become an asset now instead of a pain in our necks."

Jayden had scarcely ended that call before another came in.

"Jayden, Layda isn't here," Marley said, his voice cracking.

CHAPTER FIFTEEN

Marley Ferrel had driven right up to the dumpster, and for the past twenty minutes he'd sat there in his rental car. No one showed up—not that he expected anyone to at this point. He called his granddaughter and told her that he would wait for a few minutes more and then he'd join her at Jayden's office.

"Grandpa," she said after they'd talked for a little longer. "I can't believe my father would really do this. I thought I'd gotten to know him a little in those few visits at the prison. He made me believe he'd changed. That he would do something this terrible is more than I can understand. Why wouldn't he let her go after he got the money?"

"I've been thinking about this, Nadia," Marley responded. "I hate that man. I won't deny that for a minute. I can't believe he would kill her, but she isn't here. So I have to wonder what else could have happened?"

"Maybe he's trying to get away with the money, and when he feels like he's safe, he'll call and tell us where to find them."

"Oh, little girl. How I hope you're right. And you might be," he said. "We can't give up hope yet, even though I have to admit I just about had. Thanks for saying that."

"I don't believe she's dead, Grandpa. Deep in my heart, I just don't believe it. As hard as it is, we've got to be patient."

"I sure hope you're right. At least that gives us hope," Marley said. He put his phone in his pocket and got out of his rental car. He used the flashlight on his phone to examine the area. He wasn't sure what he'd find, if anything, and maybe the cops would be angry with him for destroying evidence if he did happen to find something, but he didn't see any cops here now. It seemed that they weren't interested or they would have sent someone. The FBI agents knew about the ransom drop now, and he hadn't been told they would send anyone.

He walked around the dumpster. All he'd done before was look in where he'd thrown the two suitcases, saw that they were gone, and returned to his car, but this time he looked closer. He was surprised when he saw a large piece of paper hanging at the back of the dumpster. He stepped closer. It was taped to the metal. He reached for it but then drew his hand back. There could be fingerprints there.

He leaned in close. If there was anything on the paper, it had to be on the back side. His curiosity got the best of him. He pulled a handkerchief from his pocket, and being careful to touch the paper only with the cloth, he pulled it free of the metal. He carried it back to his car and laid it on the hood. There was a message there addressed to him. This message, he realized, had been written before the money was ever picked up. Actually, written wasn't the right word, for the words were formed from letters cut out of a glossy magazine.

He leaned close and read it. *Ferrell, you didn't think I was stupid enough to let my captives loose until I had the money out of the state, did you? If you did, then you are crazy. They will be released only when I and my money are safe.*

That was it. Nadia was right. They were still alive and would be released later. Relief washed over him like a cool shower. He picked the note up with the handkerchief and laid it on the passenger seat of his car. Then he climbed in and called Nadia again.

"You were right, little girl. I found a note here. It says that they will be released after he gets out of the state with the money, but I wonder if he's really just leaving the state. I can't help but wonder if he's headed for Mexico," he said.

"It's good that he left a note," Nadia said. "I'm so glad you found it. I'm going to call Jayden and tell him."

"Of course," he said. "You aren't alone there, are you?"

"No, Booker left with another parole officer, but Chief Owens is here, and his wife is too," she said. "A taxi dropped her off when she was done with her shopping."

"Okay, I'll see you shortly," he said. "Are you still watching the tracking device?"

"No. Jayden had me give it to the FBI agents," she said. "But I'm in touch with Jayden. He's about four miles behind Dad, but he's gaining, according to his device. And the FBI will have a helicopter up pretty soon and be tracking him as well." Then she gasped.

"What's the matter, little girl?" Marley asked.

"If they catch him, he might not tell us where he's holding them. And . . . and they might die," she said.

"Oh, that's right. It might be best to just let him go. Let me call Jayden," he said. "If that's okay."

"Go ahead, Grandpa," she said.

***

Jayden's phone rang again. He was sure glad he had Bluetooth because at the speed he was driving, he needed both hands on the wheel and a lot of luck on his side. He was sure it was probably Nadia calling again. On her last call, she'd told him that she wished she was with him. He answered his phone.

"Jayden, this is Marley. You can't stop Ulisses. You've got to let him go," he said urgently.

Jayden was so surprised he let up on the gas. "Why?" he asked as he glanced at the tracking equipment. Then he did a double take. Neither of them was moving.

"I found a note taped to the dumpster. He said that Layda and the other woman would be released after he got out of the state," Marley said.

"It might just be a ruse to get us to stop following him. I think he's holed up somewhere because the tracking just became stationary," Jayden said.

"Jayden, we've got to back off. It's the only chance we have left," Marley said. The urgency in his voice made Jayden take pause. Marley could be right.

"It may be too late," Jayden finally said. "He might have been stopped already. There are a lot of officers looking for him. We'll just have to make him tell us."

"It can't be too late," Marley said with anguish in his voice.

"He's no longer moving. But even if someone has already shut him down, I'll see what I can do. I'm only three minutes or so behind him."

"Okay, but we *have* to get him to tell us where they are," Marley said.

The next call was only moments after he'd finished talking to Marley.

"Jayden, Booker here. The FBI chopper is in the air. They're closing in on him right now."

"So am I," Jayden said. "But he's stationary. I wonder if someone already caught him."

"Maybe. Let me call you back," he said.

Jayden pushed faster. Three minutes later, he saw flashing red-and-blue lights ahead. He was about where the tracking device informed him that he should be. It looked like someone had caught the kidnapper. Or had they?

He realized that there was a wreck ahead. He could see a car on its top. As ironic as it seemed, he hoped that Ulisses had survived the crash.

Jayden parked his Hummer off the road near a police cruiser with its lights flashing. He and Bullet jumped out and started past the cruiser. There was a cop on his knees reaching into the upside-down car. It was hard to tell its make, but it looked like a pickup truck. Jayden ran up, told Bullet to stand down, and joined the kneeling officer. A second officer told him to move, that they were trying to help a woman from the truck.

Woman? But surely it wasn't a woman. All he could do was wait and see. He and Bullet stepped back and watched the officers. A moment later, an ambulance eased through the cruisers and stopped near the wreck.

Jayden's body was pumped with adrenaline. He had to do something. He walked to the edge of the road and around the accident scene. He once again approached the wrecked truck. Something caught his eye off the road a short ways. He turned on the light on his iPhone and stepped closer. He groaned. It was one of the suitcases. It was hanging open, and the money was gone. He then began an earnest search for the other one.

Booker called him. He and the officer who was driving him had just parked behind Jayden's Hummer.

"I'm on the far side of the accident," Jayden told him.

"Is it Ulisses?" Booker asked.

"It's a woman in the truck, but I found one of the suitcases. The money is gone," he said. "I have a feeling the other one is nearby."

Booker joined him in the search, although he looked weaker than he had at the office. They spread out but still didn't find the other suitcase. Finally, Jayden convinced Booker to have the officer take him home.

After Booker had left, Jayden watched as the crash victim was removed. Once she was out of the truck, they put her on a gurney. One of the officers came over to Jayden and told him that the woman was conscious and talking. She claimed she lost control of the truck when some idiot began throwing suitcases at her. "I found one of them," Jayden said and explained what it used to contain. "I'd like to take it," he said, and when the officer didn't disagree, he put it in the Hummer.

As he shut the door to his Hummer, a helicopter circled overhead. Some officers blocked the roadway, and then the helicopter landed on the pavement. Special Agents Andrews and Press, he guessed. The FBI men jumped out and ran toward the accident. As soon as Agent Press saw Jayden, he pointed toward him, and both FBI agents came to where he was standing beside his Hummer.

"It looks like you screwed up, Spalding," Press said. "We're told that your so-called kidnapper got away. He must have found your tracking devices and thrown them out."

"Who's in the accident?" Agent Andrews asked.

"A woman who was in the wrong place at the wrong time. Whoever took the money still has it. I found one of the suitcases over there." He pointed and then explained about the wreck and what had caused it.

"But he still has the other suitcase?" Andrews asked.

"I doubt it. My tracking device tells me it's stationary and nearby. I think yours told you the same thing or you wouldn't have landed here."

"That's right," Agent Andrews agreed.

"I guarantee you gentlemen that they didn't find the tracking devices," Jayden said.

"They?" Andrews asked.

"They, he, she—whoever called Marley and made off with his million dollars," Jayden said.

Agent Press shook his head. "Let me see that suitcase," he ordered.

"You can look at it, but you're not taking it," Jayden said firmly.

"That's okay," the agent smirked. "I just want to show you how easily your little device can be found."

"Go ahead." Jayden opened the door, pulled the suitcase out, and handed it to Special Agent Press. "Here you go. Show me how easy it is to find."

Press took it in front of the Hummer and said, "Turn your lights on. This will only take a minute."

"Sure thing," Jayden said agreeably.

After Jayden had his Hummer running and the headlights shining, Special Agent Andrews left his partner examining the suitcase on the ground and walked back to where Jayden was leaning against the vehicle. "Sorry about Duncan," he said. "He's rather headstrong."

"You think?" Jayden said with a grin. "I'm sorry."

"What are you sorry about?" Andrews asked him.

"I'm sorry you have to work with the jerk. Sort of like an arranged marriage, isn't it? Can you imagine being stuck with a woman you didn't choose that acts like him and having to stick it out for the rest of your natural life? It would be enough to drive a man to suicide—or murder."

Andrews chuckled. "Hadn't thought of it quite like that. At least I will get a *divorce* from Press one day. And frankly, I look forward to it."

"That's what I like about my job," Jayden said. "I get to choose who I work with, although I'm not picky about my clients. Of course, if I work for one that gets under my skin, I can quit if I choose. I pick who I partner with, and I chose Bullet. He's easy to get along with and never tells me what to do. Nor does he embarrass me."

Special Agent Andrews shook his head. "He is a good dog. Booker told us about the professor and how your dog took care of him—with a little help from you. Tell me, Detective. Can Duncan find that transmitter you put in there?"

"I suppose, but it'll take a while. I see he hasn't found it yet." As he said that, Press pulled a pocketknife from his pocket. "Hey, don't you cut into that suitcase." He ran up and jerked it away from the agent. "You had your chance. I didn't sew it in."

Special Agent Press said, "I told you I'd find it, and I will. Give it back."

Jayden laughed, and Press drew back his fist. That was a mistake. Bullet dove for him. "Stand down!" Jayden ordered just in time. Bullet sort of stopped his leap midair and settled down on the pavement, but he stood guard, a deep rumbling coming from his chest. "That was a stupid thing to do," Jayden said. He walked back to the back door of the Hummer to throw the suitcase in.

"Detective," Special Agent Andrews said, "would you show me where the transmitter is?"

"I'd be glad to," he said. "Would you like to see too, Special Agent Press?"

Press took one step forward, but Bullet made it clear that he was going no farther.

"It looks like you offended my partner. He wants an apology," Jayden said.

"I ought to just shoot him. He's a dangerous animal."

"Try it if you think you can," Jayden said evenly.

"Then you'd sue me," Press said.

"Only if you survived, which you probably wouldn't. Bullet, stand down," he said. Bullet relaxed and allowed Press to pass. Then Jayden showed them where he'd secreted the transmitter. "I've done it before." He shrugged. "And no one has ever found one yet."

"I'd have found it if you hadn't stopped me," Press grumbled.

"Whatever," Jayden said and pocketed his transmitter. "I'd like to find that other suitcase. Marley doesn't seem too concerned about losing a million dollars, but I don't want to lose my other transmitter."

"What are you going to do now, Detective?" Andrews asked.

"I'm going to wait until the wrecker turns that truck over, and then I'm going to find Coach Fairchild," he said. "And when she's found, I'll go after Ulisses and find him."

"Are you kidding me?" Press asked in a mocking tone.

"No, I'm not. Finding people is what I do. And I'm pretty good at it."

"If you find Miss Pierza before we do, give me a call," Special Agent Andrews said.

"I'll do that, but you know, if you would tell me why you guys are so interested in her, I could probably locate her faster," Jayden said.

"That's not going to happen," Special Agent Press said. "Come on, Colten. Let's get out of here." He started back toward the front of the car only to find his path blocked by Bullet again.

"What do you think your dog is doing? Call him off," Press said gruffly.

"He hasn't had his apology yet," Jayden said with a smirk in his voice and on his face.

"He's not getting one," the agent said.

"He'll remember," Jayden warned him. "We'll probably cross paths again, since I have every intention of finding the women, and I would rather see him forgive you now than have trouble later."

"Apologize to an ugly beast? You must think I'm some kind of idiot," Press said as he backed up and started across the street.

"You've got that right," Jayden said. "And now you hurt his feelings. You owe him a second apology. Oh, and agents, I'll need that tracking device before you leave."

"I'll get it," Special Agent Andrews said, and he walked off.

As Jayden waited for Andrews to get him his device and the wrecker to upright the wrecked pickup, he called Nadia. "Are you still at my office?"

"No," she said. "Grandpa insisted that we come back to the hotel. He got a room here too. Are you still at the wreck?"

"I am." He'd told her earlier about finding the suitcase. "I'm just waiting for them to turn the truck over. I'm hoping the other suitcase is under it. The lady in the wreck said he threw suitcases at her. The other one has to be close by."

"Are you going home after that?" she asked.

"I am," he said. "I need some sleep. But first thing tomorrow, I'm going to hunt for your mother again."

"If my father took her and Naylyn—and I still want to think that he didn't do it—but if he did, he'll let her go when he gets to wherever he's going," she said.

"Maybe, but unless you want me to quit looking, there are some other things I need to check out. But it's your call. You're the boss."

"Please keep looking," she said firmly. "Will you meet Grandpa and me here for breakfast in the morning? And then I guess we need to go talk to your police friend."

"Yes, we can't forget that, and yes, I'll be there for breakfast," Jayden said. "We can talk things over then, and I'll let you know what I have in mind—if I have something in mind by then. Right now my brain is pretty much fried."

"You do need rest. Oh, and Jayden, there's one more thing," she said, sounding very serious. "You're cute too." She ended the call before he could think of a comeback.

Jayden smiled. Ten minutes later, he found the second suitcase. It had indeed been trapped beneath the overturned pickup.

An hour later, he and Bullet were back in the house. He needed some serious sleep.

CHAPTER SIXTEEN

Bullet entered the restaurant with Jayden at eight the next morning. Although it had been a short night, he'd slept well, and he was anxious to get back on the hunt. He was also anxious to see the girl who called him *cute*. As he waited to be seated, he looked as far as he could into the dining area, but he could not see Nadia or her distinguished grandfather. A waitress stepped up to him with a menu in her hand and said, "I'm sorry, sir, but pets aren't allowed in here."

"Oh, he's not a pet. He's a service dog. I need him with me, or I could run into trouble," he said. Little did she know the way in which Bullet could get him *out* of trouble.

She did not question him though, and she smiled. "He's a beautiful dog. Just one for breakfast this morning?"

He glanced at her name tag. "Actually, Tanya, there are four, me, my dog, and two more who will be here shortly. When a distinguished older gentleman and a tall, pretty young woman come in, bring them to my table please."

Tanya smiled again. "I'll do that." She led him to a table that was out of sight of the front door. He sat down on a chair, and Bullet sat beside him on the floor. "Someone will be right with you, and I'll watch for your pretty young woman and distinguished gentleman."

"Thank you, Tanya," he said with a smile.

She moved toward the front, and a moment later a petite young waitress approached Jayden. "Could I bring you a coffee while you wait?" she asked.

Her name tag read *Kyla*. She looked like she was under twenty and was slender and pretty. "I suppose you could bring one, Kyla, but it would be wasted. Neither my partner, Bullet, or I drink the stuff." He pointed at the dog beside his chair. "But we would both like water."

She looked quite puzzled. "Does your dog drink water?"

"Well, dogs get thirsty just like people," he said with a straight face.

"I mean, you know, how would he get it out of a glass?" she asked awkwardly.

"That's a good point, Kyla," he said. "A glass would probably be awkward for him. Maybe you could bring a bowl for him and a glass for me and for the other two guests who will be here in a minute. And then if you wouldn't mind bringing us a pitcher, I could refill them all."

She looked from Jayden to Bullet and back to Jayden. "I guess I could do that. Will he be the only dog?"

"As far as I know. The last I knew, neither of my friends had a dog."

"Okay," she said, finally grinning.

"Thanks, you're very kind," he said. He got a big smile from her, and she blushed.

She brought the water, but it took her two trips. He thanked her as he wondered where Nadia and Marley were at. But then, of course, they had also had a long day and a late night, and Nadia was in pain. They probably slept in.

About five minutes later, Kyla returned. She looked at the bowl and saw that it was almost empty. "He was thirsty, wasn't he?"

"He works hard taking care of me," Jayden said. "I suppose that would make anyone thirsty."

She grinned. "Would you like to order now or wait till your friends arrive?"

"We'll wait a little longer. If they're not here in a few minutes, I may need to be excused to look for them. They're here in the hotel. I suppose I could try calling them, but I'll wait a little longer."

She nodded and said, "I'll keep checking with you."

"Thank you, Kyla," he said. "And my dog thanks you too."

She looked down at Bullet almost as if she expected him to say something. The dog looked up at her with those beautiful black eyes of his and blinked.

"He's gorgeous," she said.

"He doesn't speak people talk, but he thanked you when he looked at you like that," Jayden said. "I think he likes you."

"He looks nice."

"He can be," Jayden said. "You made a good impression on him." She walked off shaking her head and smiling.

Kyla returned in about five minutes. "They aren't here yet?"

He shook his head. "Maybe I'll call one of them. I just hope they're answering their phones this morning."

"Okay, I'll keep checking. Here are some menus for them when they come," she said and walked away. He followed her with his eyes as he pulled his phone out. She looked back at him with that puzzled expression on her face. He waved at her and grinned. She turned red and hurried off.

He called Nadia's number, but it went to voice mail. So he tried Marley's number. He answered on the first ring. "Is everything okay?" Jayden asked.

"Yes, but when I talked to Nadia a few minutes ago, she said that she'd slept in but that she's hurrying. She told me to wait in my room and that she'd knock on my door when she was ready," Marley said.

"I hope she's feeling okay. This all has to be hard on her," Jayden responded.

"That's for sure. But she's a strong girl. She'll weather the storm," Marley said confidently.

"I know she will, but I worry about her anyway."

"Of course you do, and so do I. And I worry about Layda." He sighed. "Are you waiting at the restaurant for us?"

"I am," he said. "But it's fine."

"If you want to go ahead and order, I understand," Marley said.

"No, that's okay. This waitress is taking care of me, and I'm having fun making her wonder if I'm some kind of a kook," he said.

"Well, enjoy yourself then. Oh, there's a knock on the door now. We'll be right down."

But less than a minute later, Marley called Jayden back. Jayden detected a strain in the older man's voice.

"It wasn't Nadia; it was a fellow from the hotel. He said he had a message to deliver to me. He handed me a slip of paper and told me that someone called and told him to write the message down word for word and then take it to my room. The caller told them that I'd understand the message."

"Do you?" Jayden felt a knot forming in his stomach.

"I'm afraid so, but I don't like it," he said.

"Will you read it to me?" Jayden asked.

"Of course. Wait. Maybe it's my little girl at the door now. Hang on," he said.

Jayden waited, and he could hear Marley saying, "Good morning, Nadia. I was just talking to Jayden. Let's go down and meet him. He's waiting for us at the restaurant. He has a table."

Then he could hear Nadia. "Sorry I'm slow. It hasn't been a good morning."

Then, into the phone, Marley said, "We'll be right down. I'll show you this note as soon as I get there." The tension in his voice caused the knot in Jayden's stomach to twist.

Kyla came back a moment later. "Still waiting?" she asked with a grin.

"They're on their way down," he said. "Give us five minutes, and we'll order."

"Okay, is something wrong, sir? You look worried."

"I don't know," he said. "Don't mind me. Thanks for your patience."

She looked at him with that same puzzled expression, only this time there was no smile attached. She walked off, and Jayden said to Bullet, "Something is going on, and I don't like the feel of it."

Bullet stood, put his head on Jayden's lap, and whined. "You feel it too, don't you, big fella?"

Jayden's phone rang. He looked at the screen and recognized the number of Desmond Booker. "Good morning," he said into the phone.

"Detective, I'm sorry to take so long to get back to you on this Davon Karp character, but I finally have some information on him," Booker said. "He's still on parole, but he was never a cellmate with Ulisses. However, they were in the same cell block, so they knew each other."

"That's not very comforting," Jayden said.

"That's exactly how I feel. I just got off the phone with his parole officer in Coolidge," Booker said. "He told me that Davon has an attitude but that he keeps his appointments for the most part. And the two or three times that he missed, he called in with an excuse."

"Thanks, Booker. I'm going to have to go to Coolidge and speak with him," Jayden said. "How are you feeling this morning? You looked pretty miserable last night."

"I just needed rest," Booker said. "I'm feeling better now. But I have to go have my wound examined later this morning. The doctor thinks I should have stayed in the hospital for another day or two, but I don't have time for that. I have a big caseload, and I want to keep track of my parolees. Oh, I do have some guys checking at the prison to see if we can learn if Ulisses and Davon had developed a friendship. I'll get back with you when I know something more."

"I appreciate what you're doing, but I think you should take it easy today," Jayden said. "Thanks for the information."

"Any new developments this morning?" Booker asked.

"I don't know. I'm waiting for Marley right now. He says he got a note from the hotel management. I have no idea what it's about, but Marley seemed pretty tense."

"Let me know as soon as you've had a chance to read the note, especially if it has anything to do with Ulisses."

"I'll do that." Jayden spotted Nadia and Marley being escorted to the table by Tanya.

Bullet moved his head off Jayden's lap as Jayden pushed his chair back. He stood and waited as they approached. "Your distinguished gentleman guest and your pretty lady finally arrived," Tanya announced with a wide smile.

"Thank you, Tanya," Jayden said and looked closely at Nadia.

Her face was dark with worry, but she managed a weak smile before she stepped close to him. "I've missed you," she said.

"And I you," he answered.

Then she finally managed a stronger smile. "What was that all about?"

"What?" Jayden asked innocently.

"Distinguished gentleman and pretty lady?"

"I was just describing the two of you. And I think it was quite accurate," he said. "Marley, I'd like to see that note as soon as you two are seated. From the looks on both of your faces, it must not be good."

Marley sat down across the table from Jayden as he pulled out a chair for Nadia. "She hasn't seen the note yet," he said. "She had a phone call that has her worried."

Jayden waited until Nadia was seated, and then he sat. Bullet lapped a little water from his bowl and then settled down beside the chair again. "Are you okay?" Jayden asked Nadia.

"I'm just worried," she said.

"But is there something new to worry about?" he asked perceptively. "We may not have known one another for very long, but it's been long enough that I can read your face quite well. Would you like to talk about it, or should we see what that note of your grandfather's says first?"

"The note first," she said with a catch in her voice.

"Very well," he said as Kyla approached the table.

"I see your guests have arrived. And it looks like they still don't have a dog," she said.

"I guess I'll have to share mine with them," he responded.

Nadia, as worried as she was, still managed to look perplexed. "Why would we have a dog?" she asked.

"It's a long story," Jayden said. "I'm afraid I've been teasing our waitress. Kyla, this is Nadia Fairchild and her grandfather, Marley Ferrel."

Kyla's eyes grew wide. "I know who you are!" she exclaimed. "You're the best player on the Phoenix Mercury. I watch you guys every time I can. I'm your biggest fan. What happened to your arm? I hope it's nothing serious."

"It's nice to meet a fan. The arm's not serious." Nadia smiled.

"Would it be rude to ask for your signature?" she asked with a shy smile.

"Of course not. Do you have a paper?"

Kyla tore a page off her order pad and handed it to Nadia, along with her pen. Nadia scribbled something and then handed it back.

"Thank you," the girl said. "I can't believe this. My friends are going to be so jealous."

Nadia smiled graciously and said, "You're welcome."

Kyla then asked, "Have you had a chance to look at your menus, or do you need a couple minutes?"

"Give us a minute or two, please," Marley said.

"Can I get either of you coffee?"

"I'll have a cup with cream and sugar," Marley said.

Then before Nadia could say anything, Jayden said, "Nadia is like me and my dog. She doesn't drink it."

"Okay, one coffee with cream and sugar. I'll be back," she said as she smiled and gazed at Nadia's signature. "It's so great to meet you. And I mean it when I say I'm your biggest fan."

Jayden broke in. "That's not true, Kyla. First, *I'm* her biggest fan. And second, you're not big. You are really quite petite."

Kyla grinned. "Thank you." She walked toward the kitchen.

"You aren't my biggest fan," Nadia said. "You haven't even seen me play."

"Wanna bet?" he challenged.

"You mean, you've seen us play?"

"Several times. I recognized you the moment I saw you. And Kyla is right. You really are the best player on the team," he said.

"Thanks, Jayden," she said. "You're full of surprises."

"I try to be," he said. "But I'm hurt. Kyla didn't ask for my signature or your grandfather's or even Bullet's. How do you think that makes us feel?" He winked at her. Then he saved her the trouble of coming up with an answer to his ridiculous question as he reached across the table and said, "May I see the note now, Marley sir?"

Marley handed it over. Jayden unfolded it and held it so that Nadia could also read it. It said: *Thanks for the million bucks. I'll spend it wisely. Are you worried yet? You should be. I don't always do as I say I will. But then, you already knew that.*

Nadia gasped and looked at Jayden, with fear in her eyes. "He's done something to them, hasn't he?" she asked

"I don't know, but I hope not. I think we should proceed as though he's only trying to scare you two worse," Jayden said.

"Well, if that's what he's doing, it's working." Nadia looked close to tears.

As Jayden tenderly brushed a tear from her cheek, Marley said, "I agree with Jayden. We must hope for the best. Jayden, we want you to keep looking, and when you're finished and we have Layda safely back, I'll pay you to find Ulisses and bring him back to face justice—and to face me. Will you do that?"

"Of course," Jayden said. "He won't get away with whatever sick game he's playing."

Jayden's phone rang, and he pulled it from his pocket. He read Booker's number on the screen. "That was fast, Booker."

"I told you I had some guys checking for me, and I just got a call. Davon and Ulisses were in fact very good friends while in prison," Booker said.

"That's got me thinking." Jayden told Booker about the note Marley had received. "I wonder if Davon could have had anything to do with it. Booker, I have Ulisses's phone. If I can figure out how to get it open, I might be able to see if the two of them have talked. But I would also need to have a number for Davon."

"I'll call his parole officer. He'll have it. I'll call you when I get it," Booker said. "And you take good care of that client of yours."

Jayden smiled. "I'll do that. You have my word."

CHAPTER SEVENTEEN

"What does Booker have your word on?" Nadia asked.

"He asked me to take good care of my client." He winked at her.

She smiled, reached over to him with the only hand she could move, and gently rubbed his cheek. She didn't say a word, but her touch and her eyes spoke volumes.

After a long silence, Marley asked, "How do you plan to break into Ulisses's phone?"

Nadia spoke up then. "Maybe I could try. I know this is probably hard to believe, but I studied computer programming in college, and I did a little extra on the side. I'm a pretty good hacker—but don't tell anyone."

"I'll let you try then," Jayden said.

Kyla came back and asked if they were ready to order. Nadia ordered first and then Marley. Jayden was last. He ordered a large stack of pancakes, four eggs over easy, a half dozen strips of bacon and a half pound of raw hamburger.

She wrote it down and then said, with that perplexed look in her eyes again, "Do you eat raw hamburger?"

"Not usually, but Bullet likes it, and he needs to eat too," he said with a serious face. "He hasn't had anything bloody since he chewed on the professor's arm last night."

Kyla's face went white.

Nadia said, "Don't mind him. He has a warped sense of humor."

The young waitress forced a smile. "So he didn't really chew on someone's arm?"

"Actually he did. But he didn't like the professor like he likes you. And besides, the professor provoked him," Jayden said.

Kyla forced another smile, turned, and walked off shaking her head.

"You're mean," Nadia said.

"I'm sorry," he said. "I know I have a warped sense of humor. But it comes natural. When you've seen the things I've seen, and been through the life-and-death situations I have, you learn to use jokes to relieve the tension. If it offends you, I'll try to do better."

She once again touched his cheek. "I like you just the way you are. And your jokes, warped as they are, manage to relieve some of my tension. And I thank you for that."

"As do I," her grandfather spoke up.

"Thank you, Marley sir," he said. Then he faced Nadia again. "Okay, it's your turn, Nadia. You have something on your mind that's eating at you. Would you like to talk about it?"

"It might be nothing," she said. "But my coach called. She said that the general manager of the team wants to meet with me. I have to be at the corporate office at eleven."

Jayden was relieved that was all it was. "Surely it's not anything bad. You're the best player on the team."

"I try," she said. "But I should be flying to Tulsa. We have a game with the Tulsa Shock tonight."

"That's not your fault," he said. "It's your father's. I can't imagine them holding that against you."

"I hope you're right."

Marley sighed. "I would go with you to meet with him, but I have a jet coming to pick me up as soon as we finish up with Detective Noe about the scene with Delgado last night. As it is, I'm going to be running tight. I have a meeting at my office that I can't miss. It's at noon," he said. "I'm sorry. But I'll be back as soon as I can."

"There's nothing you can do here anyway," she said. "Just knowing you care is huge."

"I plan to go to Coolidge today and do some more interviews," Jayden said. "I especially want to talk to Davon Karp. He and your father were friends in prison. He could be the one who was helping him last night," he said. "But if you need me to, I'll wait until this afternoon and go with you to meet the general manager instead."

She smiled at him. "I'd love to have you with me—I'd love to have both of you with me—but I can handle it. Jayden, the most important thing right now is finding Mom, and I think you're the only one who can do that."

"Whatever you say. But if you change your mind or if you need me, don't hesitate to call. And no matter what the general manager has to say, let me know how things go as soon as your meeting's over."

"I'll call you."

"Call me too, Nadia," Marley said, "even if you have to interrupt my meeting. I'll have my cell phone with me. And I mean it, little girl. For that matter, Jayden, I'd like you to keep me updated as well. If you learn anything of importance, I'd like to hear it as soon as you can call."

"I hate to disturb your meeting. That might bother some of the other people," Jayden said.

"I'm the boss," Marley said. "Nobody is going to complain to me about an interruption. So you'll keep me informed, won't you?"

"Yes, Marley sir, I will."

Kyla brought their meals. Bullet finished his in just over ten seconds. The others were done in twenty minutes.

"I'll cover this," Marley said.

"Let me leave the tip. I owe Kyla for being so hard on her." Jayden pulled his wallet from an inside pocket of his jacket. He laid a fifty-dollar bill on the table.

"That's generous," Nadia said.

"She deserves it."

Marley went to his room and picked up his bags. Nadia and Jayden accompanied him. As they were descending in the elevator, Marley turned to Nadia. "I think you should go to another hotel. Somehow, Ulisses figured out you were here, although I can't imagine how."

"I was just thinking the same thing," Jayden said. "I'll help you find a different place after we finish at the police department. I wonder if someone is watching you." The thought gnawed at him. "Let's leave your stuff at my office. I'll give you a spare key. We'll find you a new room tonight. That way we won't be in a hurry and can make sure that no one is tailing us."

She did not argue.

Marley drove his rental car for the meeting with Detective Noe and his partner. Nadia rode with Jayden. Noe met them in the hallway. "My partner had to leave on another assignment, so it'll just be me." He ushered them into his small space and offered them chairs. Then he said, "Mr. Ferrel, I think I got what I needed from your employees. I didn't know that it was cash in the suitcases. I only know that now because of the accident last night when the empty suitcases were thrown from the getaway car."

"We got double-crossed, which I was afraid would happen," Jayden responded. "I'm sorry I couldn't tell you everything last night. I'd be glad to fill you in now, but we are under a bit of a tight schedule." He explained why, and then at Noe's request, a recorder was turned on. Jayden gave a brief overview of the case, including the shooting while trying to arrest Lester Skiles. Noe already knew about that and the part that Jayden had played in it.

"Tell me more about the man I arrested at your office last night, Pedro Delgado," Detective Noe requested.

"He is a man with a short fuse and a long memory," Jayden said. "We suspected him in the disappearance of Marley's daughter and the player that vanished with her. When Chief Owens from the college and I discovered that Layda had actually gone out with him a few times and then broke up with him, it made us suspicious. Those suspicions were validated when we discovered that he'd stalked her and made threats against her. That's why I was looking for him on campus. He clearly had evil intentions and wasn't about to forget. But I never actually got the chance to talk to him."

"He's very angry with you, Jayden," the detective said. "It was his intention to kill you when he came to your office. He admitted that to us. In fact, he more than admitted it, he bragged about it and said that he would still get you."

"I hope he'll be incarcerated for a while," Jayden said. "I'd really hate to have to let Bullet finish him off if he were to try a stunt like that again."

"He's not going anywhere. The bail is a million dollars. I doubt that will get reduced, and I don't think he can come up with it. It could even go higher. Speaking of your dog, he did a number on the professor's wrist. They patched him up, but he still has to have surgery to fix the crushed bones," Detective Noe said with a grin. "If I had my way, they'd leave it like it is. He wouldn't be able to use his hand much that way."

"Will he be kept under a tight guard at the hospital?" Nadia asked, concern in her voice.

"He won't be escaping," Noe assured her. "He'll be arraigned this morning on several charges, all felonies. And the DA intends to ask the court to increase the bail, based largely on the threats against you and Layda Fairchild. He already has an attorney, who will argue to lower the bail, but they won't have much in the way of persuasive arguments. After the arraignment, Delgado will have the surgery. So what's your next move, Jayden?"

Jayden expressed concern about Nadia's safety and outlined what he planned for her. "After I leave her at my office, I will be going to Coolidge. I have several interviews up there," he said and gave a quick rundown of his plans.

"Nadia, I'll see if I can arrange for someone to take you to your meeting and return you to Jayden's office," Noe said.

"Oh, I can drive myself. I'll be okay."

The detective shook his head. "No, you've been attacked once with serious results. I insist. I'll have an officer pick you up and return you when you finish," Detective Noe said with finality.

"Thanks, Irving," Jayden said. "But maybe I should stay and do it myself."

"No, Jayden, you need to keep looking for my mother," Nadia insisted.

"I agree with Miss Fairchild," Noe said. "It's settled."

Detective Noe then asked a number of questions pertaining to the attempted attack by the professor the night before. He then explained that he'd impounded the professor's car from where it was found that morning parked two blocks from Jayden's office. "If I find anything that pertains to the case of the missing women, I'll call you, Jayden," he promised.

The detective then began to ask about the ransom demand and the details of what occurred in connection to that matter. When Jayden handed him the note that had been attached to the back of the dumpster, Noe asked to keep it. The proper forms were filled out for the transfer of evidence, but he allowed Jayden to keep a copy of it. Detective Noe also took the message that had been sent to Marley that morning at the hotel. The same procedures were followed in transferring it from Jayden's custody to Detective Noe's. He also copied it for Jayden's use.

"Charges have been initiated for Ulisses Fairchild rising from the events of last night, but with what you've told me this morning, we'll be filing more. With his status as a parolee and the severity of the crimes, we already have a no-bail warrant. Based on his admission to you, Mr. Ferrel, we will charge him with kidnapping. The FBI could have taken over on that, but they don't seem interested."

"So you met Agents Andrews and Press," Jayden remarked.

"Andrews seems to be okay, but Press, he's a wild card," he said. "They left here just before you came in." After a few last questions, Detective Noe was finished, and he dismissed Marley to head to the airport.

"I am running very tight," Marley said. After kissing his granddaughter on the cheek and telling her that he would be back, he turned to leave. But he stopped at the door and said, "Jayden, keep me posted."

"I will, Marley sir," Jayden said.

After Marley had left, Detective Noe said, "If I didn't know you so well, I'd wonder why you call him 'Marley sir.' But I'm sure there is a reason." He chuckled. "Funny thing is he doesn't seem to mind."

"Grandpa likes Jayden a lot." Nadia smiled warmly. "How much longer will we be?"

"You guys can go now," Noe said. "What time should I have an officer meet you at Jayden's office?"

***

Before long, Jayden and Nadia arrived at his office. He was concerned about her safety, so he showed her where he kept a couple of spare pistols and made sure she knew how to use them. She assured him that she'd shot pistols before, both semiautomatics and revolvers. She reassured him that he didn't need to worry about her. That did nothing to relieve him of his concerns. She was becoming more than a client.

Jayden gave her Ulisses's phone and access to the computer.

"I'll see if I can figure this phone out," she said. "I think I can."

Jayden was reluctant to leave, but he knew he needed to get on his way. He kissed her lightly on the cheek and then left her there with the doors locked. He headed his Hummer for Coolidge, Bullet curled up on the seat beside him.

On the way, Jayden called Chief Gary Owens to let him know the plan. As Jayden walked into the office on campus, Janelle was at the reception desk again. She eyed Bullet warily. "Are you sure it's safe bringing your dog in here?" she asked.

"Of course it's safe, as long as you don't attack me," he said, bringing a weak smile to her face.

"Chief Owens told me what he did to Professor Delgado," she said. "From what he said, it sounded like the dog was very vicious."

"That was because the professor was threatening me with a gun. Bullet only did what I trained him to do."

"Is Professor Delgado still in jail?" she asked.

"I'm afraid so. And he will be for quite a while."

"That's good. He's scary. I have one of his classes this semester, but if he doesn't come back, that will be okay with me. You and your dog can go on back. The chief is expecting you."

"Thanks for your help last night," Jayden said to the chief as the two men shook hands.

"Glad I could help, even though I didn't do much," he said. "Unfortunately, we don't seem to be any closer to finding Coach Fairchild and Miss Pierza."

"That's right, I'm afraid. At this point, I'm not sure Ulisses Fairchild wasn't bluffing. I'm not at all sure he ever had the women. He may have simply taken advantage of the fact that he knew they were missing and that we didn't know who had taken them. He saw a chance to get some money. He also delayed us, making it that much harder to find Layda and Naylyn. But in one way, we have made some headway," Jayden said.

"Oh, what's that?"

Jayden grinned. "I think we can put our suspicions of Professor Delgado kidnapping them on the back burner."

"You don't think we should eliminate him as a suspect altogether?" the chief asked.

"No, that's not what I mean at all," Jayden said thoughtfully. "I don't think he kidnapped them, but I'm not sure he didn't harm them."

The chief leaned forward, his eyes narrowed. "You think he could have done something, possibly even murdered them?"

"I think it's possible. Delgado proved last night that his temper can lead him to murder. If he'd had his way, I'd be dead. I met with Detective Noe this morning, and he said that Delgado came to my office with the intention of killing me—and says he still will."

"Hopefully he won't be getting out. But I see your point, Jayden. Perhaps we should search his office," Chief Owens said.

"And his home. The Phoenix PD impounded his car. If there's anything in it, they'll let me know.

"I'll have Lieutenant Kaiser prepare the warrants. In the meantime, what would you like to do?"

"Just for entertainment purposes, I wouldn't mind interviewing Coach Wagner," he said with a grin. "But I'm afraid I don't have time to pester her right now. I would like to interview Lorena Husman and Davon Karp. I'd prefer to start with Karp. I don't want her tipping him off, and any involvement she might have had with the women vanishing almost certainly will have been in concert with Karp. Would you like to go with me?"

"Sure, I'll do that. Let me get Tevin in here first," he said and picked up his phone.

It only took the lieutenant a minute, and he walked in the door. "Good to see you in one piece, Detective," he said. "I understand our good professor was going to shoot you last night."

"Yes, but unfortunately for him, he chose to make his threat in front of my partner." He pointed at the big gray German shepherd who was taking a short nap beside Jayden's chair. "Bullet took exception to that."

"If you ever decide to get rid of that dog, let me know," Tevin said with a grin.

"That will never happen," Jayden said. "I like to keep him close."

Tevin turned to his boss. "What would you like me to do?"

"I need search warrants for Professor Delgado's house and office," he said.

"And while you're at it—if it's okay with you, Chief—I'd love to have access to Miss Pierza's dorm room," Jayden said.

Chief Owens said, "That's a good idea. Are you thinking that she might have received a threat and kept a record of it?"

"Possibly. But I really would like to know more about her. She seems to have a rather shallow background, and our FBI friends won't tell me why they're so interested in her," Jayden said. "Maybe we can find some hints of why she's here on your campus. There could be something about her that would help me find her."

"I'll get right on it," Lieutenant Kaiser said. "What are you going to do in the meantime?"

"We plan to visit an ex-con by the name of Davon Karp, who, it seems, is a close pal of Coach Fairchild's ex-con ex-husband," Jayden said. "It could prove most interesting."

CHAPTER EIGHTEEN

Nadia entered the office of the general manager of the Phoenix Mercury. Tomas Newbold was a distinguished man of about fifty with a full head of wavy, white hair and only a few black hairs still showing. He kept his hair combed to perfection with a part on the left side, kept that way with a healthy dose of hairspray. He had a square face, ice-blue eyes, dark eyebrows, and a cleft in his chin. He was built with a stocky frame that rose to a couple of inches over six feet. He was clean shaven except for a thin, perfectly manicured gray moustache. He waved Nadia to a seat with a hand that held silver-rimmed glasses. He put the glasses back on and brushed an imaginary piece of lint from the front of his expensive blue suit coat. He peered at her for a moment with eyes that seemed to be full of judgment. The longer he held his steady gaze on her, the more she squirmed. Newbold did not have a reputation as a gentle or caring man. Nadia knew he'd been hired to make this team's owner a substantial profit, no matter what it took.

There was a knock on the door frame behind her that broke his piercing gaze, to Nadia's relief.

"Coach Korner, thanks for joining us," was the first phrase he uttered. The fact that he had greeted the coach but not said a word to Nadia made her nervous. "And thanks for having Miss Fairchild come in as well."

"I suppose you have a reason for calling us in," the coach said boldly as she seated herself next to Nadia. Her eyes strayed to the sling. But when she looked at Nadia's face, she smiled warmly. "Is it feeling better?"

The general manager had been hired only a few months ago, so both Nadia and the coach had preceded him to the team. But he knew the power he had. "How she feels is not the purpose of this meeting," he said, his steely gaze shifting from one woman to the other in a smooth motion. "I was hired to make this team more profitable."

He paused, and Nadia said nothing.

Coach Korner, however, said, "And my job as coach is to help our women win games, which is what brings the spectators in and makes the profit to which you refer. And we have a very good record this season, thanks in large part to Nadia."

The general manager leaned forward and ran a finger across his pencil-thin mustache. He let the silence stretch uncomfortably. "Yes, but it could be better," he said, looking directly at the coach.

"It takes time to build a strong, cohesive team, and I have done that. And with the ladies I have playing for me now, it will only get better," Coach Korner said. "And that includes Nadia and her outstanding ability and leadership both on and off the court."

"I am aware of Miss Fairchild's abilities," he said. "She has been an important asset to the team. She is also one of the most highly paid players, even though she's not the oldest or most experienced. Far from it."

Was he going to try to make her renegotiate her contract? Nadia wondered as her stomach began to stir.

"She's worth every penny of her salary," the coach said as if she too suspected what was coming.

"That's for me to decide," he said. "Miss Fairchild, are you aware of what the average annual salary in the WNBA is?"

"I think it's about seventy-five thousand dollars," she said almost timidly.

"It would be a little lower than that if it wasn't for your salary which is well over half again that amount," he said as if she had committed some kind of serious transgression. She held her gaze steady, however. She was not going to let this man intimidate her. "You make too much, especially considering the problems you have allowed in your personal life."

That made her angry, and she could see that Coach Korner was also upset. "My age has nothing to do with my salary. I work hard. I perform well in every game. I am the leading scorer *and* rebounder on the team. As far as my off-court problems, I didn't cause them. I was attacked in my apartment for a reason that I don't even understand. I was lucky I was able to fight him off, or I could have been much more severely injured," she said.

"How or why you got injured is of no interest to me," he said coldly. "In a few minutes, your team is flying to Tulsa. I have delayed the flight so that your coach could be here for this meeting."

"Which will considerably affect our practice time when we get to Tulsa," Coach Korner said with an edge to her voice.

"I told you to practice this morning," he shot back at her.

"Flying in just a few hours before game time is hard on the team."

"Coach, it's up to you to get the most out of your team regardless of the circumstances. Now, if you'll quit arguing, I'll continue. We'll be done here shortly." He stared her down like he dared her to argue with him again.

"I understand that, Mr. Newbold," she said.

"Then let me finish," he snapped. His eyes turned to Nadia again. "You say you perform well each game."

"I do," she agreed, not sure what this exchange was leading to but nervous that, whatever it was, it was not a good place.

He stroked that silly moustache again. It was starting to irritate her. His ice-blue eyes seemed to burn into hers. She tried not to squirm. She couldn't let him think she was weak. "Okay, so you do, huh? Is that going to be the case tonight in Tulsa?"

"She's not going tonight," Coach Korner said defensively.

"I am speaking to Miss Fairchild," he said, his face turning red. He bored those icy eyes into hers for a moment, and then they moved swiftly back to Nadia. "And you're not going tonight because, while off the court, you allowed yourself to get injured. And that is what we need to address. I spoke to the team doctor yesterday afternoon. He tells me that you will probably miss several games—for an injury that occurred when you were not playing ball."

He said nothing for a moment, so she supposed he wanted her to agree with him. She said, "That's right, but I'll be back at full strength as soon as I can. I'll work, and I'll—"

He cut her off with a quick chop of the air with his hand. "You are not worth the money we are paying you just to sit on the sidelines."

"Are you suggesting you want to renegotiate my contract? It's good for five years," she said defensively.

"If I could do that, I would," he said.

"Mr. Newbold," Coach Korner said. "She's my star player. She *is* worth what we pay her. Yes, she was injured off the court, but it was not her fault.

It could happen to anyone. And besides that, are you aware of the family tragedy she is going through right now?"

He waved his hand in the air again. "Of course I know. But that's not my problem. It's her mother's problem. And I cannot—I will not—let personal problems affect how I run this team."

"But you agree that you can't cut my salary?" Nadia asked.

He smirked, and her gut twisted itself into a knot. "That's right," he said. "But the Minnesota Lynx are willing to pay that. And they want you, even knowing you're injured."

"They're a championship team," she said as she felt the hammer beginning to fall.

"They are, and we should be. We will be. You are to report to the Lynx on Monday. You have been traded," he said, that smirk of his solidly in place.

"Mr. Newbold, you can't do that," the coach protested.

"I can and I have," he said. "But I'm not leaving you without personnel." He named a player that was currently with the Indiana Fever. "This is part of a three-way trade that I have worked out, and it will save us a lot of money. The Lynx have the privilege of paying your outrageously high salary while you sit on your thumbs and nurse your injuries, and we will be receiving a girl at the median salary but whose potential will make up for your loss."

"Don't I have any say in this?" Nadia asked even as she felt like she was going to be sick.

"Are you the general manager?" he asked with tight lips.

"No." She dropped her eyes from his in defeat.

"There's your answer. This decision is mine. You'll need to get the paperwork finalized here today," he said. "And then catch a plane over the weekend to Minnesota. And when you've had time to think this over, you may send me a thank-you note. I'm doing you a big favor. That'll be all."

She rose to her feet and slowly left the office. She didn't know what she would do. Mr. Newbold had just shattered her world. She didn't care about the quality of the team he was trading her to. Nor did she care about the change in location. She cared about finding her mother. And she suddenly realized that she cared more than she could have ever guessed possible about her private detective. She'd lived for twenty-four years without Jayden Spalding. But she didn't know how she could ever live another day without him in her life.

She'd left the door open when she'd walked out of his office. Mr. Newbold's loud voice chased her down the hall, shouting, "You come back and shut my door, Miss Fairchild!"

She ignored him.

She called Detective Noe and told him she didn't know how much longer she would be, that she would just call for a cab when she was finished.

He said, "It's okay. I'll send an officer whenever you need."

"Thank you for your kindness," she said, trying to keep her emotions from affecting her voice. "But it will not be necessary."

"Miss Fairchild," he said. "I made a promise to my good friend Jayden Spalding that I would see you safely to and from the team's office. I will not break that promise, so call when you are ready."

"If you're sure," she finally said.

"I'm sure," he said. "Now I don't know what happened in your interview, but I can tell you're upset. Cheer up. Things will be okay. Jayden will find your mother, and you will heal from what that creep Lester did to you. You'll find that life has a way of bringing you out of the pits that try to swallow you."

"Thanks," she said and ended the call.

She tried to put on a happy face when she entered the office where she would effectively end her career with the Mercury. She was instantly congratulated and told how lucky she was to be going to the Lynx but how much she would be missed in Phoenix. She smiled, thanked people, filled out the necessary paperwork, and finally escaped.

She left the building and soaked up the oppressive afternoon heat. Then, despite the detective's kind offer, she caught a cab and told the driver to take her to a mall. When she was depressed, the one thing that always seemed to help was buying new clothes. She didn't need them, but that was what she intended to do.

She didn't call Detective Noe until she had arrived at the mall and was swallowed by the crowds inside. She told him, "I needed to do some shopping, so I came to a mall."

"Which mall?" he asked.

She told him and then said, "I'll be fine. I'll catch a cab back to Jayden's office."

"Nadia, that's not a good idea. We don't know who else could be out there with the intent of harming you. Please, stay put, and I'll personally come pick you up."

"Please don't," she said. "I need to do some thinking, and I think best when I'm shopping."

She could hear the detective sigh. "What happened, Nadia? Something has you terribly upset."

"I'm fine," she said as she stepped into one of her favorite shoe stores.

"Well," he said, sounding resigned, "tell me this. How are you going to carry your bags? You only have one good arm."

"I'll manage." She terminated the call then stepped back into the hallway and found a restroom. He'd made a good point, but she had every intention of splurging.

In the restroom, she removed the sling and worked her arm for a moment. It hurt, but she could manage. She thrust the sling into a garbage can, freshened her makeup, and headed back toward the shoe store swinging her arm to loosen it up.

It seemed to be working. She was soon immersed in her shopping, taking the edge off the anger and hurt and disappointment that the general manager had thrust on her.

Her phone rang as she was trying on a pair of red pumps. She sat up, reached into her purse, and looked at the screen. It was Coach Korner. "I'm sitting here waiting for our flight to leave, and I just had to talk to you. Are you okay?" Coach asked her.

"Not really. I should be with you guys. I can't believe he's doing this to me."

"The whole team is in shock," Coach Korner said. "And they're angry. I've been trying to settle them down, but it's not working. I think we are going to lose badly tonight."

"And it will be my fault," she said.

"No, it will be the fault of our *general manager*. This move is going to do just the opposite of what he says it will. It's going to hurt us, and without you, we are going to lose a lot more games. I argued with the idiot after you left, but all he did was threaten my job. He said it was my job to coach and his to figure out how to make the team more profitable."

"Did he actually say he might fire you?" Nadia asked. "Don't risk your job for me. Please, I'd feel terrible if you lost your job."

"I won't," she said, "although I'm not sure I might not be better off looking for another position. I don't have the kinds of ties to Phoenix that you do."

"Don't let him ruin your career," Nadia said. "And please don't worry about me. I'll work things out. My biggest concern right now is not basketball—it's my mother."

"You are a great woman, Nadia. I'm devastated to lose you. Usually, I would have been consulted, but Tomas left me entirely out of the loop on this one."

"It's okay. Please, I really will be okay."

"What are you doing now?" Coach Korner asked.

"I'm at the mall. Right now I'm trying on a pair of really cute red pumps. It's good therapy."

"Sounds fun. Well, they're telling us to turn off our electronic devices, so I better go, but if you need to talk, I'm here for you."

"Tell the girls to play their best tonight. They can win without me."

"This late flight that Newbold made us take is going to hurt us. The girls are all upset, especially Jules. She doesn't even want to go on the court tonight," the coach said.

"You tell her that I want her to give it the best she's got. I want all of the team to play their hardest," Nadia urged. "Ask them to win this one for me. Don't let me getting traded mess up the rest of the team." Nadia was more depressed than ever now. She loved the team, and she didn't want them to fall apart because of her.

She turned her attention back to the red pumps. She had to get herself out of this funk. She ended up buying the pumps and a pair of black high heels for church. Then she decided to go looking for a new dress. As she walked out of the shoe store, her phone rang again. She pulled it out and saw that it was her grandfather. She almost let the call go to voice mail, but then she realized that if he couldn't reach her, that might make him worry more than ever. So she answered the call as she met the eyes of a man who seemed to be staring at her from about forty or fifty feet away.

She was used to men staring at her. It was part of the price of being attractive and tall. But she didn't like it. She looked away from him as her grandfather said, "Hello, little girl. I'm sorry I had to leave. There have been some things come up here that are going to keep me tied up until tomorrow afternoon. But I'll be back tomorrow night," he promised.

"That's okay. I'm fine," she said. "I just hope Jayden is making progress."

"I do too. How was your meeting with your general manager?"

"It wasn't fun. He's only been with the team since before the beginning of the season. He says it's his job to make the team more profitable, and he thinks I'm making too much money."

"Did he cut your pay?"

"He can't. I'm under contract."

"Don't you have an agent to deal with people like him?" he asked.

"I had one, but I let him go. I didn't want to pay a good chunk of my salary to someone else. We don't make the kind of money our male counterparts in the NBA do," she said.

"Well, you be firm," he said. "I'm getting another call. Keep in touch, Nadia. I'll be back there tomorrow night. Love you, little girl."

"Love you too, Grandpa."

She put the phone back in her purse and headed down the corridor. She glanced over her shoulder. The big tattooed man was walking behind her. She turned into a card store. He was making her nervous. She was sure it was just paranoia and he would walk on by.

She ducked behind a display and began to act like she was studying the cards there. But she was really peeking past them. The big man had stopped and was leaning against a wall on the far side of the corridor. He wasn't as tall as Jayden, but he was taller than her. She judged him to be about six four. He was wearing a muscle shirt, and she could see tattoos everywhere there was skin showing. His round face with bulging eyes was not one she'd like to see in a dark street. It was hard to judge his age because his face was badly scarred, but she guessed he was probably anywhere from midtwenties to midthirties. And he just stood there.

She shivered, wishing she'd let the police take her back to Jayden's office. It was too late for that now. Then she chided herself. She was being silly. He wasn't interested in her. She finally bought a funny card that she thought Jayden would like. She put it in the shopping bag with her new shoes and left the store, walking rapidly away. She looked over her shoulder. The big man was following her with his eyes, but he hadn't moved and a scantily dressed young woman had joined him. The girl had short hair and tattoos on her arms and legs. She was average height and wasn't bad-looking. All of that was absorbed in the short look Nadia allowed herself.

She wasn't worried about him anymore. She willed herself not to look back again. She'd come to enjoy some shopping, and that was what she was going to do.

CHAPTER NINETEEN

The search warrants were about ready. Jayden hoped they would have better luck searching Professor Delgado's office and house and Naylyn Pierza's dorm room than they'd had with their interviews. Davon Karp wasn't at the shop where he worked as a welder. His boss said that he'd gone to Phoenix the evening before to take care of some business for a friend. The manager knew nothing more than that and had no idea when Karp would be back.

Jayden and the chief decided that they just as well speak with Lorena Husman, former player on Coach Fairchild's team, but her roommate told him that Lorena had gone to Phoenix with her boyfriend and had no idea when she would return.

Could the pair have been with Ulisses when he collected the money? Jayden couldn't help but think so. He had resigned himself to another trip back to Coolidge the next day, but at least he'd be back in Phoenix sooner. That thought cheered him up. The sooner he returned, the sooner he could help Nadia get settled in a different hotel. And perhaps he could spend the evening relaxing with her, if she was okay with that. They both needed some downtime.

Jayden was sitting in the police break room eating a candy bar and sharing some chips with Bullet while he waited for the search warrants. His phone began ringing. He hoped it was Nadia calling to report on how her meeting with the team's general manager had gone. But it was Detective Irving Noe of the Phoenix PD. "Hi, Irving," Jayden said. "What's happening?"

"I wish I knew. Your girlfriend is upset over something," the detective said.

"She's not my girlfriend," Jayden said. "She's my client."

"Whatever," Irving said with a chuckle. "I saw the way you two looked at each other. That's not the way a PI would look at just any client."

"So did she say what the matter was?" Jayden ignored his friendly jab.

"No. She said everything is fine, but she wouldn't let us take her back to your office. I could tell that she was more than just a little upset. She finally called from a shopping mall."

"No! That's not good," Jayden said, coming to his feet.

"I agree," Irving said. "I was wondering if you thought I should run over to the mall and see if I can find her and then keep an eye on her."

"Yes, please do. The guy I wanted to interview here, Ulisses's buddy from prison, isn't at work. His boss said he'd gone to Phoenix last night to take care of some business for a *friend* and has not returned." Jayden began to pace.

"I'll get on my way right now. And I'll take some backup," Noe said.

"Yeah, do that. But it gets worse, Irving. His girlfriend is with him."

"The one Coach Fairchild cut from the team?"

"One and the same."

"Jayden, can you give me a description of this Karp guy?" Irving asked.

"I haven't seen him, but I've been told he's an ugly guy. He's big and tattooed all over. He had a scarred face, and his eyes bug out. He's shorter than me but not by much. And he wears his hair in a ponytail."

"Age?" the detective asked.

"Twenty-six."

"Okay, I'll head down there."

"And I'll call Nadia. I hope she'll take my call. I want her to wait for you someplace where there are a lot of people around," Jayden said.

"Search warrants are ready to go," Chief Owens said as he stuck his head in the break room doorway.

"Can they wait until morning? I've got an emergency in Phoenix," Jayden said. "I've got to get back there."

The chief stepped in. "What's going on?"

"My client is being foolish," he responded, not with anger but with worry. "She's in a mall in Phoenix. She's shopping."

"Uh oh," Chief Owens responded. "You better get some cops there. Karp is in Phoenix." He didn't need to say more. He knew what was likely happening as clearly as Jayden did.

Jayden was already heading for the exit. "I've got to hurry. I've alerted the Phoenix PD, but I need to be there."

The chief was trotting alongside of him. "The search warrants will hold. Why don't you ride with me. I can get you there much faster. I'll go lights and sirens."

"My Hummer?"

"It'll be fine here. Get what you need out of it, and we'll be on our way," the chief said.

With Bullet in the backseat and Jayden in the front with Chief Owens, they hit the road. While the chief drove at breakneck speed, Jayden worked his phone. He first tried Nadia, but the call went to voice mail. Then he called Detective Noe. "She's not answering her phone," Jayden said the moment Irving answered. "He can't take her off the mall property or—"

The detective cut him off. "I already have officers beginning to surround the mall. We'll watch every door. My partner and I and several others are going inside. I'm just pulling up now."

"I hope he hasn't already got her out of there or done something to her," Jayden said as worry turned in his stomach like a knife.

"I've broadcast his description to everyone. He'll be easy to spot. I've also alerted mall security," Irving said. "I'm just pulling up there now. Are you coming?"

"Lights and sirens," Jayden answered.

"You don't have lights and sirens," the detective reminded him.

"Chief Owens does. We're in his car, and he's tearing up the pavement."

"Good. And I suppose you have your dog."

"I would leave my left arm behind before I'd leave Bullet. If you don't have Karp collared by the time I get there, Bullet will take up the trail. He'll find Nadia."

"You'll need something of hers for scent, won't you?"

"Not necessarily. Bullet knows her, and I'm pretty sure he would look for her on command," Jayden said confidently. "This dog is brighter than a lot of humans."

"I can believe that," Detective Noe said. "I'm inside the mall now. I'll call you if we find her before you get here. If not, call me the moment you arrive."

***

Nadia, no matter how hard she tried, could not get the devastating conversation with Mr. Newbold out of her head. The shoes had helped a little. And the blouse she bought had distracted her for a few minutes. Sandy, her sales clerk, had been nice. "I know you," she'd said. "You're Nadia Fairchild. I've watched you play ball. You are amazing."

Nadia had thanked her, and for a couple of minutes, they talked basketball. She'd given the girl her autograph, but when she asked why she wasn't in Tulsa to play that night, Nadia responded, "I hurt my arm. I can't play right now."

And at that moment, it was hurting. She was regretting throwing the sling away. Maybe she should find the restroom again and see if she could find it. It hadn't been all that long, and she thought she could probably dig it out of the trash can.

"Oh no," Sandy had said. "Your team will lose without you."

"I hope not," Nadia said, and she really meant it. Nadia headed for the front of the store, her stomach twisting with anxiety. She didn't want to move to Minnesota. Not that they weren't a great team—because they were. She knew she could soon fit in up there. She'd played them enough that she had a feeling for their style of play. And she'd even gotten to know a couple of the girls, but Phoenix was her home. She'd felt so blessed when they signed her, and she'd given them her best effort from day one.

Her salary was where it was because she had been such a devoted player, and she'd earned the raises she'd been given. But apparently, Mr. Newbold resented her and didn't care how much it hurt her or the team to get rid of her. Newbold didn't even care how much Coach Korner wanted to keep her. He was the boss, and he was going to make sure everyone knew it. Nadia's injury was just the opening he'd been waiting for. At least, that was the way Nadia saw it. She simply could not understand the man.

Sandy, the petite young sales clerk, called her name. "Nadia, I just had a thought."

She stopped short of the exit and turned back, painting on a smile. "What's that?"

"We have some slacks that will go nicely with that blouse. I think there might be some in your size. They would drown me—I'm so short—but they're nice. You'd look great in them, especially the light-colored ones. Would you like to look at them?"

Why not? Nadia thought. Sandy was so sweet, and she didn't want to hurt her feelings, and anyway, another pair of nice slacks would be okay. "Sure, I'd like that, Sandy," she said.

"They're clear at the back of the store. I should have mentioned it earlier. I hope you're not in a hurry."

"No hurry. Since I couldn't travel with the team, I have time on my hands." And trouble on my mind, she could have added.

Her phone rang. It was Jayden. He had so much to do that she didn't want to distract him from his work. She ignored his call, promising herself that she would make it up to him later.

She spent twenty minutes trying on slacks, examining them, holding them up to her new blouse. She finally picked out two that went well with her complexion—and one of them went really well with the new blouse. "Sandy, I'll take these two," she said. She held up one of the slacks. "But I have to get another blouse to go with this one."

"Then let's look at more blouses." Sandy smiled.

Another ten minutes passed. Finally, Nadia found one she liked. "Okay, I think this will do."

Sandy rang her up, and as Nadia took the sack gingerly in her arm, she said, "Sandy, your boss should give you a raise. You're a great salesperson. Thank you."

Sandy smiled. "I just try to do my best."

And so do I, Nadia thought bitterly as she turned and headed to the front of the store for the second time. *But look where that got me—kicked all the way to Minnesota.* She looked at her watch. She'd spent over a half hour just since the first purchase. And while Sandy was showing her things, she'd hardly thought about her situation. But she was thinking about it now and how hard she'd worked only to be rewarded with a boot out the door.

She entered the big hallway, and her heart stopped. There was that same big guy with the tattoos and bulging eyes and the same young woman. The man was watching her like he had earlier. She tried to hide the fear that attacked her. She started through the throngs of shoppers, looking backward. The guy was coming her way. She pulled her phone from her purse and dialed Jayden.

"Nadia, is that you?" he said, giving comfort to her like no one she'd ever known.

"Yes, I did a stupid thing, and I think there's a guy after me," she said.

"Is he a big man with tattoos and bulging eyes?"

"Yes, and he's gaining on me. There's a girl with him."

"Head for the nearest exit. Fast! There will be a cop there."

"I don't know where the nearest exit is," she said, frantically looking around.

"Then go into the nearest store and tell them to let you out a back way if they have one," he said. "Otherwise, wait in there, and I'll get an officer to you."

"Okay," she said, her voice trembling. "I'm sorry, Jayden. This isn't like me. It's been a really bad day."

***

Jayden's heart was beating a mile a minute. He wondered what had happened to upset her so much. But he didn't have time to worry about that now. He needed to see that she was safe. "Are you in a store yet, and if so, which one?" he asked.

"Hey, what are you doing?" she shouted, but it wasn't to him.

Then he heard a voice, probably Davon Karp, say, "You don't need your phone. Give it to me."

"No, I won't," she said. Then a moment later, she screamed and said "I'm at—"

The phone went dead.

Urgently, Jayden called Noe's number again. "He's got her," Jayden said. "Miss Husman is with him."

"Where is she?" Noe asked.

"She tried to tell me, but he took her phone and ended the call while she was screaming," Jayden said.

"I'm on it. He can't get out of the mall with her. We'll find her."

"You've got to," Jayden said to an already ended call.

"I'm sorry," the chief said. "But I know right where the mall is. We're almost there."

"I owe you. You made great time," Jayden said.

"It's all part of the job."

"I wonder why they're after Nadia. They've already got her mother and Miss Pierza. And they have a million dollars," Jayden said.

"Who knows why criminals do what they do." The chief continued to force his way through traffic. "You know, I read a piece the other day on the Internet that made a lot of sense. This old soldier says there are three kinds of people in this world. There are sheep, there are wolves, and there are sheepdogs. Most people are sheep. They go day to day thinking that nothing bad can ever happen to them, pretending that all is well. When something does happen, they're so devastated they're unable to solve their problems. They haven't learned how to fight back."

"Yeah, that makes sense," Jayden said, grateful to the chief for trying to keep his mind occupied.

"Wolves are the people like Ulisses and Davon and that guy that attacked Nadia. They harm people just to do it. They enjoy it. They look for trouble, they make trouble, and they spend their lives trying to hurt the sheep," he said.

"And the sheepdogs?" Jayden asked, already guessing where this was going.

"That's you and me. That's cops and PIs and soldiers. The kind of people who have it in our DNA to watch out for the sheep," he said. "Why do soldiers go to war? Why do you and I put ourselves in harm's way for others? It's because that's who we are. The sheep would never survive in this world without the sheepdogs. The sheepdogs are their protectors. Not all sheepdogs are cops and soldiers. Lots of them carry weapons—not because they think they are hot stuff because they have a gun but because they know that the time might come when they need to be armed to save themselves or others. There are so many in our country today who bury their heads in the sand and pretend everything is okay." He paused. "We're almost there."

Jayden could see the mall ahead, but the chief had more to say. "Some wolves can become sheepdogs. It takes some kind of life-changing event to make that kind of transition. And such a change is rare. Can you imagine what this world would be like if there were only sheep and wolves?" He shrugged. "Obviously there are some in-between cases, but you get the idea. A lot of people rail against cops and belittle soldiers, but when they're in trouble, who do they call?" The question didn't need an answer. Both knew. After all, they were sheepdogs.

Chief Owens slid to a stop near the main entrance. Good to his word, Detective Noe had cops swarming all over. He and Owens bounded out of the car. "Bullet, find Nadia," Jayden said as they hurried to one of the main entrances. At the door, an officer asked them what they were doing with a dog.

"He's a search dog," Jayden said.

Understanding dawned in the officer's eyes, and he waved them inside. Bullet went to work. Jayden called Detective Noe. "We're in, and Bullet is searching. Anything so far?"

"No, but I've got officers checking, and more on the way."

"I'm going to take Bullet down the main hallway first. I came in the west entrance. We need to find out which way she came in. Wait, he's picked up her scent. He's trailing her. Gotta go. He's going to keep the chief and me running," Jayden said. He ended the call and shoved his phone in his pocket.

Bullet swerved from the corridor into a shoe store and began to work his way around inside. "Was there a tall, dark-complexioned girl in here?" Jayden asked a clerk. She looked fearful.

The salesgirl told him that the tall girl had purchased some red pumps and a pair of high heels. He called to Bullet and took him back to the hallway. "Search," he commanded. Bullet took off down the wide corridor. People were standing against the walls. Something was happening. They didn't know what. Like sheep, they huddled and watched with frightened eyes. The sudden influx of cops with guns had frightened the sheep. They feared that wolves had entered the flock. But the sheepdogs were here. Bullet turned into another store a moment later, a women's clothing store. Jayden and the chief followed him.

"What's going on?" a girl with a name tag that read *Sandy* asked. "Why are there cops everywhere? Am I in danger?"

"Just stay in your store. Was there a tall, dark girl in here?" Jayden asked.

"You mean Nadia Fairchild?" Sandy asked, her eyes wide.

"Yes. You know her?" Jayden asked. "Bullet, come here." The dog joined him, clearly anxious to be back on the hunt. His whole body quivered.

"I recognized her from watching the Mercury play ball. She bought some slacks and blouses," Sandy said. "Has something happened to her?"

"Which way did she go?" Jayden asked urgently. "We need to find her."

"She walked to the right," Sandy said. "Is she okay?"

"I hope so," Jayden said and let Bullet follow her trail again.

"There you are," Detective Noe said. "It looks like Bullet is on her scent."

"He is," Jayden said as Noe and his partner began to trot along with Jayden and Chief Owens.

Suddenly, the German shepherd stopped and nosed a couple of large shopping bags. "Those might be hers," Jayden said.

Owens picked them up. "There're shoes in this one. Red pumps. It's hers!"

"Search," Jayden said with more urgency. Bullet turned from the bags, and he was on the hunt again. "Don't worry about the bags," Jayden called behind him.

But a woman came out of the store nearest the bags. The chief said, "Keep these. Don't let anyone touch them." And he ran after the others.

A short ways up the corridor, Bullet took another right. For five minutes, they ran through the mall. They passed an exit, but Bullet kept going. Then they entered a department store. He weaved around between racks of clothing and then shelves with all kinds of goods. Finally, he stopped at a closed door and whined, his nose to the door.

Guns in their hands, Detective Noe pushed on the door. It gave a little but then stuck. "It's blocked with something."

"Cover me," Jayden said grimly, and then he hit the door with a powerful blow that sent whatever was holding it shut breaking up and flying. He and Bullet were the first through the door.

The search for Nadia was over. She was lying in a crumpled heap on the floor, blood pooling around her head. Jayden cried out and stumbled against the wall, holding his head. Nightmarish visions of his wife lying dead in the roadway blocked his vision. He sank to his knees in anguish. It was happening again.

CHAPTER TWENTY

"Jayden, she's alive. Help me here," Detective Noe shouted at him. With an effort, Jayden shook off the terrible memory and collapsed beside the fallen girl. "Take care of her. I'll continue looking down this hallway." Noe and the others moved away.

Once Jayden was sure that Nadia was indeed alive, he looked at where they were. It was some kind of utility or storage area. There were chairs and tables, clothes racks and other items against the wall. The splintered remains of the chair that had been propped beneath the door handle lay near Nadia. Jayden heard more people approaching the door, and he shouted out to them, "Call an ambulance!"

More officers streamed into the storage area. "Take care of her," he said as he determined that the blood was from a nasty gash on the back of her head. "And watch yourselves. The guy that did this is around somewhere, and he's dangerous. There's a woman with him. Don't let them near this woman."

These men were protectors. They knew what to do.

"Bullet." The German shepherd looked up at him. "Good job, Bullet," he said, patting the dog's head. "You found her, but you aren't through yet." He touched the floor beyond the crumpled woman. "Find *them*," he said.

Bullet looked up at him as if to say, "Find whom?"

"Find them," Jayden said as he again tapped the floor beyond where Nadia had fallen. The dog put his nose back to the floor. He growled and then headed down the hallway at a trot. Others wouldn't be able to tell, but Jayden knew that the intelligent animal had just switched from rescuer to hunter. The growl told Jayden that.

They soon caught up to Detective Noe, Chief Owens, and a couple other officers. "Is she going to be okay?" Noe asked as Jayden passed them.

"Head injury, but she should be okay," he said, praying it was true, and continued at a trot. The hallway soon ended. There were two doors, one to the left and one to the right—but Bullet knew which way they'd gone. "They went through that door," Jayden said as the other officers jogged up.

Once again, the men stood aside. Bullet stood beside Jayden, trembling with the desire to plunge beyond the door. "Wait, Bullet." The dog looked up at his master and then again pointed his nose at the door.

Detective Noe tried the knob. "It's not locked, but it's blocked like the last one was," Noe said. "Be careful when you hit the door. They could be in there."

Jayden kicked the door and sprang aside as it swung open.

"I'll kill her," a voice called from inside.

"She's your girlfriend," Jayden shouted into the room. "You won't hurt her."

"She's my ticket out of here," the angry voice called back. "I'm coming out. Don't anyone try anything, or I'll kill her."

"Okay, come on out," Detective Noe shouted.

Bullet was straining against the hold Jayden had on his collar. Jayden pulled him back a ways, out of sight of the door. He heard shuffled footsteps and peeked at the door. Pretty soon, Davon Karp appeared. He had a girl held tightly against him with one muscled, tattooed arm. The other arm held a small revolver, which was pressed against her forehead.

Davon stopped at the doorway. "Put your guns on the floor, or she dies."

"Yes, do it," Lorena Husman threatened. "He'll kill me if you don't."

Jayden quickly sized the situation up. He was standing now so that Bullet was behind him. Lorena didn't look scared. She didn't even have a catch in her voice. She was faking it, trusting the cops to do what her violent boyfriend said. Her eyes met Jayden's briefly. He saw no fear, only hatred.

One by one, the cops put their guns on the floor and stepped back. Jayden leaned over and did the same. This man had no intention of shooting his girlfriend. The pair started through the door and up the hallway. "Behind you!" Jayden suddenly yelled as he released his hold on Bullet.

Instinctively, the con, who was clearly not a smart man, glanced back, and the gun slid away from the girl's head. Bullet sprang through the air and had the man's gun hand before he could even turn his head back. The gun dropped, and Jayden's foot connected with the man's hand, below where Bullet was biting it. The weapon flew across the room and hit the wall. Bullet took Davon to the floor, and for the second time in as many days, bones crunched and flesh tore. A would-be killer screamed.

Jayden watched for a moment. Then, after he believed that Davon would no longer be a danger to them, he ordered Bullet to release him.

Lorena was cursing and lunging at Jayden. "Let him go!" she screamed as several strong arms seized her and pulled her back.

"They're all yours," Jayden shouted as his eyes met Detective Noe's.

Noe knelt over the con, but suddenly a knife appeared in Karp's uninjured hand and was slicing through the air at Noe. Bullet was faster. Before the knife's flashing blade met Noe's exposed face, Bullet caught the other of Davon's wrists. This time, he tore at the man's wrist with such force that not only did the knife fall away and bones crunch, but blood began to spurt. The big con struggled to free himself, but there was no escape from the German shepherd's powerful jaws.

Lorena kicked and screamed and cursed. "He's killing him," she cried. "Make him stop."

Jayden's impulse was to let Bullet finish the job, but that would be wrong. "Bullet, release," he said.

Bullet gave one more violent shake of his head and then opened his mouth and slipped back. "I'm going," Jayden said, leaving others to tend to the felon and his severed artery.

He ran up the semidark hallway between all kinds of junk. Paramedics were lifting Nadia onto a stretcher. Jayden waited until she was strapped on, and then he bent over her. Her head was bandaged, and some of the blood had been cleaned up. "Sweetheart, I'm here," he said softly.

Her eyes fluttered open. It took a moment before she was able to focus. When she finally did, she said, "My red pumps."

"They're in good hands." Jayden chuckled. "You're going to be okay." Then he turned to a paramedic. "The perp has a torn artery. He's around the bend. You'll see the officers there in the hall." Then he turned back to Nadia.

"I'm sorry. I really made a mess of things," she said.

"Not your fault," he told her. "I want to know what upset you so badly today, but let's get you to the hospital first."

"I'm fine," she said predictably.

The paramedics were moving the gurney along the hallway. Jayden and his bloodied dog kept up with them. "You always say you're fine, but you need medical attention."

"Maybe." She shook her head, seeming to clear the fog. "Jayden, what did you call me?"

"When?" he asked innocently.

"You know when."

He grinned. "Does it offend you?"

That made her pain-filled face smile weakly. "No. Say it again."

"Nadia," he said.

"No, that other one."

"Miss Fairchild?"

"No. *Sweetheart*," she said.

"What did you just call me?" he asked.

"You're impossible," she said. "But I guess I'm a sucker for impossible."

"Jayden," someone called from behind them.

He turned back. "What's the problem, Detective Noe?" he asked as the officer sprinted toward him.

"We need your help. Miss Husman says she'll only talk to you."

"I'll be right there." Jayden turned back to the woman on the rolling gurney. "I'll meet you at the hospital, and you can tell me what's going on." He asked a paramedic which hospital she was going to, and then he spoke once again to Nadia. "I'll recover your red pumps and catch up with you at the hospital." And before she could say anything else, he turned and trotted back to where Detective Noe was waiting.

Another gurney, this one empty, was being pushed at a run through the department store toward the utility hallway. "I don't know what the hurry is," Jayden grunted. "I'd feel bad if one of those paramedics tripped and got hurt trying to save a creep like Davon Karp."

Irving chuckled. "He'll make it, but he did lose a lot of blood. And look at that dog of yours. He needs a bath. He's a bloody mess. So are you."

"And you're not?" he asked.

"Point taken," the Phoenix officer said, glancing down at the blood on himself.

"Where is Miss Husman?"

"She is in the office of the department store. Just follow me. She's asking for you. That's the only reason I pulled you away from Nadia. I have no idea what she's going to tell you."

"Whatever it is, I'll take it with a grain of salt," Jayden said.

"Yeah, I understand."

Miss Husman was sitting in a hard-backed chair with her head down. She was handcuffed with the cuffs in front of her. Chief Owens was standing near her, and another officer was behind her. A security officer was leaning against a wall.

Lorena looked up when Jayden walked in. "Are you Detective Spalding?"

"That's me. Are you Lorena Husman?"

"Yeah," she said. "I need to talk to you."

"What's on your mind?"

"You're probably wondering why Davon and I needed to talk to the Fairchild woman," she said.

"The thought crossed my mind." Jayden looked around, pulled up a chair facing her, and sat down. He pulled out his cell phone. "I'm going to record our conversation on my iPhone," he said. "Do you have a problem with that?"

"No, I'm not going to lie to you. Record away," she said in a low monotone.

He soon had it ready, and then he said, "Okay, what did you want to tell me?"

"Davon got carried away. It's not his fault. He was only trying to help me. It was all Nadia's fault," she said.

"Really. How so?"

She squirmed and rolled her shoulders. "She's been telling lies about me. It's her fault that her mother kicked me off the team. All I wanted to do was ask her why she said those things. It really hurt me. But when we tried to talk to her, she got mad and started swearing at us, so we had to take her someplace private."

Where Davon could hit her over the head with his gun, he thought. "What kinds of lies had she told her mother?" Jayden asked, trying hard to appear unbiased. In truth, the hesitation along with his general impression of the girl made him very suspicious. But he'd play along for now.

"Well, for one thing, she said that I was using drugs," Lorena said. "And that's a lie."

"Did she ever say why she thought you were doing that?" Jayden had a feeling that when he was finally able to search her dorm room, he would find drugs. But that was for later.

"No, she knew I wasn't. She was making it up. She was spreading it around, trying to make me look bad."

"I see," Jayden said, although he didn't see at all. "Perhaps you can give me a list of people she told. That way I can check with them. You know, just to verify your accusations. I need to be thorough." He waited, thinking about the accusation that Nadia had sworn at them. He knew that was a lie. He suspected the rest of what Miss Husman was saying was also untruthful. He continued to wait for her to speak. Finally he said, "Go ahead. Tell us who told you that she'd accused you of using drugs."

"Well, let's see . . ." she said. She seemed to be thinking deeply. "I don't remember all of them, but there were a lot. Oh, yeah, one of them is one of the other players on the team."

"And who is that?" he asked.

"Naylyn Pierza," she said.

"Who else?"

"Another one is a girl by the name of Jane Tribold. But she moved back home. She quit school."

"Where is she from?" he asked.

"I don't remember. But we had some classes together and were friends. She was upset by what Nadia told her. She told me that I needed to know what the coach's uppity daughter was saying about me." She reached up to her face with her cuffed hands and rubbed her eyes with the back of one hand.

"Okay, who else?" he asked.

"I can't think right now. I'm kind of upset. I'm worried about Davon. That dog nearly killed him," she said.

"You're telling me that you can't think of any others because you're upset and worried?" Jayden asked.

"That's right," she answered quickly.

"All right then, we'll come back to this. You be thinking about more names," he said. "Because the two names you've given me won't help me verify what you're saying, will they?"

"I guess not," she said.

"Well, while we're talking, I'd be interested in how you and Davon found Miss Fairchild in this mall," he said. "Surely you can remember that as it's so recent."

She shifted nervously on her chair. "He was just helping me," she finally said. "We followed her when she got in that taxi. It was easy really. It was Davon's idea. He's a really smart guy."

"Yes, I can see that. He's so smart that he pulled a gun on her and forced her to go with you two into that utility hallway and then hit her on the back of the head with that same gun. So smart that he did things that will send him back to prison for a very, very long time," he said. "And of course, you helped, so you'll go to prison too. He must really love you to help you like that." He was only assuming that Davon had pulled the gun on Nadia and hit her with it, but the look in Lorena's eyes told him that he'd assumed correctly.

"It was her fault," she stammered.

"I see. And would you like to explain how you are going to replace the red pumps she just bought and you caused her to lose?" he asked.

She looked puzzled for a moment. "Oh, you mean the bags she dropped? We didn't make her drop those bags."

"I see. So you don't think you're responsible for the shoes. Well, let me tell you this. Miss Fairchild is very upset over those shoes. She would also like her phone back."

"It's in my purse. Did you guys bring my purse?" she asked, her eyes directed toward Detective Noe.

"It's right here," he said, pointing to where it lay on a desk. "I'm going to look in your purse for her phone. Is that all right?"

"Yeah. I don't need it. We just needed her to not talk on it until she told us why she said those awful things about me."

Noe pulled a phone out. "Is this it?"

"That's mine. Put it back."

"No, I'll need it," Jayden said. Lorena cursed at him as he accepted it from Irving and put it in his pocket. Detective Noe pulled a second phone from the purse.

"That one is Nadia's," Jayden said. "I recognize the case." The detective handed it to him. He pocketed that one as well and then said, "Moving along now, Lorena. Let's talk about what you know about Davon helping Ulisses Fairchild kidnap his ex-wife."

CHAPTER TWENTY-ONE

Nadia was still in the emergency room when Jayden walked in. "There you are," he said with a smile.

"Hi," she said. "Where's Bullet?"

"I thought I might be pushing it bringing him in the hospital." He leaned down and kissed her forehead. Then he said, "Chief Owens kept him out in the parking lot."

"Oh," she said.

"I would have been here quicker, but I had to give the poor dog a bath. I used a utility sink in the mall."

"You have a little blood on you too," she said.

"Not much now. I bought a new shirt in the mall. I'll need to go home and change pants though. How do you feel?"

"I don't know," she said. "They've got so much stuff in me that I can't feel much of anything."

"It looks like you're all stitched up. Are they going to let you go?"

"They want me to stay for an hour, and then someone will need to come get me. They said I can't drive. Can I go with you?"

"Of course," he said. "But we'll actually both have to ride with Chief Owens. I left my Hummer in Coolidge."

"Why?" she asked.

"Chief Owens used lights and sirens. How do you think we got to the mall so quickly?"

"Oh, so you don't have a car here in Phoenix?"

"That's right, except for the old clunker I use for undercover work. It's at my house."

"Did you find my purse?"

"Yes, it was near where you were when that creep knocked you out," he said. "And we recovered your phone from Lorena Husman."

"Who?" she asked.

"The girl who was helping Davon Karp. Karp is your dad's prison buddy," he said.

"I knew that," she said. "After he got me in that hallway, he told me that my father insisted that I fire you and quit looking for Mom." She shivered, and a tear slid down her face. "He told me that my dad said we would never find Mom."

"He didn't say anything about where she might be?" Jayden asked.

She shook her bandaged head. "No, and it made me mad. It's my own fault I got hit over the head. He'd put his gun away. It was tucked in his belt. I kicked him, and he grabbed me and threw me down. I don't know what I was thinking. There was no way I could fight the guy. He's all muscle, tattoos, and empty head. I did manage to get back on my feet. The girl grabbed me from behind, and the guy said something about if I didn't quit searching for Mom, he'd find me again and it wouldn't end well for me."

"I suppose you got away from his girlfriend," Jayden said.

"Oh, yeah, that was easy. But then the guy pulled that gun out and pointed it at me again. He'd already threatened to shoot me. That was why I didn't make a run for it. I think he would have," she said. "Anyway, somebody pounded on the door and asked who had locked it. The guy told the girl they better split. He said that there had to be a back way out. I turned and tried to grab the chair. I guess that's when he hit me. Everything went black. I take it there wasn't another way out?"

"Nope, there were rooms down the hallway, but no exit," he said.

"The girl, who is she?" Nadia asked.

"She says you know who she is. She told me you're the reason your mother kicked her off the basketball team. She says you told people she was using drugs."

"I have no idea what you're talking about," Nadia said.

"I didn't expect you would. Miss Husman is under arrest. Detective Noe is taking her to jail. You're the one I'm worried about. We've got to get you someplace safe so that I can go back to Coolidge," he said.

He explained that he was going to search Husman's dorm and Karp's apartment. "That's more important than ever now. I'm also going to search Naylyn Pierza's dorm room. Now that you're safe, I've got to get back to searching for your mother. I think Karp may know something, and there might be something in Naylyn's room that will give me a clue as to what's happened to the two of them."

They talked for a moment longer. Then Jayden said, "I'll have Chief Owens take me home so I can change, and then we'll come back, pick you up, and then head back to Coolidge."

"Is my purse in the chief's car?" she asked.

"It is. Oh, and here's your phone," he said as he pulled it from his pocket. "I think you have some missed calls."

"Jayden," she said, "the keys to my car are in my purse. Why don't you drive the car here. Then when they let me go, you can drive me to Coolidge."

Jayden was about to argue, then he thought better. "That's a good idea. I want to keep you where I can make sure you don't get in any more trouble."

"I'd like that."

"Oh, but there is one problem," he said. "Where would Bullet ride?"
"There's a space behind the seats that he can squeeze into," she said.

"That's settled then. I'll have the chief drop me off at your car then head back to campus, and in an hour, we'll follow. Don't run away again." He pointed a stern finger at her. "And on the drive, you can tell me all about your problems with the general manager."

"It's awful," she said.

"We'll talk about it later. Rest. We have a ride ahead of us, and we may have to stay in Coolidge tonight. I don't know if we'll have time to conduct all the searches we need to until morning. But I want to get started tonight."

"I'll need a bag with some clothes and stuff," she told him. "And so will you."

"I keep what I need in my Hummer. I never know when I might be overnight or longer. I'll pick up your bags from my office." He tenderly touched her cheek. "I'll be back soon."

As Jayden and the chief drove to the hotel to get Nadia's Jaguar, Jayden spoke with Detective Noe. Due to the severity of Davon Karp's injuries, it would be another day before he could be interviewed. Noe had more news. "And Miss Husman demanded a lawyer. Let me know if you need me to help with them. Since the crimes against Nadia occurred in Phoenix, I'll be following up on that. So I'll do whatever else you need me to."

"Thanks," Jayden said.

As he was driving the small red Jaguar back to the hospital, Jayden got a call from Nadia's grandfather. The first thing Marley said was, "I have a favor to ask, Jayden. Will you keep track of my little girl? I'll come back in a day or two, but I have some things going on with my business that need my attention badly. I would feel better if I knew Nadia was with you after what she told me happened at the mall. Will you do that?"

"I will, Marley sir," Jayden said. Then he told Marley what he'd learned so far and what his plans were. "Nadia can help me search," Jayden said. "I'll do whatever it takes to keep her safe. You have my word on that."

"And one more thing, Jayden," Marley said. "See if she'll tell you what had her so upset that she went off on that silly shopping spree."

***

With three of them in the little red Jaguar, it was packed tighter than a can of sardines. Bullet sat in the spot in the back with his head poked between Jayden and Nadia. It was close quarters, but it was doable. Once the sleek little machine was on the road, Jayden looked past Bullet's head and said, "Okay, Nadia, tell me what the general manager wanted."

"There's not much to tell." She closed her eyes. "He thinks I make too much money. He says Phoenix can't afford me but the Minnesota Lynx can."

For a moment, Jayden was too stunned to say a word. But finally he managed to splutter, "That's insane, Nadia. Doesn't he know that I would rather you stayed in Phoenix?"

She leaned forward and looked past Bullet. "You hardly know me."

"I know you well enough to know that if you go to Minnesota, I'll have to go there too," he said. "I promised your granddad that I would keep track of you, and I mean to do just that."

"You'd do that for me?"

"I know it sounds farfetched, but yes, I would. How soon do you have to be there?"

"Monday morning."

"Nadia, what is that fool thinking?" he asked. "You can't even play yet, and when you can, the Mercury need you."

"He doesn't seem to think so. The whole team is upset, and Coach Korner is downright angry," she said.

"Isn't the GM fairly new?" Jayden asked.

"This is his first season with us," she said. "He says it's his job to make the team more financially stable. I wasn't aware there were any problems, but apparently, getting rid of me and bringing in someone at a lower salary will make things just peachy."

"Well, I think it stinks. It would take me some time to build my business up there, but I can do it. I gave your granddad my word," he said.

She leaned back. "Is that the only reason you would follow me to Minnesota?"

He looked over at her. "No, but it's part of it."

"And the rest is?"

"I guess the only way to say this is to be straightforward," he said. "I know we barely met, but I think I . . . well, I hope this doesn't freak you out, but I like you a lot. I'd like the chance to get to know you better."

"It doesn't worry me. You see, big guy, I want to get to know you better too, but I hate for you to have to leave your work here. I could come back and spend the off-season in Phoenix."

Jayden thought about that for a minute. It might be the only thing that would work. Moving to Minnesota for someone he really didn't know all that well would be a bit extreme. After all, they'd only met two days ago. But the thought of her moving made his heart hurt. "I guess we can see what will be the best. I just want to be able to see you after I find your mother. And I'm not going to stop until I find her."

"There is some good news," Nadia said softly.

Jayden looked past the dog, who seemed to be taking it all in, looking from one to the other as they spoke.

"I'm not going to Minnesota," she said.

"But I thought you just said you have to be there Monday." He was puzzled.

"It will mean the end of my professional basketball career," she said. "But Mr. Newbold isn't going to dictate my life."

"Are you serious?" Jayden asked. "That's kind of extreme. I mean, you've worked hard to achieve your dream. You can't just pretend it doesn't matter anymore."

"I've thought a lot about this since he dropped that bombshell on me. He'll be furious. But I don't think I'll go. I don't know what I'll do now, but I'll find something. I love basketball, but perhaps I could find a coaching job or something. I don't need a lot of money to live. In fact, I have enough money saved to last me awhile already. Although, I would go crazy just sitting around, so I'll look for a job just as soon as we find Mom," she said. "I do have a college degree. Maybe I can coach high school basketball, but I don't want to move. Phoenix is my home."

For a moment, it was silent as the red car streaked as fast as Jayden dared drive toward Coolidge, where he hoped to get some answers on where Ulisses might be keeping Nadia's mother, if he had taken her—and Jayden had doubts about that. Suddenly, a thought struck him. "Nadia, are you sure that's what you want to do?"

"Yes."

"You know that office in my reception area?" he said.

"What about it?" she asked.

"I need someone to sit behind that desk. I've been thinking about it for a while. I get so far behind on my paperwork. I make good money, and I can afford it."

"Then why don't you?"

"Well, it's like this. I'm fussy. I won't hire just anyone. I want someone who's smart and beautiful and who has dark hair, smooth olive skin, and dark brown eyes." He glanced past his dog. She was smiling.

"You *are* fussy," she said.

"That's not everything. She has to be tall and athletic," he said, trying to keep his face deadpan. "And I want a good LDS woman. Can't be a guy. Someone who's willing to travel with me when that becomes necessary, and well . . . I guess that about covers it. You see my dilemma?"

"Are you taking applications?" she asked.

"I guess I should."

"I'll apply."

"You're hired," he told her, and they both laughed. Then he got serious again. "Nadia, you're a great ball player. Even if you were to go to Minnesota, you could work for me when you were here in Phoenix. We could get to know each other better, even if you were gone a lot."

For several minutes, she didn't speak. But finally she said, "I do love basketball. Maybe I should reconsider."

"Let's think about it, but the job is yours, part- or full-time, whatever you decide." He thought about how he would miss her, and yet he felt good that she would have a reason to come back to Phoenix whenever she could.

"For right now, let's let the future work itself out. We have work to do. We've got to find Mom."

"What if this Mr. Newbold guy fishes his brain out of the sewer and tries to get you to come back?"

She shook her head. "I don't think he will, but if he does, can I still work for you?"

"You know it," he said. "Okay, Miss Fairchild, let's talk strategy." And for the rest of the drive, that is exactly what they did.

***

Chief Owens and Lieutenant Tevin Kaiser met them at the campus police department.

"Is this your client?" Tevin asked.

"No. This pretty girl with the bandaged head and sling is my newest assistant," he said with a grin. "Bullet and I have help now. Nadia Fairchild, meet Detective Tevin Kaiser. Are you gentlemen ready?"

"Yes, we are," the chief said. "Are you up to this, Nadia?"

"If I have to, I'll sit down. I'll mostly just observe anyway," she said.

"Where should we begin?" the chief asked.

"Well, since we've had a rather nasty run-in with Lorena and Davon, let's start with one of them," Jayden said. "And since we're on campus, we could start with Lorena's dorm. Does the warrant cover her car too?"

"It does," Kaiser said. "And I already know where it's parked."

Jayden grinned. "It just so happens that I have a set of keys that I think might fit. My good friend Detective Noe of the Phoenix PD got them out of her purse. While there's still some daylight left, let's take a look at the car. And just so you know, Noe's getting a search warrant for her phone."

"Oh," Nadia said. "You're going to fire me already. I didn't ever try to hack into my father's phone, and I left it in your office. Jayden, I'm sorry."

"We'll get to that, and you're not fired," he said. "I'm not that big of an idiot."

Lorena's car was a mess. They found nothing that would help them in their search for Layda, but they did find drug paraphernalia, which Lieutenant Kaiser seized. They moved on to the dorm. There were other girls there, but when they showed the girls the warrant, every one of them said they hoped the police would find something to put Lorena in jail for. None of them liked her, and they were afraid of her boyfriend. Jayden unlocked Lorena's room with a key that was on the same ring as her car keys.

Nadia mostly visited with the girls. There were four of them. The others on that floor had either gone on dates that night or had gone to their homes for the weekend. Those four were in awe when they found out who Nadia was. She signed autographs for all of them. The girls also fussed over Bullet, who accepted their attention with good nature. In the meantime, the officers and Jayden were methodically searching the little room. They found a stash of marijuana and some methamphetamine along with various items of drug paraphernalia.

Jayden interviewed each of the four students, who all claimed to not use drugs but said they knew that Lorena did. That was one of the reasons they didn't want to be in the same dorm with her anymore. The story Lorena had told him about Nadia spreading rumors made Jayden angrier because of what they'd found. None of the girls on the floor recalled Lorena ever mentioning Nadia Fairchild, but they did report that Lorena hated Coach Fairchild. None of them could recall Lorena making specific threats though. He asked about a student by the name of Jane Tribold.

It turned out that all four of them knew Jane, that she was sort of a friend of Lorena's. A couple of them recalled her telling them that she was from either North or South Dakota. One thought it might have been Montana. Nothing in Lorena's room shed any further light on Jane. "I think it'd be worthwhile to talk to her," Jayden told the others. "Maybe in the morning we can check with the records office."

"Maybe, but it's Saturday tomorrow," the chief reminded him. "We may not be able to do that until Monday."

"Then maybe I'll give Nadia her first official assignment." Jayden shrugged. "She's really good with computers. Between us, we'll see what we can find out about Jane on the Internet."

"Jayden, were you serious about hiring her?" Chief Owens asked.

"Yep. The team traded her to Minnesota. She's supposed to report there Monday morning. She may or may not go, but either way she intends to keep Phoenix as her home, and she'll work for me when she's here."

"Wow," Lieutenant Kaiser said. "That's crazy."

Jayden shrugged, and the search went on. Other than the drugs—which did nothing to move Jayden's objective forward—the search was a bust. By the time they finished, it was quite late.

"I think, if it's okay with you fellows, we'll resume in the morning." Jayden suppressed a yawn.

"What time do you want to meet us?" Chief Owens asked. "Not too early, I would assume, since you have to drive back to Phoenix tonight and then return in the morning."

"We'll find a hotel and stay over," Jayden said. "The doctor doesn't want Nadia to drive until the pain meds wear off. Is it okay if we leave her car on campus tonight?"

The chief agreed and suggested that they stay in Florence, which was only nine miles away. They were able to book adjoining rooms in the Holiday Inn Express and Suites. Bullet, when he was described as a service dog, was allowed in the hotel. They checked in and then ate a late dinner, the first either of them had eaten since breakfast at the hotel in Phoenix.

By the time they got to their rooms after dinner, Jayden could tell that Nadia was done in. She wanted to help do an Internet search for Jane Tribold, but Jayden told her to go to bed, and she didn't argue.

"I don't think anyone could find you here," he told her, "but I want Bullet to be able to guard both our rooms. He could sleep by the adjoining door."

Jayden was also exhausted, but he decided to spend some time on the computer before turning in—the Internet had become the best friend of private investigators everywhere. So he opened his laptop, connected to the hotel's Wi-Fi, and went to work.

It turned out that Jane Tribold was from a small place called Watford in the northwest corner of North Dakota. If she had indeed gone home, he should be able to locate her there. A call to the local police there in the morning would be his first order of business.

While he had his laptop running, he checked his fake Facebook page. There was nothing new there, but he decided to leave it for a little bit longer. On a whim, he searched Davon Karp's Facebook page again. He didn't honestly think that he'd find anything, but to his surprise, stupid man that Karp was, he'd bragged about things that should be left unsaid. He had posted the day before that he had a job to do for his friend Ulisses and even went so far as to write that Ulisses had a daughter who was a professional basketball player, and that Ulisses was paying him ten thousand dollars. Davon bragged that he would do whatever he had to to get that cash.

Discouraged, Jayden logged off his computer. In his prayer that night, he asked the Lord to watch over Nadia and help her recover from her injuries. And he told the Lord that he would keep looking for Nadia's mother until he received the impression to stop. He prayed that he would find her alive.

CHAPTER TWENTY-TWO

JAYDEN GOT THE FIRST GOOD night's sleep since this case had started. He was up at seven, but he felt good. He showered, shaved, changed clothes, and spent a few minutes reading scriptures on his phone. There was power in the scriptures, and he needed additional strength if he was going to succeed in his assignment. A knock on the door that connected his room with Nadia's alerted him that she was up.

"Are you decent?" she called softly through the door.

"Most of the time, are you?" he called back.

"You know what I mean." She laughed.

"Yes, I'm dressed," he said.

"May I come in?"

"I would like nothing better."

He opened the connecting door. "Did you sleep?" he asked her.

"I took one of the sleeping pills the doctor gave me. And so, yes, I did," she said. Despite her injuries and the bandage on her head, she looked amazing.

"The bruises are fading," he said. "How do your arm and head feel?"

"They hurt a little, but I'm fine," she said.

"You always say that," he reminded her with a grin.

"Grandpa called a few minutes ago. I told him about my new job. He said to thank you, although he's livid with Mr. Newbold," she said. "He knows how much I love basketball and doesn't want me to give up yet. He wants to be my manager and intervene for me. I told him to go ahead but that it was probably too late now."

"Who knows? He's an amazing and successful man. Maybe he can help you. Should we get some breakfast?" Jayden asked. "I'll fill you in on what I learned last night about Davon Karp and Jane Tribold."

"Sure," she said. "And I'm sorry I flaked out on you last night. I just couldn't even think anymore."

They ate a leisurely breakfast. Jayden had a little fun with the waitress over ordering raw hamburger, which he fed to Bullet, just like he had at dinner. They talked about the results of his computer search. She was so easy to talk to. He looked forward to doing this many more times.

They only had a few minutes before they needed to make the short drive back to Coolidge, so they went back to their rooms and packed up. Then Jayden called the police in Watford, North Dakota. Jane Tribold was well-known in the small town. They promised to find her and have her call Jayden's cell phone.

They met the chief and lieutenant at nine o'clock and went to the dorm of the missing Naylyn Pierza. A couple of her dormmates were there, but her personal room was locked. The girls said that no one had been in the room since Naylyn had disappeared. Jayden couldn't imagine why the FBI hadn't searched her room if they were so interested in her, but he was glad they hadn't.

The chief had obtained a key to the room from the RA. They were very thorough in their search. No drugs or paraphernalia were found. There were no pictures of family or friends. But Jayden found several dog-eared, slightly crumpled pictures beneath her clothes in the bottom drawer of her dresser. One was of a handsome Italian-looking fellow. Across the picture was a signature. The name *Arrigo* had been signed in a bold hand. The second picture was of Naylyn and the Italian fellow. His arm was around her waist, and they were both smiling into the camera. Knowing that Naylyn was six feet tall, Jayden judged the man to be five eleven.

Another picture was of Naylyn and a short, plump, blonde girl with a pretty, heart-shaped face. They were standing side by side. The back of that photo was inscribed, *Me and my best friend, Mya Wissing.*

There was one more. It was of the girl Mya. On the front of that one, right below the blonde's face, was written: *To my best friend, Allyah.*

"What do you have there?" Chief Owens asked.

"I think I just figured out why the FBI is so interested in Naylyn. It's because she isn't Naylyn at all. Her name is Allyah, and this fellow here, I would guess, is her boyfriend," Jayden said as he showed them the four photos. "Something is very fishy, and our FBI friends know what it is."

"I wonder if this girl, Allyah, is wanted by the FBI and they've figured out that she changed her name," Detective Kaiser said.

As Jayden stood studying the pictures. He could be way out in left field. If he was right, then this whole case could be totally different than what they thought. But if he was right, discretion would be vital, so he kept his theory to himself. "I need to find Mya Wissing," he said. "She's the key to Naylyn's mystery. Are we about done here?"

"I think so," the chief said. "Let's lock it up and go back to my office."

"Are you finished?" Nadia asked. She and the other girls on the floor had been talking.

"Close." Jayden asked the three dormmates, "Does Naylyn have a boyfriend?"

They said she did not, that she didn't even date. Not that plenty of guys didn't ask her out—she just turned them down. Jayden also asked if she'd ever mentioned a boyfriend from her past. Once again, he got a negative response. He asked them if the name Mya Wissing meant anything to any of them. Head shakes was all he got.

As they walked back toward their vehicles, Nadia asked Jayden, "What was that about a boyfriend of Naylyn's?"

"I found some photos. My FBI friends have some serious explaining to do," he said.

"Are we going to Davon Karp's place now?" she asked.

"Not until I figure out what's going on with the photos. You and I are going to work on my laptop at the police station," he said. "I'll explain when we get there."

He got his laptop out of the Hummer, and they went inside. Chief Owens offered them the use of the computer in his squad room as well. "Do you need help, or can the two of you do what you need to?"

"Thanks, but I think we've got it," he said. "Nadia is good with computers. We'll work fast and then we can go have a look at Karp's place. I'd like to make some copies of these pictures. If the FBI finds out I've got them, they'll take them, I'm sure."

The chief made copies for himself and for Jayden. Then he said, "We'll finish up some other work, but when you're ready to go, let us know."

Nadia looked at the pictures. "This is weird," she said. "I wonder if my mother knew."

"I have no idea," Jayden responded. "But I have a feeling that this Mya girl might know. We have to find her and talk to her."

"Would you like me to see what I can find out about her on the computer, boss?" Nadia asked.

"That would be great, but please, don't call me boss. I'm your friend," Jayden responded.

"Are you firing me already?" she asked with a droopy face.

He chuckled. "You know better than that. I'm lucky to have you as my *partner*."

"A promotion?" she asked.

"I'd even let you be *my* boss if that's what it took to keep you," he said very seriously. "Even though we've only known each other a few days, I feel like I've known you a lot longer. I can't think of anyone I would rather have work with me. I trust you totally."

"Thanks," she said. She booted up the police computer and went to work. Jayden did the same on his laptop.

They worked in silence for several minutes before Nadia said, "I think I've found Mya Wissing." He moved behind her and looked over her shoulder. "She's a waitress in New York. I can't find a phone number for her."

"Does it tell you where she works?" he asked.

She grinned and looked up at him. "Right here on Facebook," she said, pointing. "And I have a phone number for the restaurant."

"Do you want to call, or should I?" Jayden asked.

"I think you should. You know how to approach people better than I do."

"I don't know if that's true, but here goes. I have it on speaker phone," he said as he punched the number on his cell. Nadia watched him as he waited for an answer. Finally, he said, "I need to speak with Mya. Is she on duty today?" He was told that she was. "Great, would you ask her to come to the phone?"

Whoever answered the phone didn't even ask for his name. "Why didn't you use her last name?" Nadia asked.

"It's more personal using only the first name. It's a trick of the trade. It makes it sound like I'm a friend." He waited for over a minute. Nadia's dark eyes were on him the entire time, and it made him tingle.

"Hello, this is Mya," a sweet but hesitant voice said on the phone.

"Hello, Mya. My name if Jayden Spalding. You don't know me, but I need your help."

"What kind of help?" she asked, even more hesitant.

"I am a private investigator with Spalding, Fairchild, and Associate Investigations in Phoenix, Arizona." Nadia grinned. Her gaze went briefly to Bullet, who was lying near the door, watching Jayden. Jayden followed her gaze. Bullet didn't seem too upset over being demoted from partner to associate. "My partner and I are looking for some information about a young woman we believe you know."

"Who?" Mya asked.

"She's a basketball player for Central Arizona College in Coolidge. She and her coach are missing, and we've been retained to find them," he said.

"I don't know anyone who plays basketball, and I don't know anyone in Arizona. I'm sorry, but I can't help you," Mya said with what sounded like relief.

"Her name is Allyah. I found a picture in her dorm room of the two of you," he revealed.

He heard a gasp on the other end of the line. "What! Allyah? I thought she was dead. She disappeared one day, and I haven't heard from her since," Mya said. "You aren't trying to con me, are you?"

"No, not at all, Mya. What can you tell me about how she disappeared? This seems really strange," Jayden said.

"I probably shouldn't say anything. It could put me in danger," Mya said with a trembling voice. Jayden waited rather than pressing her. She finally spoke again. "She was on a date one night with her boyfriend. He was murdered by his brother. She was almost killed herself. She called me to come pick her up. She was scared to death. I left her at our apartment while I went to work. When I got home, she was gone. I figured she was dead, that the brother had found and killed her, but the police never closed the case."

"It sounds like she had reason to be scared," Jayden said. "She probably ran and didn't want to endanger you by telling you where she was. When the campus police and I searched her dorm room, we found some pictures. There was one of you that you'd signed for her."

"She took those pictures?" Mya said, sounding surprised. "I thought all her stuff was still in the apartment. She even left her phone."

"I'm not surprised," Jayden said. "We also found a couple of pictures of someone named Arrigo. There was no last name. He's about an inch shorter than her and looks Italian."

"Her boyfriend," she said so softly he could barely hear her.

"So you know him?" he asked.

"I don't know you," she said with a sudden tremor in her voice.

"Would it help if I let you talk to the police chief? My partner and I are in his police station right now," he said. "His name is Chief Gary Owens."

"I wouldn't know if he was a real police chief or not," Mya said cautiously.

"Okay, I understand," Jayden said. "You can look up the number for the Central Arizona College police department and call him directly. That way you'll know I'm being honest."

"Yes, I'll do that," she said. "I have to be careful."

"Please, when you hang up, don't forget about me, because I will call you back," he said a bit sternly. "This is a very important matter. Allyah and Coach Fairchild could be in danger."

"Okay, give me a couple of minutes," Mya said.

Jayden disconnected. "If she doesn't call back, we may have to fly to New York."

Nadia nodded. "Did you just change the name of your agency?"

"Of course I did. I don't want you to ever call me boss again."

"But I thought Bullet was your partner," she said with a twinkle in her eye.

"Shh, don't tell him," he whispered. "He's an associate now, but I don't want him to feel bad. I need his trust and help as much as ever."

The phone in Jayden's hand rang. "That was fast," he said as he looked at his screen. "Oh, it's not her. It's the FBI."

"I don't know what you think you are doing," Special Agent Press began without bothering to identify himself. "My partner and I just showed up to search Naylyn Pierza's dorm room, and guess what? Her roommates say you already searched it. What business do you think you have doing that?"

"Chief Owens obtained a search warrant, and I assisted him in executing it," he said. "If you are so interested in Miss Pierza, I'd think you would have already searched it."

"Don't get smart with me, Spalding. I could arrest you for interfering in an official FBI investigation," Press said.

"I don't think so," he said, trying to add a smirk to his voice. "Now, I am expecting a call, an important one. Oh, there it is. I need to take this." Without waiting for the agent's response, he accepted the other call. "I just talked to Chief Owens. He assured me that you are who you say you are, and he gave me your cell phone number," Mya said.

Jayden looked at his screen and realized that Mya must have called on her cell phone, so he had her number now. "Thanks for calling back," he said. "Now, about Arrigo."

"Yes, I know him, Mr. Spalding," she said. "Or should I call you Detective?"

"Just call me Jayden," he said. "So I take it that Arrigo was the boyfriend of Allyah's that was murdered by his brother?"

"Yes. It was awful. I wasn't there, but Allyah told me all about it."

"I'd like to hear what happened," he said.

Nadia and Jayden listened in stunned silence as Mya recounted Naylyn's harrowing experience. She concluded by saying, "She was afraid that Nino or his father would figure out that he killed someone else in that alley. She was scared—I mean, they're Chicago mafia. Who wouldn't be? But she promised she'd lock the apartment and wait for me to get off work. Anyway, when I came home, she was gone. Her cell phone was on the kitchen table. Even her purse was still there. She didn't leave me a note or anything. I still shake when I think of it. I was sure that Nino had found her. I didn't realize the photos were gone. I just boxed her stuff up and put it in a storage unit. I didn't even think about the pictures you found. I was just so upset. I've thought all this time that she was dead."

"She wasn't dead, but she goes by a different name now. Like I said, she must have fled in terror. The poor girl." Jayden noticed some shouting in the reception area. He recognized Special Agent Press's voice. He had to hurry because the FBI would be back here in a minute, with or without permission. So he said, "Her name now is Naylyn Pierza. She claims to be from California, but I couldn't find any information about her family. When I found these pictures, I was sure she'd taken on another identity for some reason. I understand the reason now. Can you tell me Allyah's last name?"

"Kravitz. And I hope you find her," Mya said as Special Agent Press shoved the door open, but he didn't make it inside before Bullet leaped to his feet, bared his teeth, and began to growl.

"I hope so too," he said. "I'll let you know what I learn."

"Thank you, Jayden," she said. "I am more relieved than I can say."

"Call your dog off," Agent Press said darkly. "If you don't, I'll shoot him."

"Agent Press, if you go for your gun, he'll attack," Jayden warned. "He's disarmed two men in the past two days. And since you still haven't apologized to him, he'll do more than disarm you."

Special Agent Andrews said, "Duncan, step back. I'll handle this."

Press reluctantly did as he was told, and Andrews stepped into the doorway. A third agent was behind him, a solid, distinguished black man in a perfectly fitting black suit and a dark blue tie. "Sorry," Andrews said. "But we do need to talk."

"Yes, we do," Jayden said with a frown. "You men have a lot of explaining to do." He looked at his German shepherd. "Bullet, stand down." Bullet looked back at him and then quietly slipped back beside his master. "Why don't you all come in, and I'll have the chief join us."

"I'm right here," Chief Owens said as he trotted into view. "These men seem to have a bone to pick with us."

"It's not nearly as big a bone as I'm about to give them to chew on," Jayden said. The men filed around the squad room table. After everyone was seated, Jayden said, "I don't believe I've met your other partner, Special Agent Andrews."

"This is Special Agent Sherman Burrows of New York," Andrews said as he gestured toward the stately African-American.

"It's nice to meet you." Jayden nodded at him. "I suppose that you can tell us more about Allyah Kravitz and why she is in Arizona going by the name of Naylyn Pierza."

"Who told you that?" Agent Press demanded.

"It certainly wasn't you," Jayden said darkly. "And your obstruction of my search for Coach Fairchild may have put them both in danger. It would have been nice to know that the Chicago mafia was after the coach's player."

Agent Press jumped to his feet, knocking his chair over backward. Bullet also leaped up, and in less time than it took to blink, he was snarling and showing some very impressive teeth to the angry agent.

"You're going to get yourself hurt, Duncan," Jayden said. "My dog doesn't take kindly to anyone acting in a threatening manner. And he's especially offended by someone who still owes him an apology."

Agent Press curled his lips but did not make any threatening gestures. "It's Special Agent to you," he hissed.

"Duncan beats a lot of other names that come to mind," Jayden said wryly. "Sit down, *Duncan*, and I'll call him off."

Agent Press slowly picked his chair up and sat down, never once taking his eyes off the snarling dog.

"Bullet, stand down," Jayden said.

Bullet's growl ceased, and he hid his deadly fangs. The hair on his back settled into place, but he didn't move or take his eyes off Duncan.

"Call him off," the agent bit out through gritted teeth.

"He's at ease. He's going to stand right there to remind you to be a gentleman," Jayden said. "Now, Special Agent Burrows, I believe you were about to tell us about the witness protection program."

CHAPTER TWENTY-THREE

"How did you know that Miss Pierza was in Witness Protection?" Burrows asked, looking quite curious rather than upset.

"I am a private investigator," he said. "And in all modesty, my partner, Miss Nadia Fairchild and I, are very good at what we do."

Special Agent Andrews said, "We were under the impression that Miss Fairchild was your client."

"She was, but I promoted her," he answered blandly. He took a deep breath, and then looking Burrows squarely in the eye, he said, "If we had known who Naylyn really was, we might have found her and Coach Fairchild by now."

"I'm sorry. I understand how you feel, but we do have protocols," he said. "She has been in the witness protection program, but when the U.S. Marshals office told us she was missing, we knew we had to look into it. As I'm sure you know, the marshals oversee witness protection, but we have a special interest in Miss Kravitz because of an ongoing mafia investigation.

"Well, the cat's out of the bag now, so let's talk about how we might work together to find the missing ladies," Jayden said.

For the next few minutes, he briefed the agents on what he'd learned so far. "Once we find Nadia's mother and Naylyn, we'll be going after Ulisses Fairchild," Jayden said. "But right now, the priority is to find Nadia's mother, and if Miss Pierza is with her, we'll be watching for her as well. It would be helpful if we could work together instead of fighting each other."

Chief Owens spoke up. "Detective Spalding is a talented investigator. He has my full cooperation."

Special Agent Burrows shushed Press when he started to make an outburst. "I agree. From here on out, we'll work together. And that means you too, Special Agent Press," he said pointedly. "And if that means you have to apologize to Bullet, I would suggest you do it." Jayden caught a fleeting twinkle in Burrows's eyes.

"We need to get back to work," Jayden said. "We have a search warrant for Davon Karp's apartment."

"You're wasting your time," Agent Press said. "If the women have been kidnapped, someone from the Chicago mafia is behind it. And that doesn't bode well for the women's lives."

"You may be right," Jayden conceded. "But the fact remains that there was a ransom paid, and Ulisses and his buddies are trying to get me off the case. I will continue to search with that in mind."

"Very well," Special Agent Burrows said. "I think we understand one another. You search your way, and we'll search ours, but you have my word that we will share any pertinent information we find and will expect the same in return. Now, there's one other thing. We would like the pictures you seized from Miss Pierza's dorm."

"That's not a problem," Jayden said and handed them over. Neither he nor the chief bothered to mention that they had made copies.

"Also, we would like you to keep this business about witness protection to yourselves for now," Burrows said.

"Of course. So what are you going to do now?" Jayden asked.

"I didn't promise to tell you what we plan to do, only that we'll let you know if we unearth evidence that is helpful to you," Burrows said.

"That's fine," Jayden said. And he would extend the same courtesy—or lack thereof—to them. He told Bullet to stand down. "Duncan, we will be meeting again. Don't you think you should apologize to Bullet? You really hurt his feelings."

Press glared at Jayden and led the way from the squad room. After the FBI had left, Jayden said, "Nadia, your father may have been exploiting a situation that wasn't of his making. This mafia thing throws a whole new light on this. Naylyn may have been the target all along, and your mother just got caught in the crossfire. That worries me. Do you happen to have a key to your mother's house?"

"It worries me too," Nadia said as she wiped at a tear. "Mom lives in an apartment, but yes, I do have a key."

"Should I have Lieutenant Kaiser get a search warrant? I don't know why we didn't think of that before," he said.

"I'll let you go in," Nadia said. "You don't need a search warrant."

"Then let's go. Where does she live?"

"She lives in Florence. It's probably not far from the hotel we stayed in last night."

"Chief, we'll search the coach's house first. You're welcome to join us, or if you'd rather, you could go ahead and search Davon Karp's place while we do Layda's. Your call," Jayden said.

"In the interest of time, let's split up," the chief agreed. "We can meet back here and compare notes."

As they drove to Florence, Nadia said, "Jayden, I think you may be right about my father."

"Until we learned what we did this morning about who Naylyn really is, I wasn't so sure. At this point, I almost hope it was him. I'd like to think that he's less likely to do them harm than the mafia is," Jayden said.

***

After an hour of careful searching, Jayden and Nadia had not turned up a single helpful thing. Layda's purse and iPad were gone. "Other than that, I have no idea what she might have had with her when she was kidnapped," Nadia said with a catch in her voice. "Oh, Jayden, what if she never comes back?"

"We can't think that way. We're going to find her."

"I know, she's my mother," Nadia said as they left the apartment and headed for the street.

They stopped and looked back just as an elderly lady opened the door next to Layda's. Her hair was in curlers, and she was wearing a threadbare housecoat. "If you young'uns are looking for Layda, she isn't home," she said.

The two of them quickly started toward the old lady's door.

"Layda is my mother," Nadia said when they got close.

"Oh, my, of course. You're Nadia. I remember you now. My eyes aren't like they used to be. That's why I gave my car to your mother. They wouldn't let me drive anymore, and I don't have family to give it to. What happened to you? You're all banged up. Were you in an accident?"

"Sort of," Nadia said.

Jayden stepped beside Nadia. "I'm Jayden Spalding," he said, sparing her from having to explain her injuries. "I'm a private investigator. I'm helping Nadia search for her mother."

"What do you mean, search for her?" the old lady asked.

"She's missing, she and one of the girls that plays basketball for her," he said. "I don't think I caught your name."

"That's 'cause I didn't give it to you," the old lady said with a sly grin. "But I will, if you promise not to let that dog of yours hurt me."

"This dog? He's harmless," Jayden said. "He wouldn't hurt a fly."

Nadia nudged Jayden. "May we come in and talk to you for a minute?" Nadia asked.

"As soon as I tell you my name," she said, a smile displacing the wrinkles on her cheeks. "I'm Maud Overson. Now you may come in."

Maud's apartment smelled like an old person's place. It was hot and muggy. She had air conditioning, but Jayden glanced at the thermostat as he walked past it in the entryway. She had it set at eighty degrees. That was only marginally better than outside. Bullet came in with them, but the old lady didn't seem to mind.

"Would you like a cold drink?" she asked.

"We just had one in Mom's apartment," Nadia explained.

"Please sit down," she said, waving at a sofa that had seen its better days thirty or forty years ago. They had to move some magazines, but as soon as they were seated, Maud asked, "What can I help you with? My, but you are a handsome couple. Are you married?"

Nadia blushed, but Jayden said, "We're just friends."

"What you waiting for?" Maud asked. "Don't make the same mistake I did, Nadia. I had a handsome young man like this freckle-faced boy. I didn't think I was ready to settle down, so I told him to give me a little time. Well, he went and married some other girl, and I never got another chance. So don't you let this one get away."

"I appreciate the advice," Nadia said. "But we are just friends. He's helping me find Mom."

Undeterred, Maud said, "And I'll give the same advice to you, young man. I can't remember your name."

"It's Jayden, and we were talking about your car," he said, glancing at an embarrassed Nadia. "Please tell us about the car you gave Layda. What make, model, and color is it?"

"Jayden, Jayden. Got it. It's blue. It's a Chevrolet. Really old, but it runs good. I never did drive it much," she said. "But I had it serviced every three thousand miles. It only had about twenty thousand miles on it."

"How old is old?" Jayden asked.

"Well, let me see now. I've had it for around thirty years, I think."

"I don't suppose you remember the license plate number, do you?"

"Do you remember yours?" she shot back. But before he had a chance to tell her that he actually did, she said, "See. You're as forgetful as this old girl."

"I think you have an amazing memory," Jayden said. "Is the car parked in the lot behind the apartments?" Jayden asked.

"Oh no. She and some pretty girl about the same complexion as you, Nadia—" She didn't finish her thought. "She was almost as pretty as you. Anyway, she drove away in it. I never saw it after that, so I suppose Layda gave it to the girl since I don't think she had a car. I saw her here with Layda a few times, but she was never driving. She was always riding with Layda. Could she be the player that's missing?"

"Did my mother mention her name?" Nadia asked.

"She might have. But I'm not too good on names. I couldn't even remember his a moment ago, but I think hers started with an *n*, sort of like your name," Maud said.

"Could it have been Naylyn?" Nadia asked.

Maud fussed with one of her curlers. "Yes, that could be it."

"What's my name?" Jayden asked mischievously.

The old gal cackled. "You thought I would forget a second time, didn't you, Jayden?"

"You caught me," he said. "Did Layda ever say anything about her and Naylyn going on a trip?"

"No, she didn't. Now that I think of it, she usually tells me when she's going to be gone for more than a day or two. If she is, she leaves me a key so I can water her house plants. Are they all droopy, Nadia?" she asked with concern.

"They were, but I watered them," Nadia said.

"Maud, what day was it that Naylyn drove the car away from here?" Jayden asked.

"Well, let me think. I'm pretty sure it's been several days." She wrinkled her already wrinkled brow. "I remember now. It was the same day that Layda didn't come home. It was in the afternoon. I think it was Wednesday. No, it was Tuesday. Yeah, I think that's when it was." Jayden stood up and thanked Maud for her hospitality. "If you happen to hear from Layda, would you call me?" he asked, handing her a card.

"I sure will, Jayden," she said. "You see, I won't forget your name again."

"What's my dog's name?" he asked as he moved beside Nadia toward the door.

"Now you're just trying to trick me, young man. You never told me." She wagged a finger at him and then stood up.

"I hope I'm half as sharp as you when I turn sixty," he said. "My dog's name is Bullet."

"Bullet. Bullet. Got it. But I'm not sixty. I'm eighty-five."

"You've got to be kidding me," Jayden said. "I would never have guessed that."

Maud touched Nadia's hand. "Now I mean it, dearie. Don't you let this one get away from you. He's a keeper." Then she said to Jayden, "You take better care of this girl. Don't let her get hurt again."

"I'll try, but she's a little reckless at times," he said quite seriously.

They stepped out in the hotter but sweeter air a moment later. Jayden sucked in huge lungfuls of it.

"She's a sweet lady," Jayden said, "but that place could use a little fresh air."

Back in the Hummer a minute later, Nadia turned to Jayden. "It sounds like Mom wanted Naylyn to have Maud's car."

"I'm sure that's the case," he said.

While they were driving back to Coolidge, Detective Noe called. "I finally had a chance to talk to Davon Karp. He swears he had no intention of hurting Nadia. He says he got a call from an old buddy from prison—he finally admitted it was Ulisses—and all he was supposed to do was scare her to convince her to quit looking for her mother."

"That's not quite what his girlfriend said," Jayden remarked blandly.

"I mentioned that to him, but he said he hadn't told her what his real purpose was. He says Lorena really did believe that Nadia was spreading rumors about her," Detective Noe said. "He claims Nadia was the one who started the fight and that the only way he could stop her was to knock her out. And he adamantly denies that he had anything to do with the kidnapping. He says he didn't even know there was one. Frankly, I don't believe him. I suspect he might know where Ulisses is, but if he does, he isn't going to say. I'll tell you, that guy's a real piece of work."

"That's for sure. Is that all?" Jayden asked.

"Not quite. I saved the best for last. Karp is heading back to prison when he gets out of the hospital. By the way, he won't gain full use of his hands again—so much for being a body shop man or a mechanic. Your dog does good work. Anyway, the gun he was using was stolen, as was the car he was driving. Did you find anything that connects him to the kidnapping or that might help you find Nadia's mother?"

Jayden explained that the campus police were taking care of that search and that he and Nadia had searched Layda's house and talked to her neighbor. He mentioned nothing about who Naylyn really was or that they now doubted that Ulisses had actually kidnapped the women.

After that call, Jayden dialed Special Agent Burrows's number. "I don't have much, but I thought I better tell you about a car." He explained about Maud's old Chevy.

"I wonder where that car is now," Burrows mused.

"I have no idea, but I was going to ask Chief Owens to put an attempt to locate it on the air. Maybe some officer has seen it."

"All right, thanks, Detective. We don't have anything to report yet, but I'll let you know when we do."

***

Back at the police headquarters on campus, the chief and his lieutenant were waiting for them.

"Did you get anything?" Jayden asked after reporting what they'd learned.

"Just this," the chief said with a grin. "It seems Mr. Karp has a bad memory when it comes to numbers because he wrote Ulisses's new cell phone number on a slip of paper. It was on his kitchen table along with about a ton of dirty dishes and empty take-out boxes."

"Ah, a way to track Ulisses down," Jayden said. "But I don't want to alert him that we have this number." Jayden tapped the paper with his finger. "I think I'll just sit on it for the moment. For now, I'm focusing on the mafia angle."

As they were talking, Nadia's cell phone rang. "Hi, Grandpa. Are you doing okay?" She listened and then said, "I'm fine. I'm not using my arm much, and my head is feeling better." After another pause, she said, "Why don't I have you talk to Jayden. He'll bring you up to date." She handed off her cell phone.

"Hello, Marley sir," Jayden said. "We're making progress, I think." Then he recounted all that they had done and learned. In his case, he disregarded the FBI's request to not mention who Naylyn actually was. But he kept it brief and asked Marley to keep it to himself.

After they'd discussed the ramifications of the new information and the new phone number for Ulisses, Marley said, "How's your new employee working out?"

"Great, but I told her that she's not to call me boss. I consider her my partner," he said. "The only trouble is that I downgraded Bullet to associate, but he seems okay with that."

"Jayden, since my little girl is now part of your team, that means that she can't be a client anymore. And that means you don't get paid," Marley said.

"That's okay. This has become personal," Jayden said as Nadia looked at him with a question in her eyes.

"It's not okay with me," Marley said. "I would like to be your client now."

"No, you don't have to do that, Marley sir," Jayden said.

"It's not what I *have* to do; it's what I *want* to do. Please, will you work for me? I'd like to have you find my daughter, and when that's done, you can go after Ulisses."

"I'll do it anyway," Jayden said.

"I'm paying you, and that's final. And by the way, I haven't been able to reach the nincompoop that traded Nadia to Minnesota, but I intend to. She told me I could act as her agent now. Okay, let me talk to my little girl again."

While Nadia was talking to Marley, Jayden opened his laptop and began to search for any information he could find on the Chicago mafia and on Nino Benini in particular. He discovered that even evil men like the Beninis use social media. Nino, he learned, was the eldest son of Santo Benini. The father was a sixty-year-old man who claimed to be a businessman. No mention was made of the specific business he ran. Surprise. Surprise.

Santo had a thick head of gray hair with a neatly trimmed moustache. His eyes were brown, and in close-up photos, Jayden swore he could see evil lurking in them. He bragged about the business sense Nino had. Pictures of the two of them appeared quite often.

A second son was mentioned in several postings. Arrigo was a handsome young man, taller by several inches than his father or his brother. According to both his father and his brother, Arrigo had chosen to drop out of the business, which they both said was his choice. However, they lamented that he had made unknown enemies in New York, where he had moved to. Sadly, his family indicated, he had been gunned down by an unknown gunman. A reward of one million dollars was offered if anyone could find the killers and bring them to justice.

Nadia had finished her phone call, so Jayden shared what he'd learned.

"They kill their own son and brother and then act like they are all broken up over it and offer a reward that they'll never have to pay," Nadia said angrily. "They are contemptable." She sat beside him as he continued to search.

"Hey, look at this," Jayden suddenly said. "There's also a reward offered by the FBI to anyone who can bring Nino and his father to justice. As if anyone would dare try to collect it."

"There's one witness who could put them in jail," Nadia said. "That is, if she's still alive. Naylyn must have been living in pure terror." Nadia shook her head sadly. "Hey, it's almost two, and we haven't eaten." The chief and his detective had gone home earlier.

"Let's go get something," Jayden said. "Then I think we should start showing the pictures of Nino Benini and his father to anyone we can think of, both here in Coolidge and in the surrounding area."

"Do you think they may have taken Mom and Naylyn?" she asked with fright in her eyes. "If they did, then Mom and Naylyn are dead."

"I'm sorry, but we have to consider it," Jayden said.

"I know, and it scares me," she said.

"Let's have lunch first," he suggested. "Then we'll see if anyone recognizes them. If we finish in time, I'd like to go for a run. And then we might want to drive back to Phoenix. We can take your car back if you're up to driving it, find you another place to stay, and then maybe, if something doesn't break, we can go to church together tomorrow."

"I'd like that," she said. "Church, I mean. But Grandpa says he wants us to go ahead and start searching for my father if we get some time soon. He says he doesn't care about the money he lost. He just hopes we can persuade my father to tell us where Mom is."

"Okay, we can do that," he said.

"My grandfather insists that he is going to pay you . . . us, I mean. He says he doesn't care what it costs."

"We do have the new phone number. I could see if I can get a GPS location on it."

"What happens if you find out where he is?" she asked.

"I have a lot of friends in the PI business around the country. If we can't nab him ourselves, I know guys who would do it for us. But we would have to talk to him ourselves as soon as we can if that happens. We need to persuade him to tell us where the ladies are—on the slim chance that he actually knows."

"What if he knows but won't tell?" she asked, her voice shaking.

"We'll face that if it comes to it. But remember, no matter what, once we locate him, he's a wanted man again," he said. "Desmond Booker is anxious to get him back in custody."

"I'll call Grandpa while you find us a place to eat. I know he'll want us to go ahead with the GPS thing."

CHAPTER TWENTY-FOUR

"Is this okay?" Jayden said as he pulled into a place called the Sunset Café.

"Sure," she said.

"What did your grandpa say?"

"He says to go for it."

"Okay, maybe we can start that before we start showing pictures around of Nino and Santo Benini."

"Whatever you think," she said. "And there's something else. Grandpa called the Minnesota Lynx head office and explained what is going on. He told them he's my agent and that there's no way I can get there by Monday due to my injuries."

"How did they respond to that?" Jayden asked.

"They didn't like it. You see, they were told that I was injured and couldn't play for a while, but they were led to believe it was only two or three days. They were expecting to use me by the end of the week. They said to let them know as soon as I can get there and am able to play again. He left it at that. So at least I have a little time."

"That's good," he said.

"Jayden, I hate being a sissy, but I don't think I dare drive yet. Would it be okay if we stayed here? I'm sure we can find a place to go to church, unless you have to be back to your ward."

"No, and since you don't have to leave for Minnesota right away, I think it's a good idea. I'll call that same place we stayed last night and make a reservation."

Jayden went through all the motions before he was allowed to bring Bullet into the café.

"What do you do if someone absolutely refuses to let him come in?" Nadia asked.

"I thumb my nose at them and go elsewhere."

After they'd ordered, Jayden made reservations for adjoining rooms again. Then they enjoyed a leisurely meal. They hadn't quite finished when Nadia's cell phone rang. "It's Jules. I haven't heard what happened in Tulsa with the game," she said to Jayden. Then to Jules, she said, "Hey, girl. How's it going?"

"I'm fine," Jules said, "but how are you doing? Is your arm still in a sling?"

"I'm afraid so, but it's feeling better."

"Are you about packed up for your forced move?"

"I haven't had time, and anyway, my grandfather called them and explained that my injuries were worse than they'd been led to believe. Their general manager is angry that he wasn't informed that I couldn't play soon. Anyway, they agreed to give me a few more days."

"I wish our wonderful GM would come to his senses and keep you here," Jules said.

"That won't happen," Nadia said. "I had to sign papers with the head office that effectively ended my relationship with the team, but since my grandpa smoothed the way for me, I am not going to show up Monday in Minnesota. I'll see what happens after that."

"Is that really a good idea?" Jules asked.

"I don't have a choice; my mother is still missing, and . . . well, I need to be here," Nadia said. "Grandpa is acting as an agent for me right now. He's a smart man, a very successful businessman. I don't actually have to go to Minnesota, you know. I don't know how your contract reads, but mine says that the team can trade me, but if I choose not to accept the trade, my contract is void."

"Does that mean you can't play for Phoenix anymore?" Jules said, sounding quite sad.

"Not unless they offered me a new contract."

"Then I hope they offer you one. We need you. We got humiliated in Tulsa. It was our worst loss this year. And it was because we didn't have you. Of course, I think we were all down. I'm not sure we played our best," Jules said.

"I'm sorry. Maybe the new girl will give you all a boost. But either way, I'm afraid I'm through. And I'll just have to see what works out with my new team," Nadia said. "Maybe they won't want me after this delay. I guess I'll see."

"Nadia, this breaks my heart," Jules said. "I'm almost crying right now, and I will be as soon as this call is over. What will you do now if they don't take you?"

"I told you about the private investigator who is looking for my mother."

"Yeah, you had stars in your eyes," Jules said.

"Well, yeah, I guess that's sort of true. He gave me a job," she announced. "Even if I go to Minnesota, I can work for him when I'm not playing ball."

"I'm glad you can at least have a job with him, but I still think this stinks," Jules said.

"It does, but please, don't say a word of this to anyone. I don't want Newbold to know what I'm doing. Of course, the Lynx might call him and give him trouble for not being honest with them about my injuries. Who knows what will happen? Thanks for calling. And give it your best, girl. I hope you know you'll still be my best friend."

"Of course I do, but I sure don't look forward to playing against you!"

Nadia chuckled. "We have to work now, Jules."

After Nadia was off the phone, Jayden said, "I've been thinking. I need my equipment from my office. Let's go back there as soon as we finish lunch. I'll try to locate Ulisses from there. If I'm successful, depending on where we find him, I'll work on getting someone to arrest him."

"You already made reservations in Florence," she said.

"That's right. If you need anything from your apartment, we can swing by there. We'll both need church clothes. Then we'll come back here and start showing Nino Benini's picture around," he said. "Is that okay with you? If it's not, I'm open to suggestions."

"It's fine with me," she said.

An hour and a half later, they were back in the office in Phoenix. "That's your desk," Jayden said as they walked in. "Why don't you get a feel for it. And if you need something else to make it work, then we'll get it."

***

Thirty minutes had passed when Jayden came out of his office and stood admiring Nadia as she worked at her desk. She had her arm out of the sling and was working at the computer. She looked up and smiled at him. "I like it here," she said. "Even if I can only work part-time, I will enjoy it. Now, I've been fooling around on social media. Almost all of my teammates have posted on Facebook or Twitter or both. They're all angry at the GM."

"As they should be," he said. Then, without missing a beat, he added, "Your father's in New Orleans."

She stood up, her eyes wide. "Are you sure?"

"Yep," he said. "Should we call Desmond Booker and then decide how to proceed?"

"Sure, let's do it," she said. "Look at Bullet."

Jayden did and chuckled. "He's wondering what you are doing at that desk. Come here, Bullet."

Jayden knelt and began to pet him. He looked up and motioned for Nadia to join them. She knelt down and put her good arm around Bullet. Then she laid her head against his soft, gray coat. He twisted around and licked her face. She laughed.

"Nothing more need be said," Jayden told Nadia as he stood up. "He likes you, and he would defend you to the death, even if I'm not around. I'll teach you some of the commands I use, and you'll soon be able to get him to do whatever you want him to."

Nadia continued to stroke Bullet and speak sweet nothings to him as Jayden called Booker.

"Jayden, how are things?" the parole officer asked. "Is Nadia feeling better?"

"A little, but I need to see to it that she doesn't overdo it," he said as Nadia looked up at him and smiled. "She isn't my client anymore."

"What? Did you find her mother?" Booker asked in surprise.

"I wish. No, she's my new partner. We're working for her grandfather now," Jayden said.

"Your . . . your partner? But she plays ball."

"She'll work with me whenever she can. Now, about this call. We've located Ulisses."

"How did you do that?" Booker asked. "You've got my head spinning."

"I'll explain it in detail some other time, but I can't leave Arizona right now. Nadia and I have some other leads we need to follow up on," he said. "Ulisses is sitting in a hotel in New Orleans as we speak. I'm just wondering what the best way to get him into custody is."

"I'll take it from here," Booker said. "Since I have a warrant for his arrest, I can get it done, and I mean quickly."

"Thanks. I need to run back to Coolidge. But in case he leaves the hotel, I'll drop by your place with the GPS equipment, give you a crash course on running it, and then he's all yours," Jayden said. "Of course, Nadia and I will want to know where he stashed her mother if he even took her—and frankly, I have my doubts now. Regardless, if possible, I'd like to get some of Marley's money back."

"I'll take care of it," Booker said.

"Good. We'll head for your office," Jayden said. "See you in a few."

By the time Jayden and Nadia got to Booker's office, he already had officers scrambling in New Orleans. Jayden spent a few minutes showing him how to keep track of Ulisses. He explained about the phone Ulisses was using and how the stupidity of Davon Karp clued him in on it.

After that, Jayden and Nadia hit the road back to Coolidge. They were still about twenty minutes from Coolidge when Booker called. Jayden put the phone on speaker. Booker was jubilant. "They caught Ulisses. He's in custody. Well, let's say he's under guard in a hospital. He pulled the same stunt his buddy Lester Skiles did and shot it out with the officers. None of them are hurt, but Ulisses took a bullet to the stomach. He'll be going into surgery in a few minutes."

"Maybe I better head down there," Jayden said.

"No, you do what you planned. My supervisor already approved me going there myself," Booker said.

"Okay, great. I just hope he can talk to you, and that he will, for that matter."

"I can be persuasive. I do have some good news. Most of the money was in his hotel room."

Nadia had leaned toward Jayden. Her eyes were glistening. She touched his arm lightly. "Mr. Booker, this is Nadia. Will you do something for me?" she asked.

"I sure will," he said enthusiastically. "What would you like me to do?"

"Tell my father that I don't hate him and I want him to get better but that it would mean everything to me if he'd tell you where Mom is," she said.

"You don't hate him?" Booker asked in amazement as Jayden looked at her with pride.

"Of course not. He's my father. But that doesn't mean that I think he shouldn't go back to prison. That's where he needs to be," she said, but then she began to sob.

"She'll be okay," Jayden said. "Keep us informed."

The rest of the way to Coolidge, Nadia was very quiet. She was hurting, and Jayden couldn't blame her. He did something during that time that he was not very good at—he resisted cracking any jokes. A number of them came to mind, but he suppressed them.

They were just driving into Coolidge when she finally spoke. "Jayden, what if he won't tell us where Mom is or if he really doesn't know?"

He reached over and took hold of the hand that was not restrained by her sling. "We'll cross that bridge when we come to it. We do have another angle to work. In the meantime, we pray, remembering that in the end, it's in God's hands."

"But what if it ends badly?" Fresh tears began to trickle down the smooth olive skin of her cheeks.

"Then we'll let God help us get through the hurt. But let's keep a positive attitude."

"No matter what happens," she said after a period of silence, "something good has come out of this."

He squeezed her hand and then reached over and brushed her tears away.

"I met you. And I know Mom would say that's a good thing. I don't know if I could have gone through this without you, Jayden. I know that Heavenly Father led me to you. You will stick with me no matter how hard it gets from here, won't you?"

A witty comment came to mind, but he again suppressed it. "You know it," he said.

"Where to now?" she asked.

"Let's go show Nino's and Santo's pictures around town. I don't think they've been here, but we need to make sure," he said. "Maybe the FBI is doing that, but I'm not going to depend on them. Your father's secrets are for Desmond Booker to unbury now. I know I can depend on him."

"Yes, I'm sure you can."

"Nadia," Jayden said as they stopped at the first convenience store they came to, "this job sometimes requires going into places that you and I would never enter for social reasons."

"Like?" she said, cocking an eyebrow.

"Like bars."

"Oh." She wrinkled her nose. "That's okay. We can always air our clothes out."

"And air your memory too," he said. "Sometimes you see things that you don't want to see and hear things that offend your nature. You don't have to go into those places though. I'll go in alone if you prefer."

"And leave me alone in the car?" she asked.

"I wouldn't do that. Bullet would stay with you."

"I'll go wherever you go," she said firmly. "Believe me, Jayden, I've heard and seen things that are shocking. Remember, I play ball. That's actually one of the things I like about Jules. She's offended by a lot of the same things I am."

"Okay," he said. "I just wanted to be sure."

For the next hour, they went into business after business with no positive results. However, that all changed when they stepped into a saloon called the Gallopin' Goose. Business was just starting to pick up as it was after five and people were coming in following their work day.

"Have you seen either of these men in here in the past few days?" Jayden asked the bartender after he'd finally managed to get Bullet admitted to the establishment.

"Sure have," the bartender, whose name was Nigel, said.

"Which one, or was it both?" Jayden asked as he and Nadia exchanged a quick glance.

"This one here," the tall, slender African-American fellow said. His finger touched the picture of Nino Benini.

"When?" Jayden asked as the bartender pulled a cloth from his shoulder and nervously began to wipe the bar with it.

"A couple times," Nigel said. "I didn't like the looks of the guy. He seemed, well, dressed too fancy for this place. He wore expensive clothes and lots of rings on his fingers and his ears. He had a watch that probably cost more than my car."

"When was the first time?" Jayden pressed.

"I think it was Monday night. No, Tuesday night. I'm not sure."

"Did you happen to speak to him?" Jayden asked.

"He called me a liar when I told him I hadn't seen the girl he was looking for."

Nadia grabbed Jayden's arm and held tightly. Jayden's stomach began to do gymnastics. "What girl?" he asked.

Nigel's eyes darted from Jayden's face to Nadia's and back again. "He had a picture. It was a pretty girl. Dark skin, not like mine," he said with a shaky grin. "More like hers." He nodded toward Nadia. "I told him I hadn't seen her, and he called me a liar. He told me I must have seen her around town because he had reason to believe she was here. He told me that she was over six feet and that she had black hair."

"You didn't recognize her?" Jayden asked.

"I didn't say that," Nigel said. "This town isn't a big place, and we see people, not only in here but in stores and such."

"So you did recognize her?" Jayden asked.

"I'm not sure, to be honest with you. The girl I thought the picture resembled has light-brown hair, not black," Nigel said. He seemed to be getting more nervous. He was scrubbing at one spot on the bar so hard that Jayden was afraid he'd wear the cloth out.

"What did you tell this man?" Jayden asked, gently waving his picture of Nino.

"Are you a cop?" Nigel asked.

"No, we're private investigators, and we're concerned about a young lady who I think must be the one you are thinking about."

"I'll tell you what I said. I told him I didn't know her and I'd never seen her." Nigel leaned across the bar and stopped fidgeting. "He told me that if he found out I'd lied, he'd be back. He said nobody lied to him. It was not so much what he *said* that worried me. It was the look in his eyes."

"Are you scared of him?" Jayden asked.

"Not really. I keep a loaded pistol right here under the bar," he said, reaching down.

"Don't get it out, but I think you should keep it close," Jayden said. Nigel nodded. "Now, let's see then. He came in another time?"

"Last night." Nigel began scrubbing again for all he was worth. "He had another picture."

"Same girl?" Jayden asked.

"No, it was—well, it was her," he said, shifting his eyes to Nadia. "You play for the Mercury," he went on, "but I didn't tell him that. And I could honestly say I hadn't seen you. I mean, you know, I've seen you in the paper and on TV, but not in person. But I know it was a picture of you."

Jayden glanced at Nadia. She was pale and trembling. "Did he threaten you again?"

"No, he didn't," he said. "I'd be careful if I were you, miss. He seems like a real dangerous guy."

When they left the saloon, Nadia was shaken up. "Why was he asking about me?"

"I wish I knew," Jayden said.

"I'm scared, Jayden."

"You'll be fine," he said.

"What do we do now?" she asked. "And don't say I'm your partner and ask me what I think. I don't have any idea."

"That's okay," he said with a smile. "After all, you're still in training." That made her smile, albeit weakly. "Let's go to Florence. I'd like to see if he's been there as well. And we might also check places like Casa Grande."

Nino had been in Florence, and he'd asked the same questions on the same days.

"Let's go visit your mother's neighbor before we call it a night," Jayden suggested.

"Why?" Nadia asked.

"I don't know for sure. I just wonder . . ."

Maud was home and seemed happy to see them. "Have you found your mother yet?" she asked Nadia.

"Not yet," she said.

Maud invited them in. They sat down and declined coffee, but each of them accepted a glass of water. "Is there something else you wanted to ask me?" the old lady asked perceptively.

"I have some pictures here," Jayden said. "Have you seen either of these men?"

The old lady's gray face turned white. "Yes." Her voice quavered. "This one." She pointed at Nino. "He came by last night and knocked on Layda's door. Then he knocked on mine. That man's eyes—they were, well, empty. When he looked at me, it was like he didn't have a soul." She shivered. "He asked where my neighbor was. I told him I didn't know. He called me a liar. Then he showed me a picture of you, Nadia. I nearly fainted. I told him I had no idea who you were. He said bad things happen to liars. Then he left."

"Maud, why didn't you call me?" Jayden asked.

"I wanted to. But I, ah, I washed your card. It was ruined. I couldn't read it," she admitted. "But I don't think I would have dared. I was too afraid he'd know I was lying."

"That's okay, Maud," Jayden said. "Here's another card. If you see him again, call me. We're staying in Florence tonight, so we can get here quickly."

She nodded and brushed at an errant gray hair. "Why does he want to know about you?" she asked Nadia.

"We don't know," Jayden answered. "But we're looking for him. When I find him, I'll get some answers. Did you see what he was driving?"

"It was a new car, shiny and white," she said.

"Rental car." Jayden nodded.

When they left Maud's place, Jayden was on alert for a shiny, new, white car. He saw several but couldn't tell what the drivers looked like.

"Do you think he's watching us now?" Nadia asked.

"I have to assume it," he said.

"If he's looking for Mom, then it means that he hasn't found her or Naylyn, don't you think?" Nadia asked hopefully.

"Possibly." He didn't say what he was really thinking. He feared for both women, but he also wondered why Nino was looking for Nadia. "It's important that Booker finds out from Ulisses where they are. He could have taken them. Or . . ."

"Or what?"

"Nothing. I'm just trying to come up with another explanation," he said. "Let's go have some dinner. And I guess I should call the FBI."

While they were waiting for their meals to arrive a few minutes later, Jayden dialed Special Agent Sherman Burrows's number.

"Have you learned something?" the agent asked as soon as Jayden had identified himself.

"Yes, Nino Benini is in town," he said. "But I suppose you already knew that."

"No, I didn't," Burrows said. "Why would he be in town now?"

Jayden told him what they had learned. "He was here last night, and he is asking about Nadia now. He even went to her mother's apartment."

"You're on to something, Detective," he said. "If he is looking there now, it may mean that he hasn't gotten hold of Allyah. Frankly, Jayden, we expected to find a dead body, if we found her at all. The Benini family doesn't kidnap. They kill."

Jayden shivered at those words that mirrored his unspoken thoughts.

"We'll come back. We've been split up looking all over the state. I'll call the other men, and we'll come to Coolidge," he said. "Maybe you're right about Ulisses Fairchild after all."

"It's kind of looking that way," Jayden said. "And that leads me to the other reason for my call. Ulisses is in New Orleans."

"How do you know that?" the agent asked, sounding more than a little surprised.

"I'm good at what I do," Jayden said smugly. "He's in a hospital down there. He shot it out with the cops that went to arrest him. They're all fine, but he took a round to the stomach. His parole officer, Desmond Booker, is going there tonight. And incidentally, he still had most of the million-dollar ransom Marley Ferrel paid."

It was silent on the line for a moment. Then Special Agent Burrows said, "Okay, I'm going to New Orleans. I'll send Andrews and Press your way to look for Benini. And, Jayden, I underestimated you. I owe you one. Good work."

After that call, Nadia called her grandfather with the phone on speaker. To say that he was not happy about a dangerous man asking around for Nadia was an understatement. "You be careful, little girl," Marley said. "You keep Jayden and his dog nearby."

"I will," she said. "Now, Grandpa, there's something else. Jayden found my father. He's in New Orleans."

"No kidding? That's great. He is one smart young man. If he ever decides to give up what he's doing, he has a job waiting for him at my company," he said.

"I think he likes what he's doing, Grandpa," she said.

"That's right," Jayden broke in. "But thanks for the vote of confidence."

"Is someone going to arrest Ulisses?" Marley asked.

"They already tried," she said and explained what they knew about his attempt to shoot his way out of the arrest.

"Looks like I need to go to New Orleans. I'll make him tell me where Layda's at," he said. His anger was so hot that Nadia could almost feel her phone melting.

"Grandpa, they got most of your money back," she said.

"That's nice, but it isn't what matters. I want your mother back."

CHAPTER TWENTY-FIVE

Jayden's priorities shifted. It was up to Desmond Booker and Sherman Burrows to get answers out of Ulisses. Although he supposed he could go down there too. He brought it up that night as he and Nadia watched TV together in his room. "If Booker or Burrows aren't successful with your father, then I think it's up to you and me. We could go down after church tomorrow."

"And meet my grandfather there," she said. "I don't think he can be talked out of going."

After the movie was over, they went to their separate rooms and went to bed. Bullet positioned himself near the adjoining door.

***

Nadia was having a hard time sleeping. As badly as her father had treated her, she felt bad that he'd been shot. Then there was her mother. Surely her father hadn't become so evil that he would fail to disclose what he'd done to her mother—if he had done anything. She just didn't know what to think at this point. If Mom was still alive and her father knew where she was, Nadia prayed that he would tell them.

She finally drifted off sometime around one o'clock, but it was an uneasy slumber, and two or three times over the next hour, she woke up, looked at the clock, and then drifted off again. Her dreams were troubling. She dreamed at one point that she was at her mother's funeral and that her father was also there, speaking of what a wonderful woman she was and how much she would be missed. Nadia woke up in a cold sweat.

Nadia slipped out of bed and went into her bathroom. When she came out a couple of minutes later, she was seized by strong hands and a cloth was shoved in her mouth before she even had a chance to scream.

She struggled, but her captor whispered, "I will kill you if you don't tell me where Allyah Kravitz is."

So he didn't know. That probably meant . . .

"You're coming with me. If you cooperate, I may let you go, but you must tell me where she is." He was shoving her toward the door as he spoke. He opened it and pushed her to the right in the hallway. They were on the ground floor, so he was heading to the rear exit, and it was unlikely that anyone would see them at this time of night. He continued to shove her, and she didn't resist because she didn't know where his gun was, but she was sure it was where he could get it easily. If this was Nino Benini, he had killed before, and she knew he would not hesitate to do so again.

When they reached the rear exit, she decided that if he got her outside, and she couldn't tell him where Allyah was, he would kill her. So she suddenly stomped on his foot, but it had no effect other than to hurt her bare foot. He wrenched her injured arm, and she tried to cry out, but the rag in her mouth was lodged tightly and wouldn't budge. She did the only other thing she could: pray.

***

Jayden was jarred awake from a deep sleep when Bullet began to pull the blankets off the bed. For a moment, he was disoriented. "What are you doing, Bullet?"

The dog growled. Jayden came fully awake and alert. He had trained the dog not to bark in hotel rooms, but his growl was vicious. Jayden swung his legs out of bed, ran to the adjoining door, unlocked it, and looked inside. Nadia was gone!

"We gotta go," he said as he dragged his pants on and shoved his hotel key into his pocket. Then he opened the door and peered into the hallway. His heart nearly stopped when he saw Nadia, clad only in her pajamas, being dragged through the door at the end of the hallway.

He ran toward the front door with his dog at his side. He burst through and turned toward the back of the building. "Bullet, find Nadia," he said, hoping and praying that the dog would understand.

Like his namesake, Bullet leaped forward, instantly at a full, silent run. Jayden also ran, but in bare feet, he didn't make good time. He'd faced a lot of enemies, deadly ones, in his day, but never had he been seized by fear like he was now. It was not for himself. It was for someone he cared for.

***

Nadia struggled as Nino shoved her through the parking lot. She saw a white car with the rear door hanging open, and that was the direction she was being forced to go. She was in serious trouble.

They were almost to the car, and her heart was pounding unmercifully. Nadia didn't hear a sound until she was suddenly knocked to the side and a gray streak took Nino by the back of the neck. The force of the attack bore her abductor to the ground. He screamed in pain. She fell to the ground herself, but as she was scrambling away, she could see Bullet tear flesh from the back of Nino's neck. The mafia man, screaming in pain, twisted and managed to pull a gun from his pocket.

"Bullet, he has a gun!" she screamed.

Her breath was wasted. Bullet knew exactly what he was doing. Before Nino could point the weapon at him, he released his now ragged neck and took Nino's wrist in a crushing grip. The gun dropped to the pavement. Nino struggled, trying to reach it with his other hand. Then Nadia heard, "Stop moving, or he'll kill you, Nino." She had never heard Jayden's voice sound so deadly.

"Get him off!" Nino screamed in anguish, ignoring Jayden's advice and thrashing and kicking wildly.

Nadia had finally gotten to her feet, and with wide eyes, she watched the battle. There was no way this could end well for the hit man. Already, in the past three days, Bullet had made short work of attackers. Jayden stood watching for a moment. Finally, he said, "Off, Bullet."

The dog let go of Nino's wrist.

"Don't move, Nino," Jayden said. Jayden had his 9mm handgun trained on him. But Nino already had his eyes on Nadia again. He scrambled clumsily to his feet and lunged at her.

Jayden held his fire because Bullet was having none of it, and Nadia knew that Jayden wouldn't take the chance of shooting the dog. This time Bullet went directly for the attacker's throat. Once again, he bore the hit man to the ground, but before he could tear open Nino's carotid artery, Jayden once again called him off.

Even though Bullet let Nino's throat go, he kept his face within inches of Nino's eyes. Nino lay still for a moment and then, once again, made a stupid choice. He struck Bullet with his uninjured hand. The ferocity with which Bullet attacked this time was terrifying. He didn't go for the throat but took the big man's face in his powerful jaws. Jayden had to command twice before the dog would let loose. When he did, Nadia turned and retched.

Sirens could be heard in the distance. Bullet backed away at Jayden's command. "Good work, Bullet." He patted the big German shepherd's head. Nadia wiped her mouth with the back of her hand as Jayden knelt beside the mafia hit man, whose face was torn to shreds. After a moment he stood up and took Nadia in his arms. He held her as police cars roared into the parking lot and slid to a stop a few yards from where Nino was lying.

"Is he dead?" Nadia asked, still trembling.

"No, but I think he may lose his eyesight," he said. "The fool should have done what I said. I can't believe he tried to come after you after the damage Bullet had already done."

***

Jayden and Nadia walked into a chapel in Florence for an eleven o'clock sacrament meeting. They had managed a couple of hours of sleep after spending the early morning hours being questioned by local police and Special Agents Press and Andrews.

Bullet had needed to be cleaned up, and Jayden and Nadia had needed showers. They'd put on the church clothes they had picked up in Phoenix and talked to Special Agent Burrows on the phone about Ulisses.

Nadia's father, who was in critical condition, had spoken only briefly with Burrows and Desmond Booker. What he'd told them left Nadia sick at heart. He'd laughed at the officers and told them that Layda was dead. He would not expound.

Jayden had asked Nadia if she was up to going to church.

"Just to sacrament meeting," she'd said. "I can't talk to people right now."

So that's what they did, and they left just before the meeting was over so that they could beat the congregation from the chapel. They drove straight back to the hotel, where they found Press and Andrews parked in front. The two agents got out and approached when they parked. Something about their faces made Nadia's stomach clench.

Press stayed back a little bit. Andrews went straight to Nadia. "I'm sorry, Nadia, but Ulisses was right. Your mother and Miss Pierza are dead."

She collapsed into Jayden, who kept her from dropping to the pavement.

"Let's go inside, and you can tell us about it," Jayden said.

In Jayden's hotel room, Nadia sat wiping at her tears. Jayden knelt beside her and put an arm around her shoulders. Then he looked up at the agents. "Okay, tell us what you know," Jayden said.

Nadia couldn't make herself look up, but she heard Andrews say, "Their bodies were found early this morning on a rural road southwest of Flagstaff. They were in a car that had rolled down a steep embankment and caught fire. It had been there for a while. A couple of rabbit hunters spotted it."

Nadia began to sob uncontrollably.

Jayden, however, asked, "If the bodies were burned, how do you know it's them?"

"Well, it'll take autopsies to confirm, but an iPad was recovered from the scene. Layda's name was on the cover."

"I see," Jayden said. "What was the car they were in?"

"The license plates came back to Layda's neighbor, Maud Overson."

Nadia sat with her head between her knees, her tears soaking her beige dress. Her world had just come crashing down around her.

Jayden took Nadia into her room and had her lie down. Then he went back into his room and spoke with the FBI agents. "Was there any other identification on the bodies?"

"Things are burned pretty badly, including the bodies, but it had to have been Layda and Naylyn," Special Agent Andrew said.

"Have you spoken to Special Agent Burrows?"

"Yes, we called him while you were in your meeting," Andrews said.

Press was strangely silent. And Bullet didn't pay any attention to him. For that matter, neither did Jayden.

"Has he talked to Ulisses again?" Jayden asked. "He must have had something to do with the crash."

"This is where it gets strange," the agent said. "When Ulisses was told that the burned bodies had been found, he went crazy. He cried and tore the tubes out of his arms. They had to restrain him. He claimed that he *hadn't* killed them nor had he kidnapped them. When asked why he told them she was dead, he said he just wanted everyone to worry, especially his former father-in-law."

"Was Marley there?" Jayden asked.

"No, but he arrived shortly after they spoke with Ulisses. Marley went in and spent a little time with him too. Ulisses was sedated, so he couldn't talk to Marley, but Marley told the agents that he wasn't sure Ulisses had killed them. He says he thinks that if it had been his ex son-in-law, Ulisses would have gloated, not fallen to pieces," Agent Andrews explained. "And that does make sense."

Just then, Nadia stumbled through the connecting door.

"Hey, I thought you were going to rest." Jayden gently put his arms around her.

She let him hold her for a moment and then pulled back. "I want to see the bodies," she said.

"Why? "Jayden asked, rocked.

"I've got to know for sure. What if it isn't really them?"

"But you may not want to see them in that state, and you won't be able to recognize them anyway."

"Jayden, she's my mother. I know her. I know what kind of jewelry she wore. I can tell by that," she insisted.

"It's a long drive," he said.

"We'll take you, and we'll get you there faster," Special Agent Andrews suggested. "I don't think either of you should be driving."

"Bullet will have to come too," Jayden said, looking directly at Special Agent Press.

"I've been a jerk," the agent said, dropping his head. Then to everyone's total amazement, he looked at Bullet and said, "I'm sorry, Bullet." Then he reached a hand out. Bullet did not bare his teeth. The agent patted his head.

"I told you all he needed was an apology," Jayden said. "Thanks."

***

Jayden watched Nadia's face as she bent over the burned corpses. They hardly looked human, but their limbs were intact. She looked at both of them for just a moment. She shook her head and backed away, holding her mouth. Once outside the room, she said, "Neither of those two are Mom."

"How can you tell?" Special Agent Andrews asked.

"The rings. Mom always wore a turquoise ring I gave her that I bought from an old Navajo woman. Those bodies had rings but not ones Mom had even owned. And did you notice that neither body is very tall?"

Jayden had noticed that. "She's right," he said. "It's not them."

CHAPTER TWENTY-SIX

As soon as they finished examining the bodies, the FBI agents returned to Florence and let Jayden and Nadia out at their hotel. They packed their bags and got in Jayden's Hummer. They had decided to go back to Phoenix while they waited for Booker to get more information from Ulisses if he woke up. They were between Florence and Phoenix when Nadia's phone rang. She'd been dozing. It took her a moment to dig it out of her purse. When she did, she looked at the screen. It wasn't a number she knew. She answered with some trepidation. "Hello, this is Nadia Fairchild."

"Nadia, it's your mother."

She moaned and fainted.

Jayden grabbed the phone and said into it, "Who is this?"

"I'm sorry. This is Layda Fairchild. I was just talking to Nadia. Is she okay?"

"She just fainted," he said. "We've been searching for you. Is Allyah with you?"

"If you mean Allyah Kravitz, the answer is yes. And we're both fine," she said.

"Where are you?"

"I can't say. I'm taking an awful risk just talking to you. I helped Allyah get away. The man who killed her boyfriend is after her. He wants to kill her."

"Why are you only calling now?" Jayden asked.

"We were afraid that if we called someone, Nino would figure out where we were, but I can't do this anymore. I saw the news that my former husband had been arrested for kidnapping us and that he'd been shot."

"That's right," Jayden said. "But you and Allyah don't need to worry about Nino Benini anymore. He's in custody."

"He is?"

"Yes. Allyah is safe now. Where can we meet you?"

"Wait. I don't even know who I'm talking to," she said.

"My name is Jayden Spalding. I'm a private investigator. Nadia hired me to find you," he said as Nadia stirred. He looked at her and smiled. "Yes," he said to Nadia, "your mother is alive and well."

"She's really okay?" Layda asked.

"She's fine." Then he spoke into the phone again. "When and where can we meet? Oh, and tell Allyah to call Special Agent Burrows. Does she have his number?"

"Just a second," Layda said. He could hear her say, "Do you know Special Agent Burrows's number?"

"I do," he heard a timid voice say.

"She does," Layda said.

"Good," Jayden said. "As soon as you tell us where to find you, she needs to call him."

***

Nadia, Jayden, Marley, and Layda were relaxing at Layda's apartment a couple of days later. They had a lot to be grateful for. Not only was Nino in custody—and blind—but his father had died in a shootout with the FBI when they attempted to arrest him. Ulisses was going to live and would be spending several more years in prison. Marley had most of his money back, and he and Layda were committed to working out their differences.

"There's one thing I'm still puzzled about," Marley said to Layda. "How did your iPad get to the place where those two car thieves went over the cliff?"

"We were in a hurry when we went to get on the bus in Casa Grande. I forgot and left it in Maud's car," she said. "Naylyn was scared to death, and for that matter, so was I. I know now that I should have called someone. I'm sorry for all the trouble I caused."

"But you saved Naylyn's life, Mom," Nadia said.

"I guess. But I can't believe I left my iPad in the car. I even left the keys in the ignition."

"And to think that the two burned bodies were a couple of men, not even women," Marley said. "A couple of car thieves. I'm sure glad it wasn't you, daughter."

Nadia's phone rang just then. "Hello," she said.

"You're in a lot of trouble, Nadia," came an angry voice. "I just got a call from the GM in Minnesota. You were supposed to be there by now. He said someone claiming to be your agent called and made excuses, but that's not good enough."

"Maybe I just won't go at all," she said calmly. "They weren't happy to hear that I was injured more severely than you told them and that I couldn't be playing in just a couple of days. You should have told them the truth, but I suppose if you had, they wouldn't have agreed to the deal."

"That's a bunch of nonsense. I traded you to them. You *have* to go, and you have to go now."

"Read my contract," she said and ended the call.

When Nadia's phone rang again a little later, it was Coach Leticia Korner. "Nadia, are you seriously considering not going to Minnesota?"

"I don't know what I'm going to do, but I don't want to go," she said. "They weren't happy when they learned that I was injured worse than Mr. Newbold had told them. They thought I could go to work by the end of this week. I'm not sure they even want me now. Newbold claims it doesn't matter, but to them it does. He told me I had to go right away. I told him to read my contract, which says that if I'm traded, I don't have to go, even though I lose my position with Phoenix. I'm sorry if it's causing you a headache."

"It's not your fault, Nadia, but you're right about the Lynx being upset about Newbold withholding information. I guess he didn't tell you everything. The whole trade just crashed around that idiot's head. And I'm the one that's got to win games despite it, even though I don't even get the new girl now. What would it take to get you back?"

"They won't have me," she said.

"That may not be true. I just talked to the owner," the coach said. "If he were to fire Newbold, you'd come back, wouldn't you?"

"Are you serious? Of course I would. But that would mean a new contract, and it would have to be negotiated with my new agent, my grandfather."

"Tell him to get after it. I'm quite sure Newbold will be gone in a few days."

"I'll tell Grandpa. And, Coach, thank you." Nadia ended the call and looked at Jayden.

"So am I to understand you might be sticking around after all?" Jayden asked with a grin.

"That's right. The trade is off, but I'll still need Grandpa to try to get me a new contract with the Mercury."

"In that case, I can use you part-time, Nadia. And I hope you'll consider it because I really need the help, and frankly, I want to spend more time with you. I've grown kind of fond of you the past few days."

"I'll work when I can if the team takes me back. If not, it will be full-time."

"They'd be fools not to take you back," Jayden said.

"It's up to Grandpa now, I guess."

"Don't worry. I'll get it done," Marley promised. "They won't dare say no. Believe me, I can be persuasive."

Tears filled Nadia's eyes. "You guys are too good to me."

"Hey, I have an idea, Nadia. You still can't play for a while, even if they take you back," Jayden said.

"They will," Marley broke in.

"So what's your idea?" Nadia asked.

"I'd like to ask you out on a date, if you'll go with me."

"Of course I will," she said with a grin. "Where did you want to go?"

"I was thinking about a ball game. Since you can't play for a while, it would be kind of fun to show up to a game of the Phoenix Mercury with their star player on my arm."

ABOUT THE AUTHOR

Clair M. Poulson was born and raised in Duchesne, Utah. His father was a rancher and farmer, his mother, a librarian. Clair has always been an avid reader, having found his love for books as a very young boy.

He has served for more than forty years in the criminal justice system. He spent twenty years in law enforcement, ending his police career with eight years as the Duchesne County Sheriff. For the past twenty-plus years, Clair has worked as a justice court judge for Duchesne County. He is also a veteran of the US Army, where he was a military policeman. In law enforcement, he has been personally involved in the investigation of murders and other violent crimes. Clair has also served on various boards and councils during his professional career, including the Justice Court Board of Judges, the Utah Commission on Criminal and Juvenile Justice, the Utah Judicial Council, the Utah Peace Officer Standards and Training Council, an FBI advisory board, and others.

In addition to his criminal justice work, Clair has farmed and ranched all his life. He has raised many kinds of animals, but his greatest interests are horses and cattle. He's also involved in the grocery store business with his oldest son and other family members.

Clair has served in many capacities in the LDS Church, including full-time missionary (California Mission), bishop, counselor to two bishops, Young Men president, high councilor, stake mission president, Scoutmaster, high priest group leader, and Gospel Doctrine teacher. He currently serves as a ward missionary.

Clair is married to Ruth, and they have five children, all of whom are married: Alan (Vicena) Poulson, Kelly Ann (Wade) Hatch, Amanda (Ben) Semadeni, Wade (Brooke) Poulson, and Mary (Tyler) Hicken. They also have twenty-five wonderful grandchildren and a great-granddaughter. Clair and Ruth met while both were students at Snow College and were married in the Manti temple.

Clair has always loved telling his children, and later his grandchildren, made-up stories. His vast experience in life and his love of literature have contributed to both his telling stories to his children and his writing of adventure and suspense novels.

Clair has published more than two dozen novels. He would love to hear from his fans, who can contact him by going to his website, clairmpoulson.com.